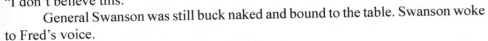

"They're not here. They're in Arka:

"Ah, they're listening in on the lin
said Joseph.

"But a few weeks may be too late,"
"I don't believe this."

General Swanson was still buck naked and bound to the table. Swanson woke to Fred's voice.

"Hello? Is somebody there?" asked Swanson.

"What do you what?" asked Fred, frustrated.

"Are you an alien?"

"No."

"Good. Then you can free me," said Swanson.

"No," replied Fred.

"Why not?"

"Because I don't want to."

"But why? You're human like me, aren't you?" asked Swanson.

"Actually, I'm not," said Fred.

"Are you the talking dog? Or the monkey?"

"Neither."

"Then what are you?"

Fred couldn't resist. "Your worst nightmare."

Just then, a man and a woman in business suits walked in the door. Fortunately for the lady, the man was no gentleman. He walked in the door first and the bucket of water fell on his head, dousing him.

"Yes!" shouted Fred, bending his elbow and thrusting it backwards in a sign of victory. "It finally worked."

"What the hell!?" said the man, removing the bucket from his head. The woman behind him was chuckling at his wet suit, but they both fell silent when they looked up and saw the naked and blindfolded general, spread-eagle across the table.

Fred mistook their stunned quiet for something else.

"Welcome. Here, shake hands," said Fred, joy buzzer at the ready. Neither man nor woman moved. "Would you like to smell my flower?" He asked the woman. She just stared blankly at him.

"Hello? Are you human? Are you here to rescue me?" asked Swanson. "Help me before they use an anal probe!"

"I don't need a drink this bad," said the man.

"Me neither," said the woman, as they both turned tail and sprinted out of the bar.

Fred ran out after them. "Wait! Come back! I have gum!"

"SLICK... ENTERTAINING." -Paul Di Filippo, ASIMOV'S
"HUMOR, OUTRAGEOUS ADVENTURES, & SOME CLEVER PLOT TWISTS." -Don D'Ammassa, SCIENCE FICTION CHRONICLE

Amanda,
Happy Fools'
Day!

FOOLS' DAY

A TALE FROM BULFINCHE'S PUB

Patrick Thomas (signature)

PATRICK THOMAS

PADWOLF
PUBLISHING

PADWOLF PUBLISHING INC.

WWW.PADWOLF.COM
WWW.MURPHYS-LORE.COM

Padwolf Publishing & logo are registered trademarks of Padwolf Publishing Inc.

MURPHY'S LORE™: FOOLS' DAY © 2001 Patrick Thomas.

Murphy's Lore, Shot o' Gold logo, Bulfinche's Pub, Nuclear Magic, Mystacaut,
The Eternity Club and all prominent characters are © and ™ Patrick Thomas.

Cover art © 2000 Michael Apice

Book Edited by Diane Raetz
Copy Edited/Proofread by Ian Randal Strock

ISBN-10: 1890096113 ISBN-13: 978-1890096113
Printed in the USA
Second Printing

For all the Tricksters that I've been blessed and cursed to know. Thanks for the laughs.

The gathering loomed, stood on one foot leaning against the wall and tried to look cool. "They" were on their way, leaving behind hearth, home and the kitchen sink. They traveled from the four corners of the Universe, where most of them had at some point been forced to sit in punishment, wear a cosmic dunce cap and then go to bed without any desert.

Every year the Tricksters gather. The last year had passed like gas, but quickly excused itself. If I had my way, we would have shut off the lights and pretended nobody was home. Sadly, this wouldn't work, as they would have stood outside on the front steps and insisted on constantly ringing the bell. Or worse, walked around the place and started looking in the windows.

It's been said that the whole of the journey is not merely the destination but also the road taken. With these guys, the road would be taken, literally, then hidden, sold to the highest bidder, never to be seen by its friends or family ever again.

-John Murphy, Bartender at Bulfinche's Pub

The little hand on the clock was on seven and the big hand had just passed the twelve. Both my hands were resting on the bar top. Except for Fred pacing in the corner, I was looking out over an empty pub. I had gotten up early for nothing. Nobody had shown yet. Somehow, even the ordinary people walking by on the Manhattan streets outside knew to avoid us today. Or it could be the fact that most people don't start drinking this early on a work morning.

If only they knew, the time of day wouldn't matter and I probably wouldn't be able to handle all the business.

I had always heard the saying that all the world loves a fool. If that were true, love should have been thick in the air, but instead all I smelt were Fred's hooves. That particular aroma was laced with the lingering stench of fear and paranoia.

Justified emotions, considering who was on their way here. Not exactly A-list people. I doubt most of them even made a Z-list. Some of them don't technically qualify as people, but each of them is an expert, a master of their craft. Individually, each could do more damage than a tornado. Together, the havoc they could wreak made brave men tremble and sane people leave town.

Sadly, I fall in neither the sane nor brave category. The only reason I was still around was I drew the short straw and got stuck working today. My name's Murphy and I tend bar here at Bulfinche's Pub, a little place at the end of the rainbow.

Three hundred and sixty four days out of the year I wouldn't trade my job for the pot of gold my boss used to buy the place. Today is April 1st, the one day I'd give up my post for a third class bus ticket to parts unknown. Except for Fred and me, the entire staff, even Hercules, demigod and bouncer, had fled Manhattan. Nobody was foolish enough to leave a forwarding address. Our regulars knew enough not to come within a mile of the place today. Many had gone into hiding.

Why should April Fools' Day strike such fear into mortal hearts? I can answer that in three words: The Trickster Guild. Every Fools' Day they gather together and for the last few decades Bulfinche's has hosted the event. Normally a party, even the wild ones we throw, wouldn't be cause for alarm.

Fools' Day is no mere party. Sure, the beer flows like wine, but drunkenness is a side effect, not the main event. The competition for the guild's highest honor is. Winner gets the title of the year's Lord High Trickster, better known as the High Yuk. Plus a year's supply of ear wax. It was a side effect from a prank years ago and they just keep passing it around.

The criteria is simple. The Trickster who pulls off the best prank between the first stroke of noon on March 31st and the last stroke of midnight on the 1st , New York time, wins.

Last year's winning scam, courtesy of Hermes, put NORAD on DE-FCON 2, convinced that an invasion of alien spacecraft had already begun. Peacetime is DEFCON 5, war is DEFCON 1. Hermes tried to explain the details, but things like radar shadows escape me. On a more daily basis, Hermes seems to be constantly amused by stealing my wallet.

I hate mornings as a whole, but Paddy Moran, my boss, insisted I be up and around before the break of dawn to greet his brethren and serve them drinks and breakfast. As our cook, Demeter, had taken Shellie, Nellie and Brian–Paddy's adopted kids–and headed for the hills of Connecticut last night, the meal fare was a cold buffet of meats, fruits and baked goods.

Everything looked delicious, but I wasn't biting or otherwise ingesting anything I hadn't made myself. Just because the prize was for the greatest prank, doesn't mean little pranks like doctoring the food would be forgone. It was bad enough Hermes had replaced my shower soap with the kind that turns black when it makes contact with water. I won't even mention the Preparation H in my toothpaste tube. Did a heck of a job on my plaque buildup though, and my gingivitis is almost gone.

Normally we run a breakfast program for the homeless and hungry, overseen by Father Mike Ryann and Rebecca, who is homeless herself. For their own safety, today it was moved up the street to Father Mike's parish, Our Lady Of The Lake.

The TV over the bar was tuned to an all-news channel. I figured maybe some of this year's pranks would be showing up. So far, nada. Then again, the NOARD incident was never made public, unless you count a distorted version put out by one supermarket tabloid.

There was nothing to do but wait and wonder.

The world was created in six days, each lasting from a few hours to a few trillion years. God looked out upon his handiwork and saw that it was good, mostly. Satisfied, he sat down to rest in the chair I prepared for him with the inflated ox's stomach. The sound that bellowed forth echoed across all creation. God blushed. That was the first thunder. And the first whoopee cushion.
-Coyote, Native American trickster god

Jeremy didn't know what to make of the Coyote in the bathroom. He was fairly sure that they didn't allow pets in the Capitol. Well, maybe seeing eye dogs, but the young boy didn't see any blind person with the canine. On top of that, the Coyote was acting unlike any other animal Jeremy had ever seen before. He was going up to each toilet in the bathroom, dropping a roll of toilet paper into it and going up on his front paws and flushing so the roll of toilet paper clogged the commode. But, it was when the Coyote looked up at him and spoke that Jeremy knew this was no ordinary dog.

"Excuse me," asked the Coyote, "Do you need to use the toilet?"

"Yes," said the eight-year-old Jeremy timidly.

Both his parents and his teachers had taught him not to talk to strangers, and while he didn't know the Coyote, something about the situation seemed to demand his reply.

"Well, then you had better go now, because this is the last working toilet in the building," said the Coyote.

"Why? Are all the toilets broken?" asked Jeremy.

"You might say that," said the Coyote with a most unusual expression for a canine. He was smiling.

"Why are they all broken?" asked Jeremy, as he went into the stall and took care of the business that he needed to. Normally, he couldn't go in front of anyone else, but the Coyote didn't seem to be like a real person.

"My fault," admitted the Coyote, introducing himself. "I've made sure none of the toilets in the building work. It's very important for the next stage of my plan."

"What plan?" asked Jeremy, as he zipped up and flushed.

"Well you see, a little boy, not much younger than yourself, recently said a prayer to me to help him. As I don't get many prayers anymore, I take the few I do get very seriously. It seems that today the House of Representatives is voting on a bill that, if passed, will kick him and his tribe off of their reservation. The same land the government forced them onto over 100 years ago, they now want to take back. When the government gave it to his people, they thought it was only desert, but ten months ago they found oil. So the government figures they can take back the land and move them to another desolate parcel. While the land the reservation is on may be barren and not exactly the prettiest piece of land in the world, for him it's home. He doesn't want to leave it. So in desperation, he said a prayer to me. I plan to help him."

Jeremy was a bright boy and while he managed to get past the idea of a talking coyote, he couldn't see the logic in his actions.

"But what good is clogging toilets going to be in helping the boy keep his home?" asked Jeremy.

"It is not the clogging of the toilets in and of itself. That is part of the greater plan. You see, that particular bill is the next one up for vote. I've arranged a little spell which will have some unsettling consequences for anyone who decides to vote for it. A moment after anyone thinks to vote yes, their intestines will be thrown into an uproar and control of their bowels will no longer be their own."

"You mean they'll get diarrhea?" asked Jeremy.

The Coyote laughed. "Closer to dysentery. It will be so bad that, if they don't find a bathroom, they will cover themselves in their own feces. I've made sure that there is not a bathroom to be found."

"But won't their insides eventually run out of food to turn into poop?" asked Jeremy as he watched the Coyote put the roll of toilet paper into the last working toilet and push the plunger.

"Nope, part of the spell makes sure there is always something in the bowels for them to lose. Care to come with me to watch the festivities?" asked the Coyote.

"I don't know, I'm supposed to get back to my class. My teacher is waiting outside the door for me. She couldn't come in because this is the men's room," said Jeremy.

"You're here on a field trip to learn how government works, correct?" asked the Coyote.

Jeremy nodded.

"Well then, this is the perfect opportunity to see your government in action and to get an idea of how things really work. See, in order to get anything done you need to have something to hold over the heads of the people in charge of the law. Sometimes it is public opinion, sometimes it's a large donation. This time it will be something a little bit more personal."

Coyote convinced the boy to join him and together they snuck past his teacher and into the observation gallery overlooking the chamber of the House of Representatives.

"But how will they know to change their vote?" asked Jeremy, as five congressmen left the floor in a rush to find restrooms. These were the ones who actually bothered to think about the vote before it happened.

"Simple, I circulated a memo yesterday to all the members of Congress.

Sadly, today that memo has disappeared from all their desks and they will never be able to find any proof that it existed. But, I made sure every one of them read it. Sooner or later they will catch on, and then this will no longer be a problem," said Coyote.

On the legislative floor below them the votes were beginning to be called for. The representatives who were pro-bill were, one by one, fleeing the legislative floor before they could cast a vote. Soon the Congressmen and women, who were leaving in search of a bathroom, became a stampede. They very soon learned there were no working toilets to be found.

"How come that one older congressman voted yes with no problem?" asked Jeremy.

The Coyote looked closely at the older man. "Ah. He's already wearing an adult diaper. He has this kind of problem on a regular basis. Should be fun to watch him sit down."

By now the hallowed halls of congress were stinking like a backed-up outhouse. Jeremy's teacher, who finally figured out he had left the bathroom, ran toward him. The woman was in obvious distress, not even noticing Coyote's presence.

"Jeremy, come quickly. We have to leave now. The other kids are already headed for the bus," she said frantically, grabbing his hand and pulling him toward the exit.

"Why?" asked Jeremy, cracking a smile and winking at Coyote.

"The reason's not important. Just move it."

"Wait, I forgot something," Jeremy said pulling his hand free and running back to Coyote. "Looks like it's working."

"Yep," said Coyote.

"Look, if I pray to you, could you help me out?" asked Jeremy.

"With what?" asked Coyote.

"A couple of bullies and getting out of a math test."

"Sure. I have to be in New York later today, but I can help you in a few days, if you like," said Coyote.

"Great! How do I call you?" asked Jeremy, as his teacher grabbed him again.

"Jeremy, leave that mutt alone," she ordered, covering Jeremy's eyes as the representative from their home district let loose all over himself. She let go with her other hand to pinch her nose closed in an effort to block out the stench.

"Just say my name three times," said Coyote.

"What?" said the teacher.

"It was the Coyote," said Jeremy.

"This is no time for joking. Follow me," she said. Jeremy stood back long enough to finish his conversation.

"Coyote?" Jeremy whispered.

"You got it."

"Thanks. Bye," said Jeremy succumbing to his teacher's superior force and being pulled away. The teacher again covered his eyes as she ran him past a gaggle of recently browned Congresspeople.

One woman was crying out, "Somebody help us. Call a doctor. Please!" It was the same congresswoman that the tribe had asked for help in the first place. Coyote gave her the same answer she gave them.

"Shit happens. Get used to it."

Whoever said women should be seen and not heard was an idiot. Woman should be seen, heard, touched, caressed and kissed. And those are just the ones you don't like.
                    -Pan, Lord of The Satyrs

"What's he got that I haven't got?" asked the annoyed man, as he stared down his large and uppity nose at the less fortunate who were forced to fly in coach. The separating curtain was uncharacteristically open. Usually its thin fabric served as the great divider between the haves and the have-nots.

From his perch in first class, Donald Washington gave silent thanks to his creator for having the wisdom to keep him out of such lowly places and making him one of the haves. Donald had never once questioned his creator's wisdom in having created him in the first place, which in and of itself revealed a lot about the man. Maybe something about his creator too.

"I don't know what you mean," said the flight attendant, barely able to keep her eyes off the coach section herself. She was the one keeping the curtain open. "We treat everyone equally here, sir."

"Equal, my eye. I paid for a first class ticket. That little man back there you are all paying so much attention to only has a coach ticket. Despite this, the lot of you are treating him as if he was royalty. It's just not right," whined Donald.

Donald may have been a snob, but nobody could fault his observation skills. The "little man", whose name was Pan, was being waited on hand and foot, although hand and hoof may be more appropriate. It wasn't just the entire female flight attendant staff, but a small number of the female passengers that were seeing to his needs. A seventy-something woman seated next to him was feeding the "little man" grapes, while a flight attendant was kneeling on the floor beside his chair and giving him a manicure. There was a male flight attendant who kept trying to weasel his way in, but Pan kept pushing him away.

Donald couldn't understand any of it. This guy was nothing special, certainly not tall, dark and handsome. More like short, hairy and homely. Donald doubted he was over five-foot-one or -two. He wore a brown goatee and he obviously wasn't a kid. A baseball cap, with a logo of a shot glass with a rainbow going into it, covered his head. The "little man" was so crass that he hadn't taken it off during the entire seventeen–hour flight from Athens to New York. No class, no couth. The typical loser, too stupid to wipe a perpetual grin off his face. Donald just shook his head in disgust.

"Sir, I'm sure you're just imagining it. Here have a hot towel," said the flight attendant, dropping it in Donald's lap, before she abandoned her post to rush back to the coach section. The little man seemed so tired she just had to help him somehow.

"Can I rub your shoulders for you?" she asked.

"With what?" asked Pan.

"Anything you want," she replied, putting two of her best attributes so far forward they almost touched Pan's face.

"Your hands will be fine," said Pan. "For now."

The flight attendant's entire body shivered and she let out a soft moan.

Realizing the flight attendant was a lost cause, Donald moved on to complain to his wife, Susan. Susan didn't pay Donald any more mind than did the flight attendant. She was also too enthralled with the little man in coach to even turn her head when her husband spoke. Donald noticed a twinkle in Susan's eye that he hadn't seen in years. Donald was so wrapped up in his own world that he credited it to their two week vacation in Greece. Not that he cared. The marriage had moved beyond that, or rather his half of the partnership had.

Donald hadn't had marital relations with his missus in over eight years. Not that he was celibate, by any means. A man like Donald has his own ways to handle these things. He had simply hired two secretaries who enjoyed spending their days at the office on their knees or on their backs. At least that's what he thought.

Donald had wanted to bring one or even both of them along, but couldn't figure out how to justify it to Susan. Susan may have been dense, but she wasn't stupid. Rubbing his infidelity in her face would be the same thing as asking for a divorce and that was one thing he would never do. Not that he didn't want to; Donald just wasn't willing to pay the price.

Donald didn't love Susan, nor did he claim to. Things had been different, years ago. Donald had thought he loved Susan. That's why he married her. In those days, he had been like that bozo in coach. He didn't have two nickels to rub together. The idea of having Susan sign a prenuptial agreement had been pointless. How he looked back now at that horrible mistake and cringed. If he ever left her, Susan would take half of everything that he owned, which was far too much. All things considered, it was far cheaper to keep her.

Frustrated, Donald reclined his seat and put the wet towel on his forehead. They were still a long way from New York and he was determined to get some sleep. Donald's eyes had barely closed, when the flight attendant was back, this time bumping into his shoulder.

"Excuse me, sir. Sorry to disturb you," apologized the flight attendant, in a merry little voice. He then heard the little man's voice.

Donald's head shot up, like a cork fired from an underwater cannon. "What's he doing here? He's a coach passenger and this is first class."

"He needs to use the bathroom," said the attendant.

"What, are the coach bathrooms broken?" asked Donald, in a nasty tone.

"But, sir, this gentleman is not feeling well and he needs a larger bathroom."

Standing at her side was the grinning little man, with a conga line of women behind him. Closer up, he looked even less attractive then he had from a distance. He was hairy. It was the only way to describe him. It was brown, coarse hair. Pan's face was rugged, with two bright green eyes set above a crooked nose. Pan also had a warm smile, which was now aimed at Donald's wife. Susan was smiling back. The twinkle in her eye had grown even larger.

"Sir, please don't cause any trouble. How about if we give you free drinks for the rest of your flight," offered the flight attendant, not taking her eyes off of Pan.

"But, I already get free drinks. I'm in first class. That's my point," countered Donald.

"We'll throw in free headphones," offered the flight attendant.

"Thanks, but I already have some," said Donald in his best snotty voice. It was impressive.

"The restroom back there was too cramped," said Pan. The seventy-something woman squeezed by, pinching the little man's butt. A twenty-something blonde model type did the same. Pan returned the favors. "I'm going to be needing more room."

"For what?" asked Donald, as the women lined up outside the bathroom, but none of the women were going in. As they walked by, each stopped first to caress some part of Pan's body. The male flight attendant came by and squeezed Pan's butt. Pan kicked the man in the shins and told him to get lost. It only seemed to turn the guy on even more.

Donald had begun to wonder if the airplane cabin had suddenly become very hot. The women were undressing and seemed to be practically panting. Maybe something was wrong with the dinner they had been served.

"Community service," said Pan with a smile. "So what do you say, buddy? You're not going to give me grief, are you?"

"This area is for first class passenger only. If the coach bathrooms are too small for you, too bad. You should have thought of that before you bought a ticket," said Donald smugly. "And I'm not your buddy."

Pan turned to the assembled ladies, with a grin. There was no reason to deal with this jerk when he could have others do it for him. "Sorry, my lovelies, but this gentleman refuses to let me through. There is nothing I can do. Sorry," said Pan, shrugging his shoulders.

A moan rose up from the assembled females and it was not the kind any of them were hoping for. A flurry of clothes, peanuts and drink glasses were thrown Donald's way.

"Shut up!" shouted one.

"Leave him alone!" demanded another.

"Please let him by," begged another on her knees. Donald couldn't help but notice that her blouse was unbuttoned down to her waist and she was wearing no bra. No skirt or pants for that matter. "I'll do anything," she promised with pouting lips. She was young and beautiful. Donald could barely keep himself from groping her, as he thought to himself that she had the most amazing knockers he had seen in a long time. He was fantasizing about hiring a third secretary, when the seventy-something woman with the grapes came over.

This one was not as pleasant or so understanding as the woman on her knees. She began hitting Donald over the head and shoulders with her large, grandmotherly purse. "Keep your trap shut, sonny boy!"

The blows knocked him to the aisle, his hands covering his head. It felt like she had a brick in the bag. The flight attendant reluctantly pulled her back, allowing Donald to attempt to get to his feet. The woman in the unbuttoned shirt was still on the floor and walked toward him on all fours. Donald froze like a deer caught in the glare of two magnificent headlights, unable to stand. The woman grabbed him in a hug, putting his face in the valley between her twin peaks.

"Please," she begged again. He forgot about his wife, he forgot his name. He would have given her anything she asked of him, but before he could answer the grandmother started to attack him again. He dove back on the floor and covered his head with his hands to ward off the blows of the pocketbook. The flight attendant again managed to stop her. Donald pulled himself up to all fours.

It was then that he noticed the little man's legs. They were bent at an odd angle at the knees and his feet seemed set further back then was normal, almost like an animal's. Pan also walked and stood in an odd way. Donald watched as Pan leaned over and whispered in Susan's ear. Donald thought he made out the words, "If you can get him to keep quiet, you can be first." Susan's whole body shivered as he rubbed her neck. He thought he saw Pan's tongue caressing his wife's ear and neck, but he knew that was impossible. She would never allow it. Susan had told him years ago she hated that.

His attention was brought back to the flight attendant who was holding the grandmother back, but just barely. "I don't see why you are making a big deal over this. A bathroom is a bathroom and you can't really stop someone from using one."

"I can't?" said Donald, looking at her name tag. "Well, Donna, I can write a letter to the president of this airline and complain," he said, crawling back into his seat. "And I'm suing that old bit—"

"Dear," interrupted his wife. "This man just needs to use the bathroom. How can you make such a fuss over nothing? Are you that heartless?"

Donald sat up and looked at his wife, unable to believe what he was hearing.

"Heartless? I don't believe this. My own wife siding with some yokel."

"Dear, I was only being charitable. It would be the right thing to do," said Susan. As she spoke her body seemed to be curling up with sexual energy. Susan moved almost like a kitten and she was licking her lips. It had been two weeks since Donald had any. The woman in the shirt had got his mojo working overtime to the point where even his own wife was beginning to look good. Thoughts of joining the mile high club flashed through his mind. To achieve that meant he was going to have to humor Susan. It looks like he would be needing the bathroom later on for himself.

"How about just not making a stink?" asked his wife, stroking his arm, or so he thought. Donald couldn't see that in addition to his arm, Susan's little finger was rubbing the front of Pan's pants and that the woman on the floor had stood and already removed Pan's shirt.

"All right," conceded Donald.

The little man went right by the line of women. The door was around a slight corner, in an alcove that lead to an emergency exit. As he went around it, Pan disappeared from sight but Donald assumed he went into the bathroom. A couple of the ladies followed him and also disappeared from sight. Pan stuck his head out from around the corner and seemed to wave back at Susan.

"Dear, I need to use the little girl's room," said Susan. Donald's face lit up.

"I'll go with you, dear," said Donald.

"Whatever for? I'm a big girl. I don't need your help."

"But I thought we could..." said Donald, letting the implication hang in the air.

"On a plane, in the restroom? Donald, we're not teenagers," scolded Susan, as she stood and squeezed by him.

She went straight to the front of the line and into the restroom. Donald eyes went wide and he motioned for Donna the flight attendant.

"Excuse me? Did my wife just go into the bathroom with that annoying little man?"

"Let me go check on that for you, sir," said Donna.

"Before you go, I could use a drink," said Donald. "Could I have a whiskey?"

"Sorry, we're all out," she said curtly and rushed up to the front of the line. She rounded the corner. There was a curtain there, designed to give the flight attendants privacy, if they decided to take a rest during the long flight.

Donna pulled it closed, separating the area from the rest of first class. The rest of the women moved to the other side of the curtain. Donald thought this was odd behavior. Wondering if he was the only one, he looked around first class. The lights had been dimmed in the cabin so people could sleep and, besides himself, the flight attendants and the women in Pan's conga line, everyone else was taking advantage of the opportunity to get some rest. He couldn't see into coach as the curtain had been pulled closed again.

The male flight attendant tried to join the group behind the curtain. He was barely inside for five seconds before he was forcibly pushed out, a bra somehow ending up on his head.

"Stay out!" screamed Pan. The man walked away, pouting. When he walked by, Donald stopped him.

"Are all those women in the same bathroom as that little man?" asked Donald.

"Well, the bathroom was not quite big enough for everyone," said the man, hesitating. He still was hoping he'd get a change to go in. "He's not feeling well and they are all helping him out. They are all concerned for his well being."

"There is nothing funny going on?" Donald said suspiciously.

"No."

"What about that bra you're holding?" asked Donald.

"Someone's carry-on luggage opened up."

"I guess that explains it. My wife would want to help him out. She's like that. Susan used to be a nurse, before we got married," said Donald. He wife had turned him down, but that didn't mean he still couldn't get some action. "Hey, what happened to that little number in the open shirt?"

"She's in helping out."

"Thanks. One guy to another, I was hoping to join the mile high club," said Donald, with a wink.

"Me too," said the guy, sighing and looking wistfully at the curtain. It seemed to be rhythmically rustling.

"Does that happen a lot?"

"More often than you think." The male flight attendant left to go check on the coach passengers.

Donald got up to see if he could figure a way the get the woman in the shirt to the first class bathroom on the other side of the plane. As he pulled the corner of the curtain the old woman greeted him with a faceful of purse.

"Stay out!" she ordered.

"But I have to use the bathroom," lied Donald.

"Use that one," she said, pointing across the cabin.

"Someone's in that one," he said.

"Then go use the one in coach," she said.

"Now hold on a second..." said Donald.

"No, you hold on. I've had more pleasure in the last ten minutes than I've had in the last ten years and I haven't even taken my girdle off yet," she said.

"Granny, what are you talking about?" said Donald. He mind could not grasp the concept of a women in her seventies as a sexual being, so if was as if she was speaking gibberish. Pan was not so encumbered.

"You ruin this for me and I will put you in a world of hurt," she said.

"Are you threatening me?" asked Donald.

"Yes," she said.

"Now listen..."

"No, you listen. Go back to your seat and stay there," she said.

"I'm looking for the girl in the open shirt," Donald said.

"She's busy. Now go sit," she said, raising up her purse.

Donald didn't want to be on the receiving end of that bag again. He was too tired and confused to argue, and Donna wasn't out here to save him again, so he just went back to his seat.

Donald tried to fall asleep, but was failing miserably. There were muffled noises coming from behind the curtain, and they were increasing in intensity. Maybe the little man was vomiting. Donald smiled at the thought.

For a second the curtain flapped open. Donald saw something that his mind convinced him must have been a trick of the light. His eyes were greeted with a bizarre vision of his wife.

Susan appeared to be naked and on top of the little man, who had finally taken off his hat. Horns, like that of a goat, were sticking out of his head. The little man was as naked as Donald's wife, but he was a freak with no feet, only hooves. The rest of the women were piled naked atop or near the little hairy man.

There was no way that troll had gotten those woman to engage in the orgy of the century, Donald thought. Donald wrote it off, convinced himself that he was only dreaming and concentrated on going back to sleep.

Don't even get me started on evolution.
-Sun Wukong, The Monkey King

Sun Wukong was surprised by the ease he had in bypassing security at Johnson Space Center in Houston, Texas. Maybe he shouldn't have been. After all, humans never took him or his kind seriously. Then again, neither did the gods, but it was too late for most of them. Sun had settled up accounts long ago. Despite his physical appearances, he was still a King: the Monkey King. All of his original tribe had long since gone, and he alone was left to walk the earth and the heavens. Sun would be gone, too, if certain gods hadn't taken him into their realm to keep an eye on him. Sun had caused them too much trouble to let him roam free, at least back then. Don't buy the PR, gods aren't all-knowing or -seeing.

These divinities made a mistake. The Jade Emperor made a big deal out of the bestowing of a title on Sun, Pi Ma-Wen. The young and naive Sun strutted around that heaven, proud to be an equal of the gods, and he performed his duties well and with gusto. His duties were the meaning of his new name, stable boy. One day he heard certain gods laughing at him and realized he had been had. Instead of an equal, he had been made the gods' fool. They had also killed his friends, lying to him that they had left.

The reason the gods took him into heaven in the first place was that this lowly monkey was more than their equal in power. Sun did not appreciate being made a fool of, so he struck back. These gods had a tree of life, which grew immortality peaches. The peaches were what kept them young and alive through the centuries. The most recent crop had been harvested for a feast for the Celestial Queen, and the god Lao Tsu had distilled some of the peach nectar into a concentrate and made immortality pills. The higher-ranking divinities were to get the pills, the more common of the gods got the peaches. Sun was to get none, even though he had helped guard the tree.

Sun devoured all the peaches and all the pills, leaving none for the gods themselves. Sun then fled the heavens, but not before burning down their tree of life, condemning the entire pantheon to eventual death.

The pantheon chased him back to his island kingdom, but Sun was so powerful that, with a small army of monkeys, he was able to fend off the gods themselves. The divine army had to flee for reinforcements several times. Finally, the gods took some of his subjects hostage and told Sun they would be executed, unless the Monkey King surrendered.

The gods had found his one weakness. Sun so loved his people that he turned himself over to die, rather than allow harm to come to any of his subjects. The gods gave their word that his island kingdom and all his subjects would be spared. Sun should have known better.

Sun was brought back to heaven in chains. The Jade Emperor ordered him killed, but the weapons of the gods, from blade to thunderbolt, were useless.

Lao Tsu came up with a plan: the monkey had stolen their immortality, so they would steal it back. If they killed Sun and ate his flesh and drank his blood, they would be immortal again, at least for a time. Tsu had the cauldron he used to make the immortality pills. It was supposed to be able to melt anything, and he put Sun in the cauldron as the main ingredient in monkey soup. After one mortal year, Tsu removed the lid, expecting some good eating. Instead, Sun Wukong leapt out, unharmed, except that his eyes had been burned red. The heat of the cauldron had melted away his chains, leaving him unfettered. Sun's magic mixed with the immortality peaches and pills had rendered him not only immortal, but invulnerable. Sun had become an eternal.

The Monkey King ran amok in the Jade Emperor's heaven, and this time he wasn't leaving until he burned it to the ground. The gods were helpless to stop him.

All seemed lost, until the Jade Emperor called upon the Buddha himself to help them. Buddha mediated a contest between Sun and the gods. In fact, Buddha became the gods' champion. Buddha had future plans for the Monkey King, so he cheated. Sun lost and was buried under a mountain for five hundred years.

He got out, of course. The Buddha needed help that only the Monkey King could provide. In short he needed a powerful con man—or rather—monkey. There was a successful quest and at the end of it, to the dismay of many a divinity, Sun Wukong was made a full-fledged god. Not that he stayed in the heavens much. Earth was much more fun.

Bypassing security at the Johnson Space Center had been ridiculously simple. Sun had simply dressed in a space suit and gotten down and walked on all fours like many of his simpler cousins. He lumbered right past the guards. None of them questioned a monkey in a space suit. Everyone assumed he was there as part of the celebration for the first American in space returning from this first space shuttle trip.

The next phase of his plan was more difficult. It involved bypassing the computer-based security and taking over the video communication systems between NASA and the shuttle. Computers had been a very new development in his relatively long life. Sun was far from an expert, but then again, neither was he a novice. With some help he had managed to acquire a computer program, originally intended for a computer game, that would do most of the work for him. All he had to do was install it. Once completed, he changed his outfit to complete the last part of his mission.

All communications to the shuttle from this point on would be obscured by static with the occasional glimpse of something truly bizarre.

"Houston, is there a problem down there? We seem to have a communication glitch," asked one of the astronauts.

"Negative on the problem, Discovery. We appear to be having some interference from sunspots. Everything here is as it should be. We look forward to having you and the Senator back."

The communications officer wasn't quite convinced and pointed out his findings to the mission commander. Though bizarre, it was no reason to abort a landing, and land they did.

Once on the ground, the shuttle crew waited for the traditional inspection before the hatch would be opened and the crew let out. Something different happened this time.

"What's that clanking?"

"It sounds like knocking," said one of the astronauts. There was a creak. "And that sounded like the airlock from the shuttle bay."

Next there were footsteps inside the shuttle, but the entire crew was already accounted for.

"Hello?" shouted the senator. "Is anyone there?"

As if in answer, Sun Wukong in an Air Force uniform, jumped out of hiding. The astronauts leapt back with a fright. No one had ever seen a man-sized species of this monkey before. There was no question that it was a real primate, not a man in a monkey suit. The length of the arms and legs was all wrong and a hole had been cut in the uniform for the tail. He was even wearing a gas mask.

Despite many of the astronauts being scientists themselves, none of them were able to identify the particular breed, and none remember that type of monkey ever being used by the space program. The mission commander stepped forward to examine the monkey.

"Hey, watch the hands, Commander," said Sun Wukong. The shock of his voice almost sent them falling to the floor. "Welcome back senator and astronauts. There've been a few changes while you were away," said Sun Wukong suppressing a smile and doing his best to look frightened.

"Who the hell are you?" asked the mission commander.

"Who I am is not important, only what you need to do. No, wait, don't come any closer. The day you went up, a military mix-up accidentally released a virus into the air. It caused those it didn't kill to devolve into primates."

"Why weren't we told?" demanded the senator.

"The president and the Joint Chiefs decided to keep you in the dark, but I had to warn you. You need to stay inside this shuttle and don't come out or else this will happen to you. If you survive."

"That makes no sense. Why wouldn't they tell us?" asked one of the astronauts.

"Simple," said Sun. "Before the virus hit, the shuttle launch was the biggest thing and brightest hope to happen in 30 years. The country is in a state of turmoil. The president decided that you were the only symbol he had to offer the confused populace. He's two steps away from having to declare martial law. They need you to get in line with the program, talk to the people. You know the drill."

"This has got to be some sort of gag," said the senator.

"I only wish it were," said Sun Wukong, "It is very serious. Here look."

He brought them over to the monitor, which in addition to picking up NASA video communications, was also tuned to the shuttle's satellite dish, which only took a few moments to align so it was able to pick up over 200 television channels. It was of course, processed though Sun's video filter.

"See for yourselves."

The mission commander turned on the television screen. The static was gone now. All of the internal communications showed all the people of NASA doing their jobs, but as apes instead of humans. A quick scan of the TV channels showed all the news programs populated by primates rather than people. The reruns were unchanged.

"Do you think this could be for real?" asked one of the astronauts and the mission commander deferred to the senior member of the team.

The senator shrugged, "I honestly don't know. The one thing I have learned is that it's best not to take unnecessary chances. For now, we stay in the shuttle and seal it off until we find out what is happening for sure."

"I agree," said the mission commander. "Double time, let's go people. Thanks," the mission commander said to Sun Wukong.

"Don't mention it, just doing my duty. I better sneak out the way I came in or they'll court martial me for sure. Make sure you seal it up behind me," said Sun Wukong, saluting and watching as the astronauts follow his instructions.

Moving away from the shuttle was a breeze. Smiling, Sun Wukong got rid of his uniform, climbed back into the space suit and just as easily as he had come, he left Houston and headed north for New York City.

The Golden Rule is usually made by those who have the gold.
-Kyna, Demigod, Demifairy

It was a beautiful morning, the kind that poets write sonnets about. The kind people in romance stories always seem to wake up to. It was a pity that this particular morning was wasted on the likes of Arthur Theodore. He really didn't care what the weather was like or whether or not the sun was shining. He only had eyes for Kyna. Not that his attention was based on love or even physical attraction. Not that Kyna wasn't beautiful. She was, although she had always considered herself a little too thin, a little too tall. She stood six feet with a very slender body. All the right curves in all the right places, just not to excess. Dirty blonde hair, rolled up in kinks, cascaded down her shoulders, tiny springs waiting to be uncurled.

Kyna's loveliness was lost on Theodore. He saw Kyna as a means to an end, as he did all people. People were viewed as commodities; what could he get from them or what could they do for him. This philosophy had worked out rather well for the man, helping build an empire on the backs of his workers, both in the United States and abroad. Hundreds of factories existed solely to produce thousands of products and make him almost a hundred million dollars.

Theodore had been married four times and none of them for love. At first it was for wealth, to get the seed money to buy his first factory. Once it was making a profit, Theodore no longer needed his first wife and he moved on to trophy wife after trophy wife. In his eyes, Kyna wouldn't have made a decent trophy wife. For one, she didn't dress trashy enough and her measurements were within the feminine norm, as opposed to that of implant-created silicone valleys. Kyna did have something he did want. Theodore was convinced that Kyna could teach him how to fly. If Theodore loved anything, it was flying. He had gotten his pilot's license when he was a teenager, and had learned to fly everything his money could buy him access to. It was wonderful, but he always dreamed of being able to fly on his own, even though he knew it was impossible. Then Kyna came along and offered to make his fantasy a reality.

Theodore was not a foolish man. He wasn't the type to be taken in by your average charlatan; the kind who charges people $300 to $500 to teach them how to fly, then tells them they can't because their heart isn't pure enough. Although Kyna did say that was part of it, she guaranteed him that after she taught him how to fly, he would soar in the wide blue yonder for five minutes. Beyond that, the purity of his heart would be the determining factor of whether or not he left the ground under his own power ever again. She didn't even ask for any money up front. Kyna promised that if he stayed earthbound, he didn't owe her a cent. It just such an attractive proposal that Theodore arranged to meet her in this deserted field outside of one of his closed factories. The pair sat beneath a shade tree with legs crossed and hands on knees.

"First you have to think happy thoughts," said Kyna. She lifted the line from Peter Pan, but Theodore didn't seem to notice. Instead he turned his thoughts to money and making more money, then parlaying that into an even larger fortune. It wasn't the emotion that most people would consider happy; it was more excitement and anticipation, which was as close to happy as Arthur Theodore had ever gotten in his adult life.

"What's next?" asked Theodore, already bored with the lesson. Like a spoiled child, he wanted to fly and he wanted to fly now.

"You throw yourself at the ground and miss," said Kyna with a smile.

"What?" said Theodore, confused and unable to grasp the concept.

"Never mind. Just a line from one of my favorite books," said Kyna.

Before they started, she had given him a pair of red high top sneakers with wings on the sides. They were an old pair of her father, Hermes', shoes. In the past, the footwear had carried her father though the skies and beyond. They still worked.

"What you have to do is get a running start and jump up into the air," explained Kyna.

Theodore was not a young man, nor was he in particularly good shape. His body had turned to fat long ago, and he hadn't run in more than 20 years. Still, he wanted to fly badly. He wanted it more than he had wanted anything else in a very long time, so he listened. Getting up a good head of steam he chugged along, his jowls and belly bouncing to the rhythm of his pounding feet. After barely six yards he was already out of breath, but he was still trying.

"Okay, jump now," shouted Kyna.

The older man obeyed, leaping forward. It looked like more of a trip actually, but for him the law of gravity had been repealed. Theodore's overweight body was lifted up and he took off into the sky. He gave a yell, but not a frightened one. It was one of joy, something very new to him. Theodore buzzed over the factory like an Air Force pilot, then chased a flock of birds into the sky, laughing like a child being tickled the entire time.

Sometimes five minutes can seem to last an eternity, but this was one of those occasions when it passed in an instant and the red high top sneakers forced him to land in front of Kyna. With the greatest reluctance, Theodore unlaced and handed them back.

"That was incredible. I must have the secret to these shoes. Can anyone make them?" asked Theodore, visions of dollar signs dancing in his head.

"No," said Kyna. "Sadly, only my father knows how to make them."

It was a small lie, as she knew how to make them as well. Kyna had created her first pair when she was barely eight years old and she had made the pair of black calf-high boots that she was wearing over her jeans. The boots, like the sneakers, sported little white wings. Kyna saw no reason to tell Theodore any of that. It would be a stupid mistake that would only up the ante, and then this con mightn't go down the way she had planned.

"Do the sneakers have to be high-top?" asked Theodore, his mind still racing with the possibilities. He was betting on himself to come in as the long shot. It was a sucker bet and Kyna was willing to act as his bookie.

"It's a good idea to always have them above your ankles. You don't want to be in the air and then slip out of them. It would be very messy."

"So how much for the shoes?" asked Theodore, getting down to business. Theodore's plan involved two briefcases, filled with $10 million in small, unmarked bills. He was prepared to spend all of it, but he had no intention of letting Kyna know that. He considered himself the master of negotiations. Despite his bulk, Theodore wasn't even near Kyna's weight class.

"I'll give you a quarter of a million dollars for them," said Theodore with a smile a snake would find charming.

"You've got to be kidding me. That's chump change for something like this and we both know it," said Kyna, acting indignant. She took the red shoes and put them under her arm and made as if to leave.

"Wait, that was just a starting point. No need to leave in a huff," said Theodore.

"Maybe I'll leave in a minute and a huff then," said Kyna, wiggling her eyebrows and wiggling an imaginary cigar.

Theodore missed the Groucho Marx reference. If he had been the side of a barn, the comment would have landed in the next county.

"How does $2 million sound?"

"Better, but still nowhere near enough."

"Well how about you give me a price?"

Kyna picked up his two briefcases, one at a time, sniffed them, held them, moved them around as if weighing them with her hands, then turned to Theodore.

"I'll take it all. All $10 million."

"How did you know how much was in there? That's incredible," said Theodore.

"It's a gift," said Kyna, buffing her fingernails on her shirt.

Actually, while Theodore was occupied with his first flying lesson, Kyna had popped the locks on the briefcases and counted the money. She was not quite as fast as her father, so counting the $10 million took her almost a minute. Theodore obviously didn't like having the haggle end so quickly, but in this case, the goal of owning the flying shoes was well worth a measly $10 million.

"It's a deal."

Kyna smiled and handed him back a pair of red high top sneakers with little wings. Using some sleight of hand, Kyna had managed to switch these and the originals, with Theodore being none the wiser.

"You realize of course, that from this point on your ability to fly is directly tied in to the purity of your heart?'" asked Kyna.

In truth, purity of heart had nothing to do with the ability to use the shoes, but if Theodore didn't believe it, Kyna's plan wasn't going to work. Theodore understood, but believed he could fool the shoes. After all, he had fooled everyone; all his ex-wives, his business partners and colleagues, his workers and the IRS. How hard could a pair of shoes be to trick? Arthur Theodore put the shoes back on his feet and got a running start. He was even more breathless than the first time but after twenty feet leapt as high as he could, getting his portly body a good six inches off the ground, before crashing down face first into the mud. Angry but undaunted, he got up, then brushed the mud from his eyes and clothes. This time he ran as fast as he could for a good thirty feet, then bounded into the sky. The landing was a rough one. Theodore crashed on the ground in a tremendous belly flop which knocked the air from his lungs and caused pain in his chest. Now he was in another race, this time to catch his breath. He won, but it took him a good five minutes. Kyna smiled as she watched him run and jump again and again, each time falling into the mud. After about a half hour of her fun, Arthur Theodore gave up exhausted and came over to her.

"It's not working."

"I told you, you have to have a pure heart. Obviously there is something that you are doing in your life which won't allow you to fly," said Kyna.

"Like what?"

Kyna shook her head, amazed at how thick the man's gall was.

"Perhaps dealings you have had with people in the past, ex-wives, workers, business partners, anybody you've cheated or swindled."

"Hey, wait a second, I never cheated anybody. I'll sue anybody who says any different," challenged Theodore.

Kyna shrugged her shoulders. "I'm not saying that you have, but the shoes aren't letting you fly. Something is obviously tying you to the ground."

"What can I do about it?"

"You have to try to make restitution to the people you may have hurt, wherever they may be. It may be in terms of attention or returning money. You have to be the judge of what it is you've done to harm people and somehow make things right again. After you've done that for every person you've ever harmed, then perhaps the shoes will work for you again."

"Thank you, thank you. I'll do that," promised Arthur Theodore. While he may not have repented his actions, he did have plans of going through the motions. That five minutes of independent flight, soaring above the earth, was the single greatest experience of his life. Better then sex, better than making a fortune. Theodore had decided he had no qualms about spending every last penny of his money trying to get that feeling back, even if it meant helping out all the nitwits and pea brains he had walked over to get where he was. He would fly again. That much he swore to himself, even if he had to dedicate his life—and he almost gagged at the thought—to charity.

"Is there anything else that I can do?" asked Theodore as he turned toward where Kyna had been standing but a moment before. She had mysteriously vanished. He looked all around the field but there was no trace of her. He never even thought of looking up where her own boots had carried her, her father's shoes and ten million dollars into the wide blue yonder.

Walk softly and carry a large cream pie. Otherwise the rube will hear you coming and run away.
-Rumbles, professional clown, former Golden Gloves boxer

It took a tough man to ride the New York City subways dressed as a clown. Not that Rumbles gave it a second thought. He had been a clown for too many years now to be self-conscious about putting on the white face over his black one. Back at the circus, children and adults alike loved Rumbles.

His gimmick was a unique one for a clown. When he first started his circus life, he decided to use his history as a golden gloves boxer to his advantage. Over a pair of sweats, he wore shiny gold boxers and a shiny gold robe with a hood. He combed his Afro-styled blue hair straight up in the air, reminiscent of a troll doll. White makeup covered his face except for around the eyes and the mouth. His left eye was blackened with make-up to look as if he had been punched. Red make-up framed his lips, either in an expression of a frown or a smile, depending on his mood. Today he had gone with a smile. To top off the outfit, he wore on his hands a pair of giant red boxing gloves, each as large as a couch cushion.

Rumbles got many strange looks because of his attire when he ventured outside of the circus. In New York City, the looks were covert. After all, it was against street etiquette to directly stare at somebody, unless you were looking for a fight. Rumbles didn't look for fights anymore. Instead, he had developed a habit of smiling and waving at the people who stared at him. Such was his skill as a performer that he was able to do it without frightening or offending anyone. Very often, he made the people laugh, which was the point of the whole thing anyhow.

It was early in the morning, still a good thirty minutes before rush hour. The subway car wasn't very crowded, and there were still a couple of seats here and there. Most of Rumbles' fellow passengers were work-force zombies, making their way to places where they earned a living. Rumbles said a silent prayer in thanks that he had never gone that route. Being a clown mightn't pay very much, but he was happy.

A young boy with a knapsack, not more than six, was riding with his mother. She had her nose buried in a newspaper so she didn't notice when he came over to talk to Rumbles. Rumbles began entertaining the kid, shaking hands with him using the giant boxing gloves. Then he pretended to get into a mock boxing match, during which every punch he threw knocked him off balance and swatted him over. Occasionally he would hit himself in the chin, pantomiming knocking himself out.

In the face of these antics, the work-force zombies came back to life for a minute, some actually applauding and laughing. Rumbles jumped up and took a bow and then pointed to his young partner and insisted he do the same. People began reaching in their pockets pulling out small change and dollar bills.

"Hey buddy, where's the hat?" asked one of the commuters in a dark gray suit with a red tie and a briefcase sitting on his lap.

"No charge. Just doing my job," announced Rumbles.

The man with the briefcase smiled and nodded his head. "Thanks."

"My pleasure."

The subway car reached the next station and stopped. The metal doors slid open. All those going ashore went and a new group of passengers climbed on. Among them were a bunch of jean-clad high school boys acting too cocky and doing it too loudly. Some of the people on the train hadn't put away their dollars yet. The youths grabbed the bills as they walked by. As the people protested, they struck threatening poses. One woman refused to be intimidated. She stood and demanded, "Give me back my money."

"What money?" said one of the boys as he pocketed the bill.

She had planned to be quite generous by giving Rumbles a five.

"The five bucks you just stashed in your back pocket," she said, getting in the teenager's face.

"I don't have your stinking money," he said, getting in her face. His breath stank.

She moved closer and put her hands on her hips and said, "Give me my money, now."

"Or what?" said the youth. His five friends were encircling her, using pack tactics, which technically made them a six pack.

At this point, street etiquette insisted quite firmly that everyone on the subway car look away. Most did, finding something far more interesting in the advertisements above the handrails or out the windows of the tunnel speeding by. Three of the six youths pulled out knives.

"Since you are being so mean and accusing us of taking stuff we didn't take, I think it's only fair that you pay reparations. Hand over your purse lady," said the boy who took the fin, brandishing a switchblade. Poor kid never even noticed Rumbles walk up behind him until the clown tapped him on the shoulder. The youth turned quickly and was startled at the sight that greeted him. He took a step back from Rumbles. The make-up and the outfit threw him off, not to mention Rumbles' sheer size. The clown was six foot two of solid muscle.

"Pardon me. I think it would be best for all involved if you put those toys away and left the lady alone. Otherwise someone will get hurt," said Rumbles in a soft voice that carried to all ends of the train. All eyes had turned back on him. Street etiquette demanded the intense observation of someone attempting suicide. It was practically a spectator sport, usually occurring on the sides of skyscrapers. The traditional yelling of "jump" was optional and didn't really apply in this case.

The teenager was embarrassed at his reaction to the clown and macho pride demanded an act of bravado to make up for the losing of face. The punk decided to go with the traditional put- down and mocking.

"Get a load of this clown. Who are you supposed to be buddy?"

"My name is Rumbles. You don't get a second warning."

"You've got to be kidding. What are you going to do? Hit us in the face with a cream pie? There are six of us and one of you. You crazy? You gotta be. We could tell that from looking at you, couldn't we?"

"Didn't your Mamma ever tell you that if you wore too much makeup you'd look like a slut?" said another of the punks with a knife. The blade gave him a feeling of power. It was a deceptive illusion, that was about to be shattered, probably along with his kneecaps.

"Hey, this guy is a nigger under the make-up," said another one of the teenagers, also with a knife, which he made the mistake of sticking in the clown's face. "You trying to be a white man, nigger?"

The underside of Rumbles' gloves had cut-outs that let him use his hands. With his left hand he grabbed the punk's wrist and bend it back. The knife clanged to the floor and the punk dropped to his knees in pain.

"Nigger is not politically correct. You should use the term African-American. Black is fine, too. When talking to me from this point on, sir will suffice. I understand you probably come from disadvantaged homes, but I figure I'd give you some higher education. Won't even cost you a cent," said Rumbles as he let go of the wrist, kicked the knife away then managed to move the woman out of the circle and behind him. One of the six ran to scoop up the knife.

The punk on his knees was helped back up to his feet by macho pride, which seemed to be having a grand old ride on the subway. "Nigger, you got one chance to walk away and just go back to Bellevue. Let them lock you up there in your straitjacket, that way you won't get hurt."

"Your concern for me is touching, but don't worry. I won't be the one getting hurt," promised Rumbles.

"We'll see."

Rumbles made a feint as if he was going to attack the leader of the group who stabbed out with his knife. Using the giant boxing glove as a pin cushion, Rumbles took the knife from him and added to the punk's momentum. The end result was a flip that landed him flat on his back and smashed all the air out of him, leaving him unable to move for half a minute.

Rumbles then tossed off the giant boxing gloves, aiming at the two punks who held knives. While they were distracted by the red gloves flying at their faces, Rumbles stepped in to take their switchblades away, then kicked each behind the nearest knee. They crumbled to the floor. The train doors opened and closed. The people on the platform moved to go in the cars on either side. Nobody inside that car got up to leave. The clown reached down to pluck the third knife from the glove where it had impaled itself and began a juggling act with the three blades. The doors closed and the 6 train moved on uptown.

The three men who were still standing rushed him, but he wove in and out among them, like water flowing down a manhole cover. None of them could touch him. Rumbles even managed to keep juggling the blades, without dropping a single knife or missing a beat. Stopping, he caught all three knives in his right hand and with a small bow handed them to the woman the youths had been assailing.

Rumbles stood still and faced the gang of teenagers. All of them had regained their footing and so had the still-present macho pride.

"Okay gentlemen, we've had some fun, but why don't we just stop here?" suggested Rumbles.

"Not a chance, nigger," said the leader, pulling out stainless steel "brass" knuckles. "Nail his ass to the wall."

"All right, but it's going to hurt you more than it hurts me," said Rumbles.

The leader snorted. "I doubt that. There's still only one of you."

"I think you should be more concerned that there are still only six of you," said Rumbles with a smile. What the teenagers didn't realize was that in addition to being a former golden gloves champion, he held an Olympic bronze medal in fencing and had more black belts than a tailor. Luckily for them, his martial arts passion was Aikido. In Aikido there are no offensive moves. The philosophy is basically to prevent your opponent from hurting himself or anyone else.

The six teenagers rushed him together, not realizing that this actually worked to Rumbles' advantage. They were bunched so close together that their attacks were more dangerous to each other than to him. Instead of coming at him from the front and sides, they should have encircled him, but they had no idea how to fight. They had always depended on superior numbers and attitude to get them what they wanted. It wasn't going to be enough this time around.

As each one threw a punch or a kick, Rumbles redirected the force until all six had been spun, knocked and battered. Rumbles then broke from his Aikido technique and he used some nerve block moves which disabled his opponents' arms and legs, effectively paralyzing them. The effect was temporary, but they didn't know that.

"You boys need to be taught a lesson. I'm going to make sure it's one you don't forget," said Rumbles. Taking the leader's steel knuckles, he stuffed them in a pocket, then stripped the six down to their underwear, returned everyone's money, then borrowed some duct tape from a construction worker who had watched with amusement. He used the duct tape to bind their hands behind their backs and cover their eyes so they couldn't see. He waited until the subway got to the 125th Street station, then ripped the tape off their eyes and pushed them out the open door. They had to hop because their legs were still taped together.

"Since you have such a good opinion of black people, I thought maybe I would give you a chance to get to know some better, up close and personal like," said Rumbles with a smile.

The teenagers looked around and realized where they were.

"Oh shi..." said the leader. Macho pride may not have died right then, but it was definitely on life support. "We're in Harlem."

"That's right. Why don't you try using the n-word here and see where it gets you?" suggested Rumbles.

The six young men tried to get back on the train, but Rumbles blocked them. The passengers on the train, most of whom had stayed to watch this drama to its conclusion, gave Rumbles a standing ovation. He took a bow, picked up his gloves, the clothes from the six punks and walked off the car heading towards the downtown train. As pleasant a diversion as this might be, he had places to go and people to see. He kept a watchful eye on the teenagers, not wanting them to actually get hurt. Rumbles knew the area well enough to know that, during rush hour, there were always transit police stationed on or near the platform. They hopped up to the police like one-legged kangaroos, begging for help, and tried to explain their story to the officers, who couldn't help but laugh.

"Let me get this straight. An evil clown did this to you, for no good reason?" asked one officer.

"That's right," said the leader, trying not to fall over.

"And he was totally unprovoked."

"Of course, of course, we were just on our way to school."

"I don't know about that. You six fit the description of the gang that's been hassling passengers on the 6 line for the past two months. I think you had better come with us for questioning."

"But..."

Rumbles had heard enough. He dumped their clothes in a garbage can and hopped in the opening doors of a downtown train. He didn't want to be the last one to Bulfinche's Pub. No telling what would be hanging over the door waiting to fall on his head.

Stoned? On Acid? Strung out? You don't know the half of it.
-Loki, Norse god of Mischief

The mountains shook with the screams of an imprisoned god. The sound was enough to make a grown man feel something between fear and the urge to burst into tears. It wasn't so much the sheer volume of the scream: it was more the agony that was carried in the sound. The screams were by no means constant. Sometimes almost an hour would pass between. This wasn't one of those times. Paddy Moran heard the screams, but they didn't make him want to move any faster. In fact, if anything, they gave him the burning desire to be elsewhere. Not that Paddy wasn't a brave man. His courage dwarfed most people. In truth, while nobody would call him a coward, some wouldn't consider him a man at all. That wasn't based on his appearance or any radical sex change surgery, but on his ancestry.

Paddy Moran was a leprechaun who had used his pot of gold to buy a bar in Manhattan; Bulfinche's Pub by name. In it, he was as close to all-powerful as anyone could get on either side of the Styx. Outside, he was maybe a little more than the average mortal, although not in height. The list of Paddy's achievements would stretch to the moon and back. Paddy had to stretch to get things off a high shelf. Paddy had helped more lives than anyone could probably ever count. There isn't a person alive who would fault him from walking away from this dark corner of Asgard and back into Manhattan. No one but him.

Paddy had a debt of honor that he intended to repay, as he did every year, by releasing a prisoner for twenty four hours. Using rock climbing gear, he rappelled down into the pit where the god Loki was chained to three stones. A serpent forever dripped acidic venom onto his face and body. This wasn't your garden-variety snake. This was a serpent large enough to wrap itself around a T-Rex and crush the life out of it. Despite its incredible size, the serpent's intelligence was minimal. Its brain was about the size of a baseball. The serpent was very content to spend day in and day out torturing the trickster god. It was more than content, it enjoyed its work. The screams of his victim were like manna, nourishing the serpent and making him stronger.

Loki hadn't always been alone in his torment. There had been a bright spot in his otherwise dismal, personal Hell and her name was Sigyn. Sigyn was Loki's wife. There was a time when she stood by his side, trying to protect him and ease his suffering by catching some of the venom. Sigyn used a large metal bowl, fashioned out of a shield, to protect Loki from the acid's bite.

These days the shield lay discarded in the corner, alone and unused. There was no one who cared enough for Loki to stand between him and liquid pain.

It had been years since Sigyn had left, since frustration at Loki's ingratitude had driven her away. No matter how much she did, she could never stop all the venom. Some slipped by her and Loki cursed her for it, instead of thanking her for the gallons she managed to turn aside. Sigyn had never even complained at the disfigurement her actions caused her hands or the agony she felt when the acid burned the skin from her fingers. Finally the abuse and lack of appreciation became too great. Sigyn left Loki to fend for himself.

All that remained of her was the memory, and it tortured Loki far more that the burning serpent drool. What they said about not knowing what you had until it's gone was never truer than it was with Loki. Sigyn's leaving taught Loki something he had never learned before in all of his punishments. He learned humility.

Loki had loved Sigyn, but so confident was he in her love for him that he never treated her well, even though she stood by his side protecting him. He never offered her a kind word or a single thank you. That would change if she ever came back, but it wasn't likely and Loki knew it. Part of his heart died that day. Something in his manner and spirit was forever changed as well. A piece of the darkness that was in his soul kicked the bucket. Sorrow, not bitterness, took its place. You could hear it in his screams.

Paddy rappelled down fifty feet of the stone pit wall, leaving a good two hundred plus feet to go. At first the serpent didn't notice him, unable to hear him over Loki's cries. Paddy chiseled free a hunk of rock, then threw it, hitting the serpent squarely in the back of its head. The blow wasn't powerful enough to hurt the serpent, nor was it meant to. Its mission was to arouse the serpent's curiosity.

It gradually turned its massive head to face the descending leprechaun. The serpent seemed to almost recognize the man with the white hair and mustache, but there wasn't enough mind to tell it from where or why. With blinding quickness, it leapt towards Paddy, jaws open, fangs glistening, venom dripping. The intent was clear. The serpent's plan was to swallow him whole, like an ordinary snake might a mouse. The strike fell far short of the wall-climbing leprechaun, so it slithered closer and stretched its long body to its limits. Paddy was still too far above it.

Opening its mouth and hissing, the serpent hoped to scare its prey into falling off the wall. While this strategy had little merit, it did allow Paddy to remove ten pounds of grade A beef from his backpack with his right hand. With a simple toss, the meat meteor flew down into the serpent's open mouth and down its throat. It was barely a crumb in terms of nourishment, but the drugs it was laced with packed a wallop. Within seconds the serpent lay unconscious on the floor of the pit. Paddy rappelled down the rest of the way. The sudden silence was eerie. The only noise left were the twin sounds of Loki and the serpent breathing heavily.

"Moran, is that you?" asked Loki doing his best to lift his head up and look around. He was chained in what would be considered a drawing and quartering position. It didn't leave much slack in his body for movement.

"Yes, Loki, it is. Ye ready?" asked Paddy, as he picked the locks on the shackles that trapped the god. In mere moments, Loki was unbound.

"I'm always ready to be free of my prison," said Loki, sitting up and rubbing his wrists, "and cause a little mischief. Thank you, Moran."

"You're welcome. Time's a wasting."

No more words were spoken as the two scaled up the face of the pit's wall. Once out, Paddy and Loki dressed themselves up in disguises. Getting Loki out of the pit was not the hard part. Getting him out of Asgard and back to Midgard, or Earth as most of us know it, was the real challenge. Luckily there, was nary a raven in sight. A good sign meaning Woden, also known as Odin, was still in the dark as to the jailbreak.

The next worry was getting past Heimdal. He was the guardian of the rainbow bridge Bifrost, which led from Earth to the home of the Norse gods. He was also a good friend of Paddy's. Heimdal and Loki never cared much for each other. Not without good reason. They're destined to kill each other at Ragnarok, the twilight of the gods. The Norse ones anyway.

Heimdal had eyes that put observatory telescopes to shame. Most of the traffic in and out of Asgard traveled over the rainbow bridge, and with good reason. It was the easiest route. Obviously, it wasn't an option open to them.

In years past, Paddy had worked out a deal. In exchange for Loki's favor to him, Paddy had arranged with Woden for Loki to be released one day every year. The day corresponded with our Halloween. This second annual release, which had been going on for just as many years, was unauthorized. If they were caught, there would be hell to pay.

To ensure that getting caught wouldn't be a worry, Paddy had arrived on a special motorcycle created by Vulcan. It was outwardly identical to the motorcycle that Mista—a valkyrie and Heimdal's girlfriend—rode, even down to the sidecar. The motorcycle had transworld technology. What that meant was that it could transport itself and its riders across the dimensions. Mista's cycle had only two settings, Earth and Asgard. Paddy, having a bit more cash than the average battle maiden, had the full transworld package, but today he only needed the Earth setting.

He dressed up in a leather jacket and battlehelm that was identical to Mista's, while Loki dressed as a warrior who might have fallen in battle. From a distance the gods of Asgard would think it was Mista with a hero for Valhalla. Heimdal would not be so easily fooled, which is why they took a long ride through Asgard, along where it bordered Hel's realm, the Norse Underworld.

Actually crossing over into the realm of the dead would be fraught with danger, but the border was far enough from Heimdal to be able to activate the transworld drive without much risk of discovery.

In a beautiful flash of rainbow colored lights, the motorcycle flashed out of existence in Asgard and back into existence on the busy streets of Manhattan, with no one being any the wiser. However, the sight got one alcoholic to enter a twelve-step program later that day.

Not only do gods play dice with the universe, the smart ones tend to load the dice.

-Hermes, Greco-Roman god of trickery, thieves, medicine and travelers

The general woke to darkness and fear, not to mention a cool breeze. The room around him was pitch black, darker than a coal mine in a black out. Machinery hummed all around him. The breeze became even colder and the general realized that he was naked, wearing no more than the day he came into this world. Part of him realized he might have just left it.

His last memory was that of a ray of light blinding him as he was lifted up off the ground, into the sky. Now he was tied down securely to something that felt a lot like an operating table. The best of all possible scenarios was still a terrible thing to consider. He thought all those fruitcakes and wackos were liars and nuts, but now realized too late that maybe there was some truth to the stories of alien abduction and UFO's he had been forced to investigate this past year.

It was the perfect end to the worst year of his military career. It started a year to the day after the accident. April 1st was not a good day for the general. Just three hundred and sixty six days ago he had been in charge of America's nuclear defense grid, one promotion away from being on the Joint Chiefs of Staff. After the happenings of last April 1st, he had been demoted, lost two stars and been given a worthless assignment.

It could have been worse. They could have put him at some radar tracking station in the Arctic. Investigating the crazies was almost as bad. It was his job to discredit the UFO's and aliens, to make sure that no one believed any of their stories. Most of them had been crap. The rest he made sure never became a problem. There had never been a conflict because he never believed. Now it appeared that the general himself was the victim of an alien abduction. General Richard Swanson was not the least bit happy with the situation. Of course, he had always dreamed of being tied up, but this wasn't the setting of his fantasies. The restraints never chafed in his imagination either.

"You can't do this to me. I'm a general in the United States Air Force. I demand that you release me," he shouted into the darkness.

No one answered back.

"I'm a very important man: people will know I'm gone. I will be missed. They will be coming after you," threatened the General.

Still no response from the darkness. A door opened and the light behind seemed to burn his retinas as if looking directly into the sun. Out of it walked something in a long gray coat with its collar turned up. He couldn't see the face, the head or any distinguishing marks. It carried a tray with shiny objects on it.

"Excuse me," asked the general politely. It was easier to make demands of the darkness. "Why am I here? What do you want with me?"

The figure in the long gray coat remained silent and went about its business as if it had not even heard. It dropped the tray onto a counter top near him and he heard the clang of metal instruments. Surgical instruments.

"Dear God. Please, please don't hurt me," begged the general. "I'll tell you anything you want to know. Please."

Again, the being in the gray trenchcoat said nothing. Instead it picked up some very sharp looking instruments off the tray, as if trying to choose the best one for what it planned to do. Eventually, it put it down and picked up something that looked like a tiny buzz saw and turned it on. A high-pitched whine sounded through the darkness. The being in the trenchcoat held it over the general's face and started to move it towards his head. With the buzzing instrument, it stepped into the light and the General saw its face; hairless, gray with two big eyes.

There was no longer any doubt: he had been abducted by aliens. The general fainted dead away. Hermes stepped back into the shadows and smiled, removing the alien mask from his head.

That was enough fun for now. Not as much fun as last year, but definitely jolly making. Deciding the general was secure enough for now, Hermes headed out. Time to go downstairs to the bar and greet the company.

Wherever the Tricksters went, mirth and chaos traveled in their wake, like drunken groupies.
   And I was stuck serving them drinks.

   -John Murphy, Bartender at Bulfinche's Pub

The morning was half gone and nothing yet. All the quiet was making me nervous. I was waiting for tumbleweeds to start rolling by. It was a situation too good to last long. I was bored enough to take a nap, but I wasn't that foolish. I'd probably wake up in a dress on a freighter scheduled to be at sea for three months straight and me without my razor.

The TV over the bar was still tuned to a news channel. Unless they had caused the weather, which wasn't out of the question, nothing had shown up yet.

The fax machine was spitting out another RSVP. This one was from Wisp. He owned a place of his own in Philadelphia called The Eternity Club. His duties there would keep him from arriving until the afternoon. Bubba Sue, a gremlin from the old south, also wouldn't arrive until the PM. Her prank came in second last year. Bubba Sue took apart Air Force One and reassembled it inside a shopping mall's car show. They had to take a wall off the place to get it out. There were a few others in the pile, including Eshu, who also goes by Legba, and a few of the boss' relatives who wouldn't arrive until nightfall.

Fred was nervous, waiting for his father, Pan, to show. Fred is sixty something years old, but in satyr years he is barely in his mid-teens and hasn't hit full puberty yet. That didn't stop Fred from taking a few swings at it whenever the opportunity arose. Poor guy kept missing, so he kept waiting for the end of puberty. When a satyr reaches that magic milestone, he is able to produce pheromones, wonderful chemicals that have the ability to rouse women to a sexual frenzy. At present, Fred was having trouble dating and was praying twice daily for his personal musk to kick in.

Fred lived in the shadow of his father. For such a small guy, Pan cast a huge shadow, and it enveloped Fred. Poor guy was trying to match his father's legend and, frankly, he wasn't up to it. Fred cared too much about people to pull some of the stunts his father is famous for. In terms of the ladies, he was at a disadvantage because his heart was already claimed by our waitress, Toni. Sadly, she hadn't returned Fred's affections in the romantic sense, but Toni considered Fred her best friend. In my mind, that made the rest inevitable, but Fred couldn't accept that yet. The fact that he was the oldest ever satyr virgin was a point of constant contention between him and his father.

Fred had decided to set a few pranks of his own. Frighteningly, Fred was deluding himself into thinking he was a serious contender for High Yuk. Poor guy had even bought a book to help him. Most of his ideas were pretty lame. He had trick gum that turned the chewer's teeth green and a joy buzzer hidden in his palm. A whoopee cushion was inflated and ready to go. The flower in his shirt squirted water and so on. The owner of the novelty shop saw Fred coming a mile away.

Fred was using a step ladder to put a bucket of water over the front door. The really sad part was he was very proud of himself for his creativity.

"This will get them," said Fred.

"I'm sure it will," I said, humoring him.

"Are you sure you don't want a piece of gum, Murphy?"

"I'm sure."

Fred bent the gag flower to his nose and sniffed happily. "What to smell my flower?"

"Nope. I've never been partial to the smell of plastic."

"Let me know if you change your mind," said Fred.

"I will," I said. Out of the corner of my eye, I saw the doggie door on the bar's side door, the one that led to our parking garage, swing up. Our first contestant had arrived.

"Hi, Coyote," I said.

"Hey, Murph. Hi, Fred. I'm the first to get here?" said Coyote.

"That you are."

Coyote didn't take my word for it and did a quick recon of the place, backing up his visual inspection with an olfactory one. Satisfied that no one was lying in wait, he came over to the bar and leapt up onto a stool.

"Give me a bowl of your best whiskey, Murph," he said. Looking at the breakfast spread, he added, "Got any buffalo jerky?"

"Yep. Demeter knew you were coming and make up a few pounds." He acquired a taste for the stuff when he and Paddy had hung out together in the Old West. I put the bowl and a few pieces of jerky in front of him.

"Bless her heart. Tell her thanks for me, will you," he said, lapping up some of the whiskey. With a paw he held a slice of jerky to the bar and bit off half. "Heaven."

"How's it going, Coyote?" asked Fred, holding his hand out. Coyote just looked at it.

"Not bad," he said, turning his head back to lap up some whiskey.

"Don't you want to shake hands?" asked Fred, almost hurt.

"Sorry. Can't."

"Why not?"

Coyote started in with a put down, but at a glare from me reconsidered. "No hands."

"Oh." Fred seemed to accept that.

The front door opened and in walked Sun Wukong, wearing a long brown trenchcoat, mirrored cop shades and a Bulfinche's baseball cap, although technically it's from our softball league. It had our trademark shot o' gold on it. Fred wore a similar one to cover his horns.

Fred turned with anticipation, ready to see the waterworks. Sun disappointed him by reaching up with a long hairy arm to hold the bucket in place until he closed the door. Fred actually crossed his arms over his chest and started to pout.

"Monkey King!" I said, giving him a royal welcome.

"Greetings!" he said, taking off the coat, hat and shades to hang them on the coat rack. He also did a quick check of the premises before joining Coyote and me at the bar.

"What can I get for you, your majesty?"

"Banana daiquiri, Murph," he said.

"Aren't you being a bit stereotypical?" asked Coyote.

"Like a Indian deity drinking fire water is helping stereotyping. You gonna try and sell me a blanket or invite me to play bingo next?"

"Depends how much wampum you got on you," answered Coyote.

"Enough to kick your scrawny hide back to the reservation."

"Not before you go screaming back to the jungle."

"Yeah?" asked Sun.

"Yeah. You man enough to put your money where your mouth is?" replied Coyote.

"Guys, I hate to be the one to point this out, but neither of you is a man," I said.

"That's right. Thank goodness for small favors," said Coyote.

"Amen to that," added Sun.

"Hey, I resemble that remark," I said.

"No offense, Murphy. For a human, you ain't half bad," said Sun.

"He's not half good either," said Coyote.

"At least I don't need a flea collar," I said.

"I don't think of fleas as a negative," said Coyote.

"What do you think of them as?" I asked.

"Portable snacks," he said, chomping down his jaws on his hind quarter to nibble on what I hoped was an imaginary flea.

"May I?" asked the Monkey King.

"Help yourself," replied Coyote. Sun began grooming Coyote, pulling off imaginary fleas and then eating them.

"I hope you didn't expect all of us to bring our own snacks," said a new female voice.

The door had opened again, this time to reveal Rumbles and Kyna. Fred stopped his pouting and watched hopefully. Rumbles held the bucket up with one of his red boxing gloves, so the pair walked in dry as a bone.

"Don't worry. Demeter left both your favorites. Lasagna for you, Kyna, and beef stew for Rumbles. Have to heat it in the microwave, though," I said.

Kyna's smile lit up the room and turned the tricksters into old softies. Kyna had grown up at Bulfinche's. Both Coyote and Sun had known her since she was a baby. They were like uncles to her. Kyna hugged and kissed Sun first, then Coyote. The furball gruffly pretended to barely tolerate it. She then graced me with some of the same. When she got to Fred, he held out his hand.

"What's this?" she asked, holding back a chuckle.

"A handshake," he said.

"That's no way to greet your aunt," said Kyna, scooping Fred up in her arms and planting a smacker on his forehead. Fred blushed. By way of explanation, Fred is more than thirty years older that Kyna, but as Hermes is both her father and Pan's, it makes her Fred's aunt. Fred only found this out recently, as apparently Pan just never told him that Hermes was his grandfather. Neither did Hermes. It's a weird family. Fred immediately turned his attentions toward hanging out with his grandfather more. Dionysus, our bartender, was thrilled by this turn of events, as Fred had been his shadow for a long time. Fred had wanted to learn from the god who taught his father the wild ways. Now it was Hermes turn to be the object of Fred's attentions.

Luckily, that's one of the easier family tree explanations in that group. Their family relations can get real complicated, between all the siblings and parents begetting with each other. They like to keep it in the family I guess. Rumbles ordered a vanilla egg cream with rum and Kyna wanted a fuzzy navel.

Rumbles made his rounds, even shaking hands with Fred. Fred was ecstatic until he realized that Rumbles couldn't feel the joy buzzer though his glove.

"Before you all arrived, I was just about to whip Coyote's butt at poker. Would you care to join us?" asked Sun.

"Sure," said Rumbles, taking Kyna's lasagna out of the nuker and putting in his beef stew.

"I'm in," said Kyna.

"So are we," said Paddy, as he walked in thought the side door with Loki. Loki was rubbing his chaffed wrists.

"Uncle Paddy!" shouted Kyna, running to grab the boss in a bear hug. The boss hugged back every bit as good as he got.

"Kyna, my dear. You're a sight for sore eyes. Beautiful as ever," Paddy said.

"I think you're just a little prejudiced," said Kyna, smiling.

"And why shouldn't I be? I used to change your diapers."

"And you still love me."

"Yes, but I still haven't forgiven ye entirely for that bad squash episode. Murph, give me a whiskey and the RSVP list."

"Coming up. What do you need, Loki?"

"Besides an acid free umbrella? How about a cold flagon of ale?" asked Loki. "And a side of oxen."

"You got it. Demeter cooked it for you but it's a bit too big to put in the nuker, so she left you this," I said, handing him a bucket sized sterno. "Cut off hunks and roast it over this."

"That Demeter is a living doll," said Loki, tearing off a fist-sized hunk of meat and devouring it cold. Understandable reaction. It had been five months since his last meal.

"Nice hat, boss," I said, handing out drinks. Paddy was still wearing the battlehelm.

"You like? Do I really look like a valkyrie?" asked Paddy, in a feminine voice.

"Only if said battle maiden had gotten chopped off at the knees," said Hermes, coming in from the door behind the bar that lead to our living quarters. Fred looked pensive, as if making a mental note to put a bucket over each door next year.

"Daddy," screamed Kyna, embracing Hermes, who swung her around in a circle.

"How's my baby?" asked Hermes.

"I'm fine. Thanks for asking," said Pan, walking in the front door. Fred was elated. The bucket fell but things didn't go as planned. It never turned over to spill its contents. It just dropped, bottom first into Pan's waiting hands. He lifted the bucket to his lips and took a gulp. "Water? Yuck, what sort of drudge are you serving these days? Murphy, fill this up with ouzo, will you?"

Paddy took the bucket and handed it back to Fred who promptly put it back over the door. "Use a glass, Murphy."

"But make it a big one," added Pan. The greetings started again. A few exchanges were particularly notable.

"Hey, monkey boy. I got a present for you," said Hermes, handing Sun Wukong a three- foot-long bushel of bananas.

"Thanks, baldy," said Sun. Hermes has been plagued with male pattern baldness for centuries. That's why he always wears a hat. Today, he was also wearing a Bulfinche's baseball cap. So was Pan. They were all the rage. "I have something for you too." The Monkey King handed him a bottle of Rogaine.

"Rumbles, good to see you," said Pan. "Where's Roy?" Roy G. Biv is another regular and a clown like Rumbles, only he does his clowning from a wheelchair. Roy became a paraplegic after a high wire accident. Last year he and Pan went at it. Pan somehow managed to weld Roy's wheels to his chair, effectively making Roy's main form of locomotion about as mobile as a rock. Roy retaliated a few hours later by spraying Pan's hairy legs with a mixture of seltzer and Nair. Left the satyr's legs as smooth and bald as a baby's bottom, just not as cute. Looked like a shaved goat.

"Roy decided to forgo this year's festivities," said Rumbles.

"That's a pity. He fit in well. I even had a special gift for him. Oh well, there's always next year," said Pan.

The bunch of them sat down at a table for a game of poker, with house rules. Those are simple to explain. Cheating is allowed and even encouraged, provided you don't get caught. It came about when Paddy's dear, departed wife Bulfinche, had gotten fed up with all the cheating at cards she was seeing and was threatening to ban poker. Bulfinche was no prude, but she hated dishonesty with a passion. Paddy came up with the perfect solution. Make cheating part of the game. Let me tell you, it makes for some unusual hands of poker.

Sun Wukong looked up from his hand at the TV news. Coyote used the distraction to paw two cards from under his chair.

"Murphy, turn this one up. It's mine," said Sun proudly.

The reporter droned on into a microphone. "As yet, we have no explanation why the senator and the other shuttle astronauts have not disembarked. One source claims it is because the crew have locked themselves in the space shuttle and refuse to come out."

"Why'd they lock themselves in?" I asked.

"'Cause they think a virus has turned the population into monkeys," said Sun.

"Not bad," said Loki, nodding approvingly.

"Keep the volume up, Murphy. I think mine's up next," said Coyote.

"The scene in Congress today is one where everything is hitting the proverbial fan. Some sort of virus appears to have struck hundreds of members of the House, causing the literal shut down of the Capitol building. The FBI denies any sort of germ warfare."

"And the real story is?" I asked. Coyote explained what had gone down.

"Very impressive," said Hermes. "I raise fifty."

"I'm out. Excuse me," said Coyote. "Nature calls."

Coyote walked over to the doggie door.

"The bathroom's over there," said Fred, pointing to the other side of the bar.

"I don't have you two-leggers' obsession with plumbing. There's a perfectly good fire hydrant outside. Besides, I've seen enough toilets for one day," answered Coyote, exiting through the swinging door.

After relieving himself on the fire hydrant, Coyote walked to the front door and scratched on it.

"Fred, would you let him in?" asked Paddy.

"Sure." Fred was still pouting that nobody had fallen for any of his jokes. When he opened the door, the bucket fell, turning the right way this time. All the water dumped on Fred's head and body.

Removing the bucket from his head, Fred said, "You did that on purpose!"

"Who me?" said Coyote, with mock innocence.

Before Fred could counter, the last expected member of our little group arrived. As he stepped in the two foot walkway that led to the door, he screamed like someone had stuck a red hot poker in his gut and twisted it. He then fell to his knees.

No one reacted. It was Fools' Day after all.

"Hey, Hex. Pull up a chair," said Paddy, not lifting his eyes from his cards.

Hex was a regular. Actually his full name is Mr. Hex, but we don't stand on formality here. Hex was a magí and a cursed one at that. A magí, popularly associated with either the three kings or the plural of magnus, is actually a mage who can use all forms of magic equally. Apparently it's a rare thing, happens only once each generation or so. He's supposed to be one of the most powerful people on the planet. He's got enough juice to go toe to toe with gods and demons. Problem is his curse. Using any sort of magic gives him pain. The stronger the magic, the worse the pain. Also, he can't use his magic to help someone else unless they ask him first. Apparently he ticked off another mage, who put the curse on him. The level of magic needed to break the curse could kill him. Not a good situation.

The only good point for him is that Bulfinche's is a neutral zone. No powers or curses work here without Paddy's say-so which means when he's here the pain goes away, even without drinking.

Hex looked up, dazed and confused. If this was a prank, it was great acting. He crawled in the door and looked up at me.

"Murphy, did I make it?" Hex asked.

"You made it just in time for the poker game," I said. "Want a drink?"

Hex's eyes went wide and a delirious grin took hold of his mouth. "I made it! I'm in Bulfinche's!" said Hex in a triumphant shout, getting to his feet. "Am I in time?"

"Hex, so far I don't get the joke. Give it a rest and ante up," said Paddy.

Hex looked up, registering Paddy for the first time.

"Paddy! I made it in time!" yelled Hex, running to Paddy, lifting him off his chair and kissing him.

"It's only a poker game, Hex," said Sun, sliding five aces out of his armpit and into his hand.

"Put me down!" demanded Paddy. The boss was sensitive about his height and hated being picked up like a child. Hex ignored him. "Stop kissing me! What are ye going on about?"

"You're alive!" shouted Hex, hugging the boss even tighter.

"Why wouldn't I be?" asked Paddy. Hex looked in the boss' eyes and put him down gently.

"Because I saw you die," said Hex.

In a normal bar, I would say tip the bartender and people would give me money. Here, I say tip the bartender and someone tries to knock me over.
-John Murphy, Bartender at Bulfinche's Pub

All the tricksters were paying attention now.

"This is a new one," said Loki, lifting an ace out of Sun's cards, while Hermes did the same to him.

"Better get ye eyes checked, 'cause I'm doing fine," Paddy said. "Now tell me the punch line."

"Paddy, you don't understand. I was there when we buried you next to Bulfinche," said Hex.

Paddy's face turned red. "Hex, invoking my dear wife's name in whatever sick joke you're pulling is going too far. I've had enough. Either end the joke or get out."

"Paddy, it's no joke. I'm from the future," said Hex.

"Time traveling? This is grand!" said Sun, "I wish I had thought of it."

"You will," said Coyote.

"It's not a joke, Wukong. It cost me a lot to come back here," said Hex.

"You live downtown. Subway is only a token," said Sun.

"So you're here to save Paddy's life?" asked Hermes, raising one eyebrow.

"No. Something bigger than that," said Hex, "I came back to save the world."

"Gotta give him credit for creativity," said Rumbles.

"Then go save it," said Hermes.

"I can't do it alone. I need help," said Hex.

"I've never heard you admit to something you couldn't handle, Hex," I said.

"I'm older, Murphy, and hopefully wiser," said Hex.

"More like a wiseass," said Paddy.

"I don't know," chimed in Kyna, "I think he's telling the truth."

"I believe him as well," said Loki.

"You just want to get outside. You've been chained to those rocks for too long," said Sun. Loki shrugged his shoulders.

"Fresh air and sunlight would be... nice," replied Loki.

"Oh, come on," said Pan, "You've come back in time? Right and I'm a virgin." Fred cringed at his father's choice of phrase. "What did you use? A time machine?"

"No. With some help, I managed to send my consciousness back to the me of now," said Hex.

"Hex, now you're insulting my intelligence," said Paddy, "I know ye well enough to know ye keep wards up to protect yourself against mystic attack. You're obsessive about it. How could ye get past those wards?"

"Simple. I couldn't," said Hex.

"Oh good. Now everything makes sense," said Coyote.

"I had to wait until the wards were no longer functioning, here in the bar."

"But magic doesn't work here," I pointed out.

"True, but there is a spilt second walking in the doorway where the wards were weakened. I knew what wards I had set and could bypass them before the null zone hit. Inside Bulfinche's, the wards couldn't kick in to boot me out."

"Let me guess. To help you save the world, you need us to go somewhere with you?" said Pan.

"Yes."

"I'm willing to go," said Loki, "It doesn't matter where. Like the monkey said, I don't get out much anymore."

"And once we get there, what happens to us? Acid wash dissolves our clothes? Potion to shrink us down to the size of ants? A spell changes us to frogs?" asked Pan.

"Besides, if the world is destroyed, what's the big loss?" added Coyote, sarcastically. "Not like you two-leggers have done any good redecorating the place. I liked it better au natural."

"The world isn't going to be destroyed. It's going to be changed into a nightmare land."

"Sounds like New York City to me," said Coyote.

"This isn't a joke!" shouted Hex.

"Right," said Sun, mockingly. "We believe you."

"Paddy, you have to believe me," pleaded Hex. It was out of character. Hex never pleaded, he was always in control. It was one of his more annoying traits.

"There is nothing you can do to convince us," said Pan.

Hex looked around and shook his head as if he was disgusted with the lot of us. Slowly, some of his usual demeanor and attitude seeped back into him. A grin slid over his face.

"Yes, there is. Paddy, what I am saying is true. *I give you my word. I promise you I am telling the truth*," said Hex, looking into Paddy's eyes.

"Like that's going to work," said Sun.

"Nice try," said Pan, "You must think we're idiots."

Hex was back to being himself. "You are, but that doesn't enter into this."

Pan stuck his tongue out. "Give it up."

"No," said Paddy. "I believe him."

"What!?" said Sun and Pan in unison.

"Have you lost what passes for your mind, Moran?" said Pan, "He's setting us up."

"Hex gave his word and made a promise. I've never known him to break either and he wouldn't start now for the sake of a joke. Hex is telling the truth," said Paddy.

"How can you be sure?" asked Pan.

"I just am. And if he's pulling a fast one, he's banned from the bar for life. Fair enough, Daniel James Robinson?" asked Paddy, using Hex's given name.

"That's easy enough to agree to. If we don't stop this, Bulfinche's will be destroyed in less than three years," said Hex.

"Maybe you'd better start at the beginning. What's going on?" asked Paddy.

"Later today, an army from Faerie will attack a BMDO installation in the 55th Wing," said Hex.

"Translation time, Hex. What the heck is BMDO and the 55th Wing? Something from a mutant bird?" I asked.

"Hardly. BMDO is an acronym for Ballistic Missile Defense Organization. A Wing is a loosely grouped missile cluster. The missiles are kept underground in scattered silos. The missiles in the 55th Wing are deployed in a fan 30 and 60 miles north of Little Rock, Arkansas. Most of the silos are disguised as farmland. The one Mab hits is at the nerve center of the 55th Wing and is an actual Air Force Base."

"Mab?" said Hermes, looked over at Kyna.

"So?" asked Pan.

"Using a sleep potion, they will knock out all the personnel on the base. Then they will steal a 40-foot Trident nuclear missile and take it back with them to Faerie," said Hex.

"That's not good," I said.

"That's an understatement. They screw up. They don't put everyone on the base to sleep. One quick-thinking Air Force captain gets a gas mask on and trails the army back to Faerie. He marks off the no-longer-hidden entrance and reports back to his superiors. Somehow he gets them to believe him. The military sends a patrol in to do recon and discover there's another land with a window into the heart of America. The people in this land have a nuclear weapon and the access to use it on the American heartland. Realizing they have a tactical advantage—namely that the Sidhe have no idea that the military is aware of their existence—the powers that be decide that, instead of opening up a dialogue, the best option is a first strike. The US military nukes Faerie."

"Damn," said Paddy. Faerie is the boss' homeland.

"The missiles kill thousands, but that's not the worst of it. The radiation and fallout warp and twist Faerie's natural magic until it becomes something dark and twisted."

"Nuclear Magic," I say.

"That's what we called it. Instead of killing, it mutates into a Mystacaut. Then the Nuclear Magic fallout starts leaking out onto Earth, through the doorways that lead to Faerie. England, Ireland and Scotland are hit worst, followed by Africa, Australia, parts of Europe and the United States, particularly one favorite drinking spot."

"Bulfinche's," said Paddy, softly.

"Exactly," said Hex. The lower level of our parking garage is a nexus, where there are several doorways into the otherworlds, Faerie among them.

"Magic returns to the Earth but in a twisted form. The creatures of night and nightmare become stronger, new forms of monsters are created. The Nuclear Magic taints Earth's ley lines and other sources of power, including that which sustains the gods. Many divinities are driven mad.

"Faerie is turned into a wasteland, unable to sustain life. Tens of thousands of refugees pour out through the doorways onto Earth. People blame the Faerie folk for what's happened, so they aren't exactly made to feel welcome. Many are herded into concentration camps. Paddy, you and the gang at Bulfinche's hide many of the refugees and protect them, starting a new underground railroad." Makes sense. Paddy worked on the original. "Problem is, the government doesn't like that. They also know that there is an opening to Faerie under the building. They show up outside Bulfinche's with an entire armored division of tanks and helicopters, plus a battalion of soldiers. They threaten to flatten the place unless you turn over the refugees."

"They can threaten all they like. Their tanks and explosives couldn't even break the windows," said Paddy, smugly.

"Right now, that's true, but you are forgetting something. Because you bought the place with your pot of gold, Faerie gold I might add, a core part of the magic that sustains Bulfinche's comes from Faerie. With Faerie dying and the Nuclear Magic taking its place, Bulfinche's power becomes only a fraction of what it is today."

"Meaning their weapons could destroy me home," said Paddy.

"Yes. Most of the staff and regulars are not here that day and the troops cut the phone lines and block any transmissions out. Inside the building you are hiding over five hundred refugees. It's a stand-off for a while. You're able to ward off everything they throw at you, but the explosions destroy the surrounding buildings. Defense uses too much of your power. You know it's only a matter of time before an attack gets through. You make a deal with Pluto to hide the refugees in Hades. Problem is getting them down to the bottom of the parking garage without the military catching on. You volunteer yourself to the officer in charge, Colonel Redmond, as a peace offering, with the understanding that he will let the refugees go free. You don't believe a word of it, but decide it's the only way to buy more time. You make sure everyone has a coin to pay Charon for the ferry ride and send the first wave out.

"You're right about the colonel. No sooner does he have you outside, than he starts bombing again. Outside the bar you're even weaker, but you're far from powerless. You stop the attack and get Colonel Redmond's throat in your hands. Even then you stick to your belief that all life is sacred and refuse to kill him. I wish you had. One of Redmond's subordinates puts an iron bullet in your shoulder. You can't concentrate past the pain, so when the colonel launches the next wave, some missiles get through. Almost all of the second wave do, and the third wave leveled all fifteen stories of Bulfinche's Pub, with one hundred twenty of the Gentry refugees still inside. Your gambit saves more than three hundred lives. Fifteen of the hundred twenty in the rubble survive.

"At that moment you don't care. Colonel Redmond has destroyed everything you had built, and in a blind rage you rush at him. Feeling the death throbs of Bulfinche's miles away, I body slide to the rumble, too late to be any good. I get there just in time to see him put six iron bullets into your head. I lose it and attack him. Unfortunately for me, nobody has asked for my help, so using magic against him isn't an option. I try to beat Redmond's face to a bloody pulp. Five soldiers pull me off before I can do any real damage. They have a dark mage who opens a wormhole for her and Redmond to escape through.

"Redmond could run, but he couldn't hide forever. Someone asked me to avenge you Paddy, freeing me up to use magic."

"Who asked?" asked Coyote.

"Actually, Coyote, it was you," Hex replied.

"I trust you succeeded that time," said Coyote.

"You better believe it. I found Redmond again and that time I killed the bastard."

"Good," said Coyote, stopping to groom his leg with his tongue. Paddy opened his mouth to give his usual speech about all life being scared, but thought better of it.

"Whose army stole the first nuke?" asked Hermes.

"Mab."

"Mom?" said Kyna. This is one of those family tree things again. In the mid-sixties Mab—who was a Queen of one of the many kingdoms of Faerie—had been dethroned and exiled. She sought refuge and asylum with Paddy. Mab and Hermes fell in love or, at the very least, lust. The end result was Kyna.

When the opportunity came to reclaim her kingdom, Mab spilt, leaving Kyna and Hermes behind. In all fairness, she did ask Hermes to fight by her side, but he declined, not wanting to live the life of a guerilla, no disrespect to Sun's relations. Kyna was raised by Hermes with the aid of the rest of the crew here at Bulfinche's.

"Yep. She plans to threaten Titania and Oberon with it, in an effort to expand her newly reclaimed kingdom," said Hex.

"Oh joy," said Coyote. "Damn two-leggers and things that go boom."

"So we have to stop her," said Kyna.

"Mab's no dummy. We are going to have to be careful," said Hermes.

"It's not like Mab would hurt her own daughter," I said. My tenure as bartender stated long after Mab left. I knew her by reputation only. Hermes and Kyna gave each other a sad look. Paddy suddenly found the tops of his shoes to be very interesting. Nobody else spoke up. "Would she?"

"Murph," said Hermes, "soon after Mab left me to reclaim her kingdom, she made a deal with a neighboring kingdom for troops. I don't have time to go into the details, but suffice it to say they required a hostage as a sign of good faith. Mab kidnapped a four-year-old Kyna and used her own daughter as the hostage. She set up no safeguards to make sure Kyna would not be hurt."

"Was she?" I asked.

"Almost," said Kyna, a sad gleam in her eye.

"Is Mab evil?" I asked.

"Mab is dangerous. She does what she thinks is best for her, without regard for consequences," said Paddy.

"She's a politician," said Coyote. "What do you expect?"

Hex plopped down in a chair and put his feet up on the table. "We don't have a lot of time. We have to get to Arkansas."

"We're going to need some help. I'll call in some friends," said Paddy, whipping out his flip-top cellular phone. "Murphy, grab a phone and help me out."

"You got it, boss," I said. Hex had a cell phone and made some calls of his own.

Hermes moved toward the door behind the bar. "I have a little something upstairs that may help us out." He left up the stairs.

Normally at Bulfinche's Pub, when Paddy calls in his friends, people and gods came running. Today we were having a problem of monumental proportions. Almost nobody was taking our phone calls. I could hear Paddy yelling at Hercules over the phone.

"Get yer muscle-bound butt back here now!" yelled Paddy. "This is an emergency."

The headset volume was high enough that I could hear our bouncer's reply.

"Sorry, Paddy. There's nothing you can say to get me anywhere near that place today. I'm no dummy. What's the scam?"

"No scam," said Paddy. "I'm serious."

"Of course you are, boss. I'm going to go now."

"Hercules, don't hang up..."

"Why? I'm not staying on long enough to let you trace this call. See you in two days," said Hercules. The click resonated in the silent receiver.

Everybody who was home hung up as soon as they heard my voice. Most knew where I was and nobody wanted to be a victim of any of the tricksters. Most of my calls went something like this.

"Hello?" said Lucas Wilson. Lucas was a blood junkie, a vampyre. He had successfully resisted his cravings and sworn off human blood, surviving on that of animals. Lucas can survive out in sunlight for brief periods with a 199 sunscreen lotion. He is also a computer programmer and hacker supreme. He had helped install several government systems and had helped us take control of a Star Wars satellite once. Sadly, the orbital lasers would be useless to us in this scenario, but Lucas' skills could still be helpful.

"Lucas, this is Murphy," I said.

"I thought you were stuck at the bar today," Lucas said.

"I am."

"Do you need an ambulance?"

"No," I said.

"Good. Bye." Lucas hung up.

Hex was having the same trouble with his friends and associates.

"Looks like you guys have pulled so many pranks over the years that on Fools' Day, no one wants any part of you," I said.

"We'll have to go it alone," said Hex.

"The nine of us against an army? Them's great odds," said Pan sarcastically.

"We can do this," said Sun. "We can outsmart anybody."

"That's right. Nobody's ever made a monkey out of you," said Coyote.

"This can be done," said Loki, coming back to life. Grabbing a pen, he began writing on the back of a placemat. "We just need plans of the base and records of personnel. We already know several things. We know what they are planning. The Sidhe are vulnerable to iron. We can assume that Shapelings have infiltrated the base. If we use all that right, we can take them out."

"We can do it without killing anyone," said Paddy.

"Moran, they are at war. They won't be playing games. Neither should we," said Loki.

"Think of it as a challenge then," Paddy said with a mischievous wink.

"That goes for you too, Hex."

"I agree with Loki, Paddy. You haven't seen what is going to happen. I have. Countless more lives will be lost," said Hex.

"We can do this without bloodshed," said Paddy. "I want your word on that Daniel James."

"I can't give it. I will try my best," said Hex.

Paddy nodded. "Now we just have to figure out a way to get intelligence on the base."

"I may have that one covered," said Hermes, walking back into the bar with a naked man tossed over his shoulder.

"What's this?" asked Paddy.

"General Richard Swanson," said Hermes.

"The general from your prank last year?" asked Sun.

"The same. He got demoted to UFO patrol."

"That's fine and good, but what is he doing in the upstairs of my bar?" asked Paddy.

"He thinks he's been abducted by a UFO," said Hermes, putting Swanson on a table, then tying his limbs to the table legs.

"That explains everything. Thanks so much," said Paddy. "Do you have to do that here?"

"Yes. It's crucial," said Hermes, smiling.

"So we can get the base layout, security clearances and such from him," said Kyna.

"Exactly, daughter dear. Up until last year, he was in charge of it all."

"Why would he betray his country just because you ask him?" asked Pan.

"It wouldn't be the first time this man betrayed his country. Watch and learn," said Hermes, putting on the rubber Grey alien mask. "Loki, you want in on this?"

"Sure. Moran?" asked Loki. Among Loki's powers is the ability to shape shift. Magic, curses and the like don't work inside the bar without Paddy's say-so; therefore, Loki needed permission.

Paddy shrugged his shoulders and nodded. "Sure."

Loki's features liquefied and molded, all the while glowing. It was all over in a second and the end result was a seven foot tall "alien" with grey skin, a big head and large eyes. Loki had even morphed himself some long flowing silver robes.

Rumbles moved to my side. As used as we are to the notion that, in Bulfinche's, gods drink among us, it can be a little frightening to see their powers at work. "We have a kidnapped US Air Force general hogtied naked to a table and nobody has even thought to lock the door." Actually, the door is almost never locked. Boss says we never know when somebody might need help, but that's beside the point. "I can't wait to see what happens next."

The pugilistic clown didn't have to wait long. Hermes waved something under Swanson's nose and the general slowly inched his way back toward consciousness.

"Murphy, come here and hold this," said Hermes, handing me a very powerful flashlight. "Keep it shining in his eyes."

"You got it," I said, putting in an extra interpretation of my own.

"Murphy, stop the finger shadows," said Hermes.

"Then give me back my wallet," I said. I hadn't even checked to see if it was missing, but I knew Hermes. He handed it back without a word.

Swanson's eyes opened, his pupils shrinking against the light. He quickly shut his eyes and twisted his head away in an attempt to reclaim darkness. From what Hermes told us last year, darkness had already claimed the general long ago. While he was a colonel in Vietnam, he showed initiative. That in and of itself was no crime, but when initiative involved the wholesale slaughtering of a village of unarmed civilians, including women and children, his offense becomes clear. Then to keep his deeds hidden, he sent the only two men who could prove his guilt on a suicide mission.

Unluckily for Swanson, one survived his plane crash and crossed over to Cambodia, where he married and had kids. A reporter in that village on an unrelated story spoke to the former pilot and got the full story, but his paper wouldn't print it unless the reporter revealed the man's name and location. The reporter knew that if that happened, Swanson would arrange for the pilot to die again. The pilot was happy and had a family so the reporter decided to leave well enough alone.

Knowing that Swanson was going unpunished was weighing heavily on the reporter's sense of justice. A year and a bit ago, he unloaded the story to us over a few glasses of beer. Hermes told him he would that care of it.

Hermes wiped out Swanson's personal fortune, leaving him penniless, with only his military pay. He humiliated him professionally with the alien invasion scam at NORAD in hopes that he would be booted out. Swanson had too many friends in high places, so he just got demoted. Meanwhile, Hermes has been slowly making Swanson's life a living hell, culminating in what was happening here today.

"Awaken, Dick Swanson," commanded Hermes.

"Leave me alone. Please," begged Swanson, trying to shut out the light I was shining in his eyes.

"Open your eyes and look at me when I speak to you," ordered Hermes. Swanson obeyed and was greeted with the sight of two aliens.

"Aaah!" screamed Swanson.

"Be silent, Earthling," said Hermes. "You have information we need."

"I won't tell you anything."

"Oh yes, you will. We have ways of making you talk," promised Hermes.

"How?" asked Swanson but he was answered with silence. "How?" he said louder but still no one replied. "Not an anal probe? It's not an anal probe, is it?"

The alien morphed Loki looked at the alien disguised Hermes. Hermes nodded. Loki put his alien hand in front of Swanson's face and I focused the light on it. The general's eye's fixated on the hand.

"Anal probe?" Loki asked. He was not as up on current culture as he might like and was confused as to the significance but was able to run with it. "Not yet. We have other ways to try first."

"Like what?"

In response, Loki's hand transformed in an instant to fingers with six inch claws which he slowly raked up and down the general's bare torso. Swanson's eyes closed in fearful anticipation, but the claws only scratched hard enough to raise lines on the skin, not break it.

"I have been anxious to examine a human from the inside. You would make an excellent subject," bluffed Loki. At least I hoped he was buffing. He was a god of evil years ago, but he had theoretically reformed. Paddy always tries to give the benefit of the doubt and he's always been right as far as I know, but the odds demand that he has to be wrong sometime. "I think I will begin with the digestive track, then remove the external reproductive organs."

The general was no dummy and was rather attached to his family jewels. Few men, especially the tied up, naked kind, could stand up to that type of threat. I admit it was a tad harsh, but it got results.

"I'll tell you anything you want! Just don't hurt me," begged Swanson.

Coyote jumped up on the side of the table and stood over the general's face, my flashlight putting a halo behind his head. "We need to know everything you do about the command center for the 55th Wing."

"That's a missile base. You're going after our nukes!" said Swanson, turning to look Coyote right in the snout. "Oh my God! A talking mutt!"

"I'm not a mutt," said Coyote, annoyed. "I have a pedigree."

"Please don't put my brain in a dog. Please!" pleaded Swanson, tears streaming down his face.

"Don't worry. You have to have a brain to qualify for our transplant program," said Sun, leaning over so Swanson could get a good look at his face.

"A talking monkey! What kind of godless experiments are you doing up here?"

"Godless? I resemble that remark," said Sun, stealing my line.

"Enough!" shouted Loki. "Give us the information or feel our wrath."

Swanson told us everything. Layout, passwords, access codes, where his wife hid her jewelry and anything else we asked.

"I've told you everything I know. What are you going to do to me?" asked Swanson. He got no answer. "Tell me. Please? You're not going to give me an anal probe are you?"

Kyna chimed in. "Why, yes we are." She reached out and pinched the general's flabby butt. Swanson let out a shriek and passed out.

I always pay my debts.
        -Padriac Moran, Leprechaun, Owner of Bulfinche's Pub

Battle plans were made. We were all going to Arkansas, except Fred. He was staying behind in hopes that he could convince anyone who stopped by to help out. He was also going to keep working the phones. He was the most harmless of the bunch, and therefore had the best chance of convincing someone that we were on the level.

Hex got dispensation from Paddy to use magic to adjust his wards so they wouldn't kick the future him out as soon as he stepped outside of the bar.

Paddy headed down into the lower level to get our transportation, what was originally a 1930 V-8 Cadillac. It had since been modified by Vulcan. It had a transworld drive and could fly. Paddy called it "Baby" and wouldn't let anyone else drive it.

The lot of us moved into the parking garage. Hermes and I were the last ones out of the bar.

"Hermes, what about him?" I asked, pointing to Swanson.

Hermes went back and blindfolded the general. "Leave him. We'll take care of him later." Paddy drove up the ramp in the Caddy. He leaned out the window. "Hermes, you and Kyna can get there faster than the rest of us on your own. Get going."

"We're gone," said Kyna. The pair ran out of the garage and leapt into the skies, holding hands. Under her own power, Kyna could probably make the flight from New York to Arkansas in thirty minutes. Hermes could do it in less than three seconds. By holding his daughter's hand, he could take her along at his speed.

"Paddy, I can bodyslide there just as fast," said Hex.

"No. We need you with us. The pair of them can take care of anything until we get there," said Paddy. "Plus, Mab might be able to sense the bodyslide or any other magical means of teleportation. Best not to give her any advance warning."

"Shotgun!" yelled Sun as he got in the passenger seat, to the grumbles of Coyote.

One by one we climbed in the car. I was in the back seat with Rumbles to my right, Hex and Pan to my left. Coyote was in the front between Paddy and Sun. Loki alone stood on the blacktop.

"C'mon, Loki. We haven't got all day," said Paddy.

"Moran, I have been thinking. Once I leave the pub, Heimdal may be able to sense that I am gone. If he does, he will tell Woden, who will not be happy. It may screw up your deal with him," said Loki. Paddy had a deal to cater Ragnarok in exchange for a very valuable payment.

"A deal I wouldn't even have if it wasn't for you," countered Paddy. "Odds are Heimdal won't notice."

"I might use this opportunity to escape," said Loki. I was actually puzzled about that myself. He spends all Halloween trying to escape, but on Fools' Day he has never even made an attempt. Paddy says it is a point of honor. The boss risks a lot to break out Loki for the day, so Loki repays the favor by returning to his imprisonment willingly.

"Ye might. Will you?"

"I... I don't know," said Loki.

"I appreciate your honesty. We don't have much time. Ye need to decide," said Paddy.

"Moran, why do you do this for me? I have never done a decent thing in my life."

"Yes, ye have."

"I only told you because you were kind enough to turn aside the acid for a few moments."

"That's not what ye said at the time. Ye were moved by my love for my wife and you didn't want another to lose his wife, as you had."

"I was delirious with pain."

"No, ye weren't. Because of ye help, I got the means to save Bulfinche."

"But you didn't."

"Only because I arrived too late. It wasn't your fault. Had I made it back thirty minutes sooner, what you did for me would have saved me wife's life. For that, I will forever owe you," said Paddy.

"Even if I make a break for it?" asked Loki.

"Even then." Paddy tossed Loki a set of keys. "These are the keys to the cycle. Ye can use it to join us or to get a jump on Woden. With the transworld drive, even Woden would have trouble catching up to ye. The choice is yours."

"I make bad choices," said Loki.

"I trust you to make the right one," said the boss.

"You shouldn't," said Loki. "I don't want to go back."

Paddy smiled. "See you in Arkansas." Loki didn't reply. His attention was focused on the set of keys in his hand. We pulled out into New York traffic and at the first light, took to the skies. No one noticed us flying among the skyscrapers, which in and of itself says a lot about New York. Coyote was sitting on Sun's lap and sticking his head out the window, letting his tongue hang out.

"You were criticizing me about stereotypical behavior?" said Sun.

"Have you ever tried it?" asked Coyote.

"Well, no," said Sun.

"Try it first, then criticize," suggested Coyote. The Monkey King shrugged his shoulders and put his head out the window.

"Monkey see, monkey do," said Hex. The Monkey King ignored him.

"Hey, you're right. This is great," said Sun, who kept his head out, laughing all the while.

Rumbles looked at the pair in the front seat and raised his eyebrows. Shrugging his shoulders, he rolled his window down and gave it a try himself.

"Cool," said Rumbles.

"Isn't it?" said Sun.

Pan looked at the three other tricksters and at his window.

"What the heck," Pan said, and joined the crowd. "I like it."

Hex was on my left, between me and Pan. "Let me try," Hex said. Pan made room. Hex must have liked it because he didn't pull his face back in.

"Man see, man do," mocked Sun. There wasn't enough room for me to stick my head out Rumbles' window so I talked to Paddy instead.

"Paddy, I agree with Loki. You shouldn't trust him," I said.

"By that reasoning, I should never have taken ye in," said Paddy, with a smile. He was right. We met when I captured him in an attempt to steal his pot of gold. At the last minute, I decided to do the right thing. Of course, at the time I didn't know that he had bought the bar with it, but that was beside the point. Paddy and the gang helped bail me out of some trouble I was having with loan sharks, and gave me a job to boot.

"I hadn't done a fraction of what Loki's done," I countered.

"Which means he needs a chance for redemption even more than ye did."

"It could cause a war with Woden," I said.

"It could. I'll admit it is a gamble, but ye can't win unless you place the bet," Paddy said, as we soared over Jersey. The stench caused everyone to pull their heads inside and roll the windows up. "So do the rest of you agree with Murphy?"

"Paddy, if it was anyone else but you, I would," said Coyote. "Bulfinche had the gift for bringing out the best in people by believing in them. Somewhere along the line, you picked up the same gift. If you were betting on someone, I know enough not to bet against you."

Everyone else agreed with Coyote.

"I still say it's too risky," I said.

"Care to put your money where your mouth is?" asked Paddy.

"You realize the odds are in my favor?"

"How much, Murph?"

"Fifty bucks," I said.

"Bet," said Paddy, reaching behind to shake my hand.

"I want some of this action, Murphy. Cover my fifty?" asked Coyote.

"No problem."

"I want a piece of this," said Rumbles.

"Me too," said Sun.

"Me three," said Pan.

"Me four," said Hex.

I did the math. Only three hundred. I could cover that if I lost. If I won, I could beef up my CD and book collection. "You're all covered."

We were in the better smelling part of Jersey now. Windows began opening again. Something about the field around the car allowed the air to flow freely and the pressure to remain constant. Some sort of quantum magic, the same stuff the chariots of the gods have used since ancient times.

"Fasten your seatbelts. I'm hitting the overdrive," said Paddy. Instead of listening, everyone put their heads back out the windows. I squeezed next to Rumbles.

"Move over," I said, joining the crowd.

Betting should be fun. Remember a few things: Never bet more than you can afford to lose. The longshot is sometimes the best bet. Always bet on people, not against. That way you don't lose twice. Oh yeah, anytime ye can put the fix in, do it.

-Padriac Moran, Leprechaun, Owner of Bulfinche's Pub

We landed on a dirt road about a mile outside the command center. We stayed below radar for the entire trip, so I assumed our landing went unnoticed. I was wrong. Leaning against a tree, waiting for us, was Loki. The cycle was next to him.

"What took you so long?" said Loki, smiling.

"Alright! Pay up, Murph," said Rumbles.

"I'll cover all bets once we get back to the bar," I grumbled.

"Bets?" asked Loki, raising both eyebrows.

Coyote answered, "About whether or not you'd be here..."

"Before we were," finished Paddy. Loki nodded.

"Thanks for the loan of the wheels, Moran," said Loki, tossing Paddy the keys. Paddy threw them back.

"Hold onto them. You're going to have to drive it back," said Paddy. If Loki beamed any more, he wouldn't need the headlight on the cycle.

It was time to get down to tactics.

What I didn't know about tactics could fill a library. What Loki knew could provide that library with more books than its shelves could hold. In short, during the planning stage, Loki was in charge. Despite my other misgivings about him, Loki was a master tactician's master and everyone else deferred to his expertise. Even Sun Wukong.

To me, it seemed to make more sense to try to sneak in, but everyone explained to me that it would be the worst move to make. Military bases are always expecting people to sneak in and make preparations for such an eventuality. The way to do it without getting caught would be to waltz in the front gate. Personally, I'm more of a tango man myself, but I wasn't leading on this one. Of course, to be able to file in the front successfully, we had to make a few changes and modifications. Hermes and Kyna had picked up a few things to help us out with that part of the plan. The pair drove out of the sky and dropped uniforms on the rest of us. Apparently, they couldn't find any uniforms that would hide Coyote's or Sun's obvious physical differences, and it would take to long for Rumbles to remove his make-up. An explanation for them had already been established. Paddy, Pan, Kyna and I changed into the uniforms. Hermes, Loki and Hex didn't.

"I'll make my own way in," said Hex, "Besides, we'll need somebody doing a recon on the inside."

"Go ahead," said Paddy, "But be careful."

"I always am."

Hex took a couple steps and, as near as I could tell, disappeared entirely. No one but me seemed to even be impressed. Hermes was going to be staying outside the base, keeping an eye out for Mab and her army. I was curious as to why Hermes and his daughter hadn't brought anything for Loki to wear.

"Loki, you don't need a uniform?" I asked.

"What, you weren't paying attention for that part of the briefing?" asked Loki sarcastically.

"I had to go to the bathroom," I said. It had taken longer than usual by about ten minutes. I had to check the rest room for booby traps.

"I don't need a uniform. I'll just make my own."

Loki morphed before my eyes. Actually, in all fairness, my eyes had never morphed and probably never would. Now Loki had taken on the form of General Swanson, who was still safely tied up back at the bar. His new shape came complete with the general's uniform.

"All right troops, fall in," said Loki, sounding exactly like the general. Even his own mother would have been fooled. Loki's or the general's.

The uniforms had determined our assumed rank. Paddy was a colonel, Kyna was a major, Pan was a lieutenant, while I was a lowly airman. As usual, Hermes had disappeared so quickly he seemed to vanish.

Loki moved behind a grove of trees where he removed some camouflage netting. Hermes, putting his larceny skills to good use, had acquired for us the traditional, nondescript, dark sedan and an olive green army jeep. He even attached tiny American flags to the front of the sedan. That or the previous owners had. "General" Loki gave us our driving orders. The jeep was to lead the convoy, driven by Pan and carrying Rumbles, Sun and Coyote. Because of my low rank, I was to drive the sedan with General Loki, Paddy and Kyna in the back.

Our caravan got under way, driving over hill and dale until we hit the main road. We followed it to the front gate of the base. It had the traditional guard house complete with the little, liftable lever arm that allowed people in and out. There were two airmen on sentry duty, whose faces grew giant smirks when they saw the passengers in the open jeep. Both airmen walked out of the guard house, flanking either side of the jeep.

"What do we have here? The circus in town?" asked the airman on the driver's side. The tag on the left side of his shirt read "D. Smithers". The other one read "F. Daniels". "Afraid I didn't see anything on the admittance list about a circus. Step out of the jeep, please, sir."

Pan did as he was instructed. Pan stood about five-foot-two, and barely came up to the airman's shoulders.

"A little short to be in the Air Force, aren't you?" asked Smithers.

"Maybe he's wearing his daddy's uniform," suggested Daniels.

"I'm tall enough to whip your ass. And the way your mama put out, for all you know I am your daddy. Keep this up, and I'll have you digging latrines," said Pan indignantly. His reaction was typical of an officer, so their jocularity went down a notch.

"We have indoor plumbing on this base, sir."

"Doesn't matter to me. You'll just have to dig me a personal latrine for every time I have to take a dump," promised Pan.

"I highly doubt that," said Smithers.

"You realize you are addressing a superior officer?" questioned Pan.

"Sir, as you should know, at a BMDO guard post, the sentries have the ultimate authority. Rank means nothing to me," said the airman.

Loki, disguised as the General, had walked stealthily up behind Smithers and asked, "Is that so, Airman?"

"Yes, it is..." said the airman, turning around to see who had walked up behind him. He stopped in mid-sentence when he saw the rank. He fumbled a salute. "Yes, sir, General. I mean, no, sir, General. I mean..."

"At ease, Airman. What appears to be the problem?"

"General, I was not informed that you and your entourage would be visiting the base today, sir," said Smithers, weakly.

"That's because it is a surprise inspection and if you knew about it, there would hardly be a surprise, now would there?" spat Loki.

"No, sir."

"This airman was also making disparaging remarks about my height," said Pan, enjoying making Smithers sweat.

I was secretly grateful that Paddy wasn't the one chosen to drive the lead jeep. The boss is even shorter than Pan and more than a wee bit sensitive about his height. He would have been more likely to lose his cool.

"Is that so, Airman?" spat Loki.

"General, Air Force regulations state that..."

"So you think that the lieutenant's height is amusing, do you airman?"

"No, sir."

"The lieutenant here lost most of both legs below the knees in a crash in Desert Storm. His lower legs have been replaced by prosthetics. Lieutenant, would you be so kind as to remove one of your boots for the airman," said Loki.

"Certainly, General," said Pan, removing a boot. Like all satyrs, he had hooves instead of feet. Hard hooves. Loki tapped the hoof with his knuckle and it made a sound like it was knocking against fiberglass. Pan put the boot back on. Smithers had begun to feel some shame.

"This man bled for this country. Unlike some namby-pambys, he didn't let his injuries stop him from continuing to serve his country. You should show some respect. I think you owe the lieutenant an apology. *Now*, Airman."

At the tone of Loki's voice, the airman snapped to attention.

"I offer my sincerest apologies, Lieutenant," said Smithers, saluting Pan.

"No harm done," said Pan, returning the salute.

"Now, please allow myself and my inspection team onto the base," said Loki.

"Sir, I can't let him in," Smithers said pointing to Rumbles.

"Why? Because he's black? I thought we got beyond that sort of thing, even here in the South," said Loki.

The airman looked stunned at the general's response.

"No, General, because he's a clown."

"So you have a problem with the USO, Airman? I suppose you have a problem with the monkey and the talking dog, too?" said Loki.

"Talking dog, sir?" asked Smithers, very confused.

"Did I say talking dog? Damn, this is classified, Airman. Speak a word and you'll be guarding an air base in the arctic for the next twenty years. You understand me, Airman?"

"Yes, General."

"Now allow my inspection team inside the base, then lock this place down. You are not going to allow anybody else on or off the base without my personal permission. That doesn't mean your base commander, that doesn't mean any of my aids. That means my personal okay. Any deviations from these orders and I will have you up on court martial charges. Do you understand, Airman?"

"Yes, General, but may I ask why?"

"No, you may not. It's a matter of national security. That's all you need to know."

"But, I'm supposed to report directly to my base commander, the colonel."

"See these stars? That means I outrank your colonel. You'll do as I say. Will it make you feel better that as soon as you allow us in, we will wait by the guard house until you call your base commander. Then it will be his problem, not yours. Do it, airman."

"Yes, General."

Stand by your friends. Stand behind your enemies. That way if anybody is going to get pushed into oncoming traffic, it won't be you.
      -Padriac Moran, Leprechaun, Owner of Bulfinche's Pub

We pulled the jeep and the sedan onto the base. We got out and stood waiting for the base commander to arrive. It didn't take long before he and his driver came to a screeching halt in their own Jeep.

"Here comes Colonel Redmond now, General," said one of the sentries.

At the mention of the Colonel's name, Paddy stiffened and his jaw clenched. Coyote growled and the overall mood of the group changed to one of outright hostility. By whatever dumb or dark luck, this was the colonel who would kill Paddy, just a few years in the future.

Colonel Redmond jumped out of the jeep and saluted the general. Loki didn't return the salute immediately, choosing instead to make the colonel stand there with his hand in front of his head. Air Force regulations dictate that when saluting a higher ranking officer, the lower ranking officer must hold the salute until it is returned or until the person they are saluting is out of visual range. Loki was playing his part to a tee. He looked the colonel up and down, then walked in a circle around Redmond, inspecting him. The colonel began to sweat and his right arm trembled. I guess Redmond hadn't had to salute anyone in quite awhile. Finally, Loki returned to the spot in front of the base commander and returned the salute.

"Hello, general, I had no idea you were coming. This is a surprise," said the colonel.

"Of course it is. Just like I told your sentries, what would good would a surprise inspection be without the surprise part?" said Loki.

"Inspection, sir?"

"You heard me," said Loki. The sentries were standing off to the side at full attention, in the same saluting position and in an extreme state of nervousness. The colonel wasn't as kind to them as Loki had been to him. Redmond ignored them entirely. "Why don't we retire to your office so we can discuss matters in a less public place."

"Of course, General, sir. Quite an interesting entourage you have with you, General," said Colonel Redmond, not bothering to hide the sarcasm that was creeping into his voice.

"Who is on my inspection team is not your concern. Following my orders is. I suggest you double time it to your office, or should I ream you out here in full view of your men?"

"No, General."

"Then move your ass," barked Loki. Redmond moved as fast as he could back to his jeep without appearing to be actually running. As an afterthought, Loki added to the sentries, "At ease gentlemen."

Not tonight. I have a headache.
-Hex, cursed magi

Hex walked the base with the presence of a shadow. He preferred moving in darkness, but could make do in daylight. It wasn't that he was invisible; he wasn't. Hex was making use of a distraction spell, which caused anyone who looked directly at him to turn away to look at something else. The exertion of using magic gave him a mild headache because of his curse, but pain was nothing new to Hex. He once told me the only time he wasn't in pain was when he was in Bulfinche's Pub. Besides, if his time quest gambit worked, he would be preventing much more pain from ever existing, so it was worth the personal agony.

Hex's recon goal was to locate any infiltration of Mab's army among the base personnel. Shapelings, or changelings, would be almost impossible to detect. Sun had the ability to see through dinguses and Paddy or Coyote might be able to smell Shapelings, but there were no guarantees. As a Magi, Hex had the ability to read umbras or auras, something all living things have. A plant's is different than an animal's, a person's is different than a god's. A Shapeling's would be visibly distinct from that of normal military personnel.

The problem was locating the Shapelings. Hex would be able to pick one out of a lineup, but the 55th Wing had more than five thousand personnel, two thousand of whom were on this base. We didn't have the kind of time that would let Hex check each person individually, and faking a fire drill or the like to get two thousand people outside would be counterproductive.

If bringing the ants out of the hill wasn't an option, Hex would go inside the hill. Reason dictated the Shapelings would need to be in a position to learn how to operate and maintain a Trident.

Hex began by checking the three underground silos that were on the base. In keeping with fate's rules regarding a search, he didn't hit paydirt until silo number three.

All the silos had two captains, sitting in front of identical control panels about twelve feet apart. In the center of a mass of computerized dials were turn-key switches. The keys were stored in a safe halfway between. The Trident would only be sent skyward on its mission of radioactive death if both captains turned their keys simultaneously. The turn-keys were too far apart for one person to do it alone. Each captain was a built-in failsafe for the other.

A typical twelve-hour shift of monitor duty was quite dull. A time to daydream or do some leisure reading. The two captains in the third silo were reading through manuals with the energy of a pair of zealots. As soon as he walked in, Hex knew they were Shapelings. Among his talents, besides the ability to play Irish drinking songs on his armpits, was the ability to do what he called a reading. It didn't involve manuals or paperbacks. Hex gets information mystically, sometimes just by walking into a room.

The real captains, a man and a woman, were asleep on a flower-filled hillside in Faerie. They had chased a gaggle of pixies in and had sat down to rest for a moment and had been rendered unconscious by the same potion Mab planned to use on the rest of the base. In their framework, the pair had only been asleep about 30 hours, but in real-world time, the Shapelings had replaced the officers over a month ago. Faerie is like that. Depending on how you enter and leave, you can live a lifetime in an instant or in an instant lose a lifetime.

The Shapelings had taken over every aspect of the mortal lives they had hijacked, down to conjugal duties with the officers' spouses. The Shapelings even made a few improvements to the forms they mimicked. The man's wife was amazed at his sudden increase in both length and girth. He seemed to double almost overnight. He also went from Mr. Quickie to Joe Endurance, treating her to eight- and ten-hour marathon pleasure sessions. Meanwhile, the woman's husband was in a month-long wet dream, as his rather averagely proportioned wife took on a figure that put any centerfold to shame. He spent the first two nights looking for surgical augmentation scars, then realized she never had a chance to have the procedure. By the middle of the third insatiable night, he stopped caring and found out he could get by on only two hours of sleep quite happily.

As the pair worked alone, there wasn't anyone else on the base who noticed any change, so the switch had worked. At least until Hex.

Walking up to the man poring over the manual, Hex whispered, "I read that one. The butler did it."

The male Shapeling looked up and started to open his mouth, but Hex was quicker on the draw.

"*Freeze,*" he intoned. The he-Shapeling was immobilized. "Shush now. My work here isn't done yet."

The distraction spell was still active, so the female Shapeling was oblivious to the third party in the silo. She wouldn't notice Hex until he made first contact.

"So, do you think the missile is really a phallic symbol and if so, what does that say about its destructive power?" Hex asked.

"What?" asked the she-Shapeling.

"I'm sorry. Too forward for the first date? I probably should have started with something like 'come here often?'"

The she-Shapeling stood and lunged for Hex's throat, but he moved aside too swiftly.

"This area is restricted to Air Force personnel. You will have to leave," she said, still unsure of how the man's throat had escaped her grasp.

"Then I guess you should join me, shouldn't you?" asked Hex with a winning smile.

"What are you talking about?" she demanded. Hex pushed her back into her seat.

"*Paralyzed*," he intoned. The she-Shapling was as frozen as her partner. The curse caused Hex's muscles to stiffen up. He had to take what he dished out, at a lesser intensity. Not fun.

The office chairs they sat on had wheels. Hex grabbed the she-Shapling's chair and pushed it fast, sprinting all out toward the wall. He stopped a millimeter short of smashing her face in. Moving her chair to the center of the silo, he turned his attention to the male. Taking hold of his chair, Hex ran around the room, spinning him like a top. The chair ended up parked next to the other one. "Now that I have your undivided attention, let me introduce myself. I am Mr. Hex."

The Shapelings' pupils went wide and the pair began to sweat.

"You've heard of me, I see. I have spent some time in Faerie, after all. Years by your reckoning, but only about five hours out of my childhood. But why bore you with details of my life? I'm sure it could never match the stories you've heard. Now, on to business. You're here to take a Trident. I'm here to stop you. Who do you think is going to win?"

The Shapelings were unable to speak because of Hex's spells.

"What? Nothing to say? That's just not neighborly. Of course, maybe you just hate to admit you're about to lose. I can understand that. Never been there myself, but I can understand it."

In the silo, there were four large steel lockers, each belonging to one of the captains on the watch duty rooster. They were large enough to hide a body or, in this case, two. Shapelings have less painful reactions to iron that other Gentry. Cold iron was like kryptonite to many of the Gentry, but not all. Some, like Leprechauns and Shapelings, aren't bothered by iron but still can be trapped in it. In this case, iron bars do a prison make. The steel contained enough iron to imprison the Shapelings.

Hex dumped the he-Shapling in the first locker.

"Nobody will find you until after this shift is done. By then, this will be over, one way or the other." Hex started to close the locker door and the he-Shapling's pupils dilated again. "Don't worry, I punched air holes in it. Hope you aren't claustrophobic."

Hex shut the lid and turned his rambling attentions to the she-Shapeling.

"I guess this is good night. I hope you'll understand if I don't kiss you good night on the first date. I just don't want a reputation as that kind of guy. I mean, if you get the milk for free, you won't buy the cow, and then I won't have my steaks. I love steak, especially barbequed. Let me tuck you in. Sweet dreams."

The door closed with the clang of a steel coffin. To quiet the pounding in his head, Hex took a bottle of aspirin out of his trenchcoat pocket and swallowed two of the pills dry. It would not get rid of the pain, but it would make it more bearable.

Don't worry. It's not the end of the world. Trust me, I'd know.
-Loki, Norse god of Mischief

With a few strange looks and many more raised eyebrows, the group of us were admitted into the colonel's office. It was laid out like an office in a low-budget war movie. There were maps on the wall indicating strategic targets and an actual red phone at the side of the office, which was obviously not intended for personal calls.

"I find your arrival here most unusual, General. I was under the impression that you were no longer in command of either BMDO or America's nuclear arsenal," said Colonel Redmond.

"That's correct. I was promoted," said Loki.

"Promoted? You lost two stars. It seems to me Project Skywatch would be a demotion."

"Yes, that's what you were supposed to think. . . or at least what most people were. Frankly, I expected more from you, Redmond. What's your security clearance."

"A-2."

"Only A-2? How sad. Even with only an A-2 clearance, you must know that the official position of the government of the United States of America on UFOs and what they know to be true are not the same thing."

"Sir? I don't understand."

"Don't play dumb with me. You've gotten the reports of the unusual activity in this area."

"Sir, I can assure you that there has been no unusual activity here."

"Really? My information is to the contrary," said Loki.

"Where are you getting your information?" questioned Redmond.

"Same places you should be, plus a few others," said Loki, as Hex walked in the door. "Speaking of which. . ."

Hex saw Redmond and went thermonuclear himself. "Redmond!? You son of a bitch. . ."

Paddy grabbed Hex's arm. "Easy. Ye are one who can never afford to lose control, Daniel."

Apparently, if Hex blew up at someone, they might literally blow up. To put it another way, if Hex told someone to go to Hell, they better be packing sunscreen, because they would be forced to go. Fortunately for Redmond, Hex took a deep breath and calmed down. Moving behind the desk, Hex planted his butt in Redmond's chair and propped his feet on the colonel's blotter.

"Get out of my chair. Take your feet off my desk," ordered Redmond.

"Nope," said Hex, kicking dirt off his sneakers.

"Who is this man? How did he get on my base?" shouted Redmond.

"You mean you don't know? This is not a good sign, Redmond," said Loki.

"Silo Charlie had been taken over by hostiles, as you suspected, General," said Hex.

"Hostiles? What are you talking about?" demanded Redmond.

Loki ignored the Colonel. "Has the threat been neutralized?"

"Of course," said Hex.

"What threat?" asked Redmond.

"Redmond, the fact that you continue not only to proclaim your ignorance, but shout it, is very disturbing. You make me wonder about your competency, or maybe you've been compromised. If that's the case, I will relieve you of your command and replace you myself until a suitable replacement can be found. Until I make that determination this base is closed. No communication in or out."

"Excuse me, General, but I'm going to have to get verification of your authority on this," said Redmond, picking up the phone and dialing a number. He put the phone down, staring at it quizzically. He didn't see Coyote standing innocently with the cord to the phone jack dangling out of his mouth. "That's odd, the phone seems to have gone dead."

"Redmond, is it my understanding that you just disobeyed a direct order by calling for verification of my authority?"

"General, you better than anyone know that we have rules and regulations to uphold here."

"And you better than anyone, Redmond, know that when national security is involved, extreme measures have to be taken. Major," Loki said to Kyna. She snapped to attention. "Get me two MPs right now."

Kyna rushed out of the office.

"General, you can't be serious," said Redmond.

"Not only am I serious, but I am officially taking command of this base. You are hereby relieved of command under suspicion of dereliction of duty and for disobeying a direct order from a superior officer. You will be held in the stockade until such time as it is appropriate for your court martial."

"General, you can't do this," said Redmond, as the two MPs came in the door with Kyna.

"Not only can I do it, but watch me. You two will take the colonel to the stockade and keep him under armed guard. His actions have comprised national security and the security of this base. He is to have no visitors and be allowed no communication unless it is okayed by me."

"I won't stand for this," yelled Redmond. He turned toward the MPs. "Place the general and his party under arrest."

The MPs hesitated, momentarily confused. Loki's commanding presence unconfused them in a hurry.

"If the colonel tries to disobey any of these directives or tries to escape, you are under orders to shoot him. Have I made myself clear, gentlemen?"

Both MPs snapped to attention and saluted, "Yes, sir, General, sir."

"Good," said Loki with a smile as he watched the MPs place handcuffs on Redmond and escort him out. As soon as they were out of earshot he added, "Damn bastard killed Paddy. Or rather, he will if we don't succeed here. Redmond's lucky I don't have him shot just for spite."

"We'll make sure he doesn't succeed this time," said Paddy passionately.

"Amen to that," I said.

"Let's get to work," said Loki. "We have to search as much of the base as possible, make sure no more of Mab's people are here. Then we need to mount a defense."

"Are you sure we don't need the Air Force troops to help?" I asked.

"Yes," said Loki. "To have the military help us against Mab would alert them to her existence, which ruins the secrecy part of our mission."

"They'd still have proof of Faerie's existence and that would leave the Gentry open to attack," said Paddy.

"We need Mab to gas the locals, Murph," said Hex. "The stuff not only knocks them out, but erases the previous day-and-a-half's memories. Our visit here is best left not remembered. We also need all video surveillance for the base to disappear since before we arrived."

"I can take care of that," said Kyna.

"Good, do it," said Loki. "Meanwhile, the rest of you get searching. We have less than two hours before Mab arrives. We better be ready. Rumbles and Murphy, the gas will nail both of you. It could even get you, Hex. magí or not, your lungs are still human. I want the three of you to have gas masks on in an hour and not to take them off for at least ninety minutes."

Kyna pulled out a briefcase she had been carrying. "Already got it covered. Gas masks for everybody."

"I don't think we all need them. Breathing is an option for the rest of us, so if we stop, the gas won't bother us," said Loki.

"All things considered, we should all probably wear them, just to be on the safe side. Some Faerie potions work through the eyes," said Paddy.

"I have enough," said Kyna, handing them out. Sun's fit him well enough, but Kyna had to make major adjustments to Coyote's. The canine divinity looked ridiculous.

Loki was having some difficulty with having his "orders" overridden, but realized Paddy was right. He even took a gas mask for himself, then stepped outside to the reception area. I followed him.

Frankly, I had been overly harsh in my opinion of Loki. Part of it may be because he is destined to kill Heimdal at Ragnarok. Heimdal's my friend; not that Loki isn't, but I only see Loki twice a year. Not a whole lot of time to get close. Heimdal is Paddy's friend, too. More than that, he's family. Heimdal used to work for the boss and live over the bar like Hermes and I do now. So if Paddy thinks Loki is alright, it's good enough for me. It was time for me to make up for past offenses, like the bet.

"Loki, you got a minute?" I asked.

"Sure," Loki said, absentmindedly fiddling with his gas mask.

"I wanted to talk to you about what happened in there."

"Then talk."

"Don't feel bad about Paddy putting in his two cents. This is a team effort," I said.

"You noticed, huh? I didn't think you were that observant, Murph," said Loki.

"It comes and goes," I confessed. Sometimes I pick up on stuff no one else notices and other times something has to hit me over the head before I see it. "Near as I can figure, you and I have one thing in common."

"Really? I can't wait to hear what it is."

"We both have a problem with authority. I fight back with the wisecracks. You have more extreme compensations. You want to be the ultimate authority. Paddy changed that for you. Don't let ego knock you back."

Loki smiled. "True, Paddy thinks highly of me, but who else?"

"Does it matter?"

"Maybe," Loki said wistfully. "Thor and Balder were the golden boys, loved by all. I was the black sheep. I never knew love until I lost it. The last few centuries I've had a lot of time to think, and my conclusion is that others' opinions may be part of why I turned out how I did."

"Getting Freudian in your old age are you? So you are saying because people thought bad of you, you became bad?"

"Maybe."

"Didn't you have to take responsibility for yourself at some point?"

"Of course. But without anyone thinking well of me, maybe I had no reason to change."

"Paddy thinks highly of you."

"He's just one person, and he's got reason to be biased. I'm not sure it's enough."

Time to confess all. "Loki, on the way here, I told Paddy I thought giving you the cycle solo was a bad idea. I figured you'd take off. I was confident enough to put my money where my mouth was. Paddy bet me you wouldn't run."

"No surprises there."

"True, but the next part might have a few. Everyone else in that car thought enough of you to bet against me. They bet on you."

"All of them?"

"Yes."

Loki shook his head and smiled. "That's good to know." Loki paused a minute, deep in thought. "I have a history of getting people to trust me and then screwing them over. What makes you think I won't do that with this info?"

"Because this time I'm betting on you, too," I said, extending my hand. Loki shook it.

"Thanks Murph. I wouldn't advise you to trust me completely just yet."

I didn't, but maybe that could change.

I'm not sure I understand. I haven't been in this country a long distance.
-Fred, satyr son of Pan, busboy at Bulfinche's Pub

Meanwhile back at the bar, Fred was fruitlessly still making calls.

"Joseph, please come to Bulfinche's," begged Fred. Joseph was better known as the Wandering Jew. A while back he had found Bulfinche's Pub and a home after two thousand years of pounding pavement. Paddy had given him a cellular satellite phone as a gift, so he could keep in touch with friends. Joseph can find the bar whenever he wants to. Today wasn't one of those times. "Or meet them in Arkansas."

"Fred, are they threatening you?" asked Joseph.

"They're not here. They're in Arkansas."

"Ah, they're listening in on the line. Got you. I'll stop by in a few weeks," said Joseph.

"But a few weeks may be too late," said Fred, but he was talking to dead air. "I don't believe this."

General Swanson was still buck naked and bound to the table. Swanson woke to Fred's voice.

"Hello? Is somebody there?" asked Swanson.

"What do you what?" asked Fred, frustrated.

"Are you an alien?"

"No."

"Good. Then you can free me," said Swanson.

"No," replied Fred.

"Why not?"

"Because I don't want to."

"But why? You're human like me, aren't you?" asked Swanson.

"Actually, I'm not," said Fred.

"Are you the talking dog? Or the monkey?"

"Neither."

"Then what are you?"

Fred couldn't resist. "Your worst nightmare."

Just then, a man and a woman in business suits walked in the door. Fortunately for the lady, the man was no gentleman. He walked in the door first and the bucket of water fell on his head, dousing him.

"Yes!" shouted Fred, bending his elbow and thrusting it backwards in a sign of victory. "It finally worked."

"What the hell!?" said the man, removing the bucket from his head. The woman behind him was chuckling at his wet suit, but they both fell silent when they looked up and saw the naked and blindfolded general, spread-eagle across the table.

Fred mistook their stunned quiet for something else.

"Welcome. Here, shake hands," said Fred, joy buzzer at the ready. Neither man nor woman moved. "Would you like to smell my flower?" He asked the woman. She just stared blankly at him.

"Hello? Are you human? Are you here to rescue me?" asked Swanson. "Help me before they use an anal probe!"

"I don't need a drink this bad," said the man.

"Me neither," said the woman, as they both turned tail and sprinted out of the bar.

Fred ran out after them. "Wait! Come back! I have gum!"

Curses suck.
  -Hex, cursed magi

Hex and I were teamed up for the next round of hide and go seek with the Faerie folk. Loki had divided us up in teams of two and sent us out to make sure we didn't have any more of Mab's agents to worry about. The order to the teams was simple. Each one had somebody on it who had the ability to tell a Shapeshifter—or someone using a glamour spell—from a normal person. In our group it wasn't me. Hex was using his abilities to search. I was along, more or less, for moral support.

Our rounds included the cantina. We were catching the tail end of lunch and the place was still fairly crowded. We walked among the tables watching people chow down. No one appeared to be watching us. So far, all the diners were human.

"Want to grab a bite to eat?" I asked Hex.

"No. I don't eat anything I don't have a hand in fixing myself," said Hex.

"But I've seen you eat and drink," I replied.

"Only at Bulfinche's Pub."

"Why?" I asked.

"One of the oldest tricks in the book is to give somebody food that belongs to another realm. Somebody who eats that food may be trapped, doomed to live forever in another land."

"Like Persephone with Hades," I said. Persephone was our chef, Demeter's, daughter. A few millennia back, Persephone was carried off by Hades. While visiting his dark realm, she ate half of six pomegranates. Because she ate half, she was bound to spend half of the year with the man who became her husband.

"Exactly. Of course, there is also the old favorite, poison," said Hex.

"You don't trust a lot of people, do you?" I asked.

"No."

"Then why is the food and drink at Bulfinche's okay?"

"Two reasons. One, by the nature of the bar, magic doesn't work, so I can't be cursed. And two, Paddy's one of the few people I actually do trust."

"But a lot of the time I'm the one serving you the drinks," I said.

"Paddy trusts you. That's good enough for me," said Hex. "Plus, in the future I get to know you real well."

"We haven't had time for me to indulge my curiosity yet. What exactly does happen to me in the future? Or is there some problem with telling me? Time paradoxes and all that?"

"My being here is going to cause a time paradox, so I'm not terribly worried about giving you too many details. You do survive the destruction of Bulfinche's Pub. In fact, you were there the day it was destroyed, but you escaped. You led the first group of refugees to Hades' realm."

"I did?"

"Paddy needed to send somebody who knew the way and also had experience with Charon. You got those entrusted to your care safely away, but you came back too late. You were actually trapped for a while in Hades' realm, but managed to get out. You joined the underground, those of us who were trying to stop the dark forces and the tyrants. You became a leader."

"So I ended up getting some sort of powers or something?"

"No, you never showed any affinity for magic, although you did use several mystic artifacts, some of which you salvaged from the rubble of Paddy's trophy room. You even saved my life once."

I was about to pick Hex's brain for more details of what was to come when he pointed to the air vents and put his index finger over his lips in a shhh sign.

"Infestation," he whispered. Right below the air vent was a table. Hex walked up to it and stepped on it, bringing one of the chairs with him. People moved their food trays quickly to get out of his way.

"Excuse me, pardon me, coming through," said Hex, barely avoiding stepping in someone's mashed potatoes. He put the chair on the table and stood atop it. Taking a dime out of his pocket, he undid the screws that held the vent cover in place. He waved me toward him, so I climbed up on the table.

"What is it?" I asked.

"Pixies. Here hold this," he said handing me the vent cover. He took what looked like a canvas sack out of his pocket and held it up about four inches in front of the air hole.

"So they're just gonna fly in the bag?" I asked.

"Hardly. I'm going to have to help them a bit. Watch. *Blow,*" intoned Hex, using a one word spell. A huge gust of wind began blowing through all the air vents. A noise like sneakers in a clothes dryer came from all the vents in the building. As the breeze kept going, one by one, tiny people with little gossamer wings began being tossed out of the ventilation system and into the bag. There must have been over twenty. Hex pulled the cord around the neck of the sack closed and the wind stopped.

"Ever consider a job as an exterminator?" I asked.

"Naw. It's more of a hobby. Doing it as a job would take all the fun out of it. Besides, cockroaches are too resourceful to be caught this way. I know pixies; one of my roommates is one. As a whole, they aren't the strongest of the Gentry and can be easily captured, once you know how," said Hex, jumping down off the table. "C'mon, we still have work to do."

A sexist? Who me?
　　　　-Pan, Lord of the Satyrs

"You smell anything yet?" asked Pan.

"Besides you, no. You know you really could bathe once in a while," said Coyote, "for all I know, your stench could be messing with their scents."

"It's my musk. Don't want to dilute it with any of that soap and water stuff. It doesn't look like there is any sign of more of Mab's people."

"So far it looks good, but we still have to check the barracks over there," said Coyote.

At this, Pan's ears picked up, for he caught the faintest hint of feminine laughter coming from the building. He noticed the sign that labeled it as the female officers' barrack.

"Well, if we have to, we have to," said Pan, taking off in a happy gallop.

Coyote chuckled, shook his head and sauntered behind Pan. Under normal circumstances, Coyote had quite a bit of a lecherous side to him, but around Pan it seemed both redundant and a waste of time. As it was still the afternoon, most of the sleeping quarters were empty, and those that weren't had only human occupants. The pair searched systematically, finding nothing. The last area left unchecked was the women's showers, which were currently occupied by eight female officers, who had plans to head into the nearest town, 25 minutes away, for some R&R. Coyote and Pan peered around the corner as the women showered.

"They're clean," said Coyote.

"Well, they will be," said Pan, "But how can we be sure?"

"What do you mean, Pan?" said Coyote, raising a fuzzy eyebrow.

"Maybe these are a new breed of Shapelings. Maybe they've found some chemical means to mask their scent. We would be really lax in our duties if we didn't examine them more closely," said Pan, staring into the steam.

"And what good would that do?" asked Coyote, more to annoy Pan than out of a desire for answers.

"I've heard that during the throws of passion, Shapeshifters have difficulty maintaining their assumed from, and that during orgasm lose all control of their shape," said Pan.

"That's a new one. I've never heard that and I've been known to try out the occasional odd shape for recreational activities. I've held the shape though climax and beyond."

"Oh, well you were in a male form, weren't you?" Coyote nodded that he was. "That's where the discrepancy arises. The orgasms have to be multiple," said Pan with a smile as he lifted up his elbow and blew into his armpit toward the shower. Switching arms, he did the same on the opposite side. This way he was assured his pheromones would enter the room before he did. "Now mind you, I don't know if this is a fact, but can we really take the risk of not finding out? Besides, you said I needed to bath, and a shower is just as good." Pan stripped off his uniform, folding it neatly over a chair, before heading toward the steamy vapors.

"You coming?" asked Pan.

"No, but I'm sure you will be," said Coyote.

Pan shrugged his shoulders and, with a big smile, joined the ladies in the shower. At first, there were a couple of shrieks, but within moments most had turned into not-so-subtle moans. There was one woman who came out of the shower with apparently no interest in Pan. She had a towel wrapped around herself, and was heading to the locker room. Coyote noticed the engagement ring on her finger and nodded. Love trumped pheromones.

Seeing Coyote, she shouted back into the shower, "Any of you guys leave a dog out here?"

There was no answer from in the shower room, but one nubile officer pulled herself away from the festivities to come out and look. She was young, voluptuous, and still soaking wet from the hot shower. Steam, in fact, was rising off her skin, and she wore no more than the day she was born.

"Oh, I love doggies," said the raven-haired beauty, dropping to her knees to embrace Coyote and pulling him close. The water from her body soaked his fur. "How's the little doggie woggie? Aren't you the cutest little fellow. Oh, no, you're a big strapping fellow aren't you?" Having the option to remake themselves, Shapeshifters usually are well, if not overly, endowed. Coyote has been known in the past to overdo it to the point where he needed to build something to help carry his manhood around with him.

The young lady continued to babble at Coyote. There was something about animals and babies that causes competent and sane adults to be reduced to a state of speaking pure gibberish. Normally, Coyote hated this kind of stuff, but as it was being spouted by a naked woman who kept pulling him closer and closer, and hugging him tighter, he began to actually enjoy it.

"Would the doggie woggie like to take a shower with me?" asked the woman, with a voice husky enough to pull a sled.

Coyote nodded his head up and down, thinking to himself that he might as well put Pan's theory to the test.

I regret ever coming down from the trees. Every so often I climb back up, but sadly I can't go home again.
                          -Sun Wukong, the Monkey King

Sun and Rumbles were making their rounds, but so far hadn't discovered any Gentry spies. They had, however, turned quite a few heads. After all, a clown in full make-up and a large independent monkey were not exactly ordinary sights on an Air Force base. Rumbles had no way of actually telling a Shapeling from an ordinary airman. Sun, on the other hand, was the key player here. By squinting and concentrating he was able to see into the mystic spectrum enough to tell if a person's umbra was human or not. All the squinting, however, was giving him eye strain, and he was getting tired. Their search was systematic. They were doing a building by building search in the sectors they were assigned. They came to a large, square, tan building, the entrance to which was guarded by two MPs. Of course, they were only doing their job when they stopped the clown and monkey from entering.

"You can't come in here," said one of the MPs.

"Actually, we can," said Rumbles, "We are under the authority of General Swanson."

"I'll have to verify this with Colonel Redmond," said the MP reading the pass that Rumbles had handed to him.

"There is only one problem with that scenario; Colonel Redmond is under arrest for dereliction of duty and possible treason," said Rumbles.

"You're kidding."

"No," said Rumbles.

"You don't look like an inspector," said the MP eyeing the pair suspiciously. "Why are you dressed like a clown?"

"Yeah, and what's with the monkey?" said the other MP.

"I'm afraid that's all classified information, gentlemen," said Rumbles.

Being military and having an authorized form in front of them, the MPs accepted this without any more questions, and even held the door open for Sun and Rumbles to go inside.

"By the way, what is R&D?"

Seeing the look of confusion on Rumbles's face, Sun whispered, "Research and development."

The MPs did a double take at the monkey. Rumbles debated whether or not to explain it was a ventriloquist act, but realized as a supposedly senior office he had no reason to explain himself.

"No one is to leave or enter this building until we come out," said Rumbles to the MPs.

"Yes, sir," they chimed in unison.

Starting in the basement, Rumbles and Sun worked their way room by room and floor by floor. They shut down the elevator so that anyone who was aware of their search would have to use the stairs. When they got to the third floor, Sun stopped short as if he had been slapped in the face with a baseball bat.

"By the Buddha," said Sun.

"What?" asked Rumbles.

"Don't you hear it?" asked Sun.

"What, Gentry?" asked Rumbles.

"No, torture," said Sun.

"Who?"

"My people," said Sun, and the Monkey King was off, running down the hall. Any semblance of a systematic search lost, Rumbles jogged after him.

At the end of the corridor was an animal research lab. Without missing a step, Sun kicked in the door. Inside the lab, a woman and a man in white lab coats snapped their heads around fast enough to give them both whiplash.

"Oh my God, one of the monkeys got loose," said the man who was the lab assistant.

"That's not one of ours," said the woman, whose name tag read Dr. Hanley. This was her lab; in it she was used to having ultimate authority. Sun's entrance shocked her, which she didn't like. "But he is a fine specimen. Amazingly large. We could easily add him to the experiment."

With one furry arm, Sun grabbed her by the front of her blouse and slammed her into the wall.

"You're not doing any more experiments on my people," growled Sun.

"It talks," said the man.

Dr. Hanley, while a bit put off by the physical nature of the confrontation, only showed apprehension, not fear. She had never feared a monkey before in her life. She wasn't about to start now. To her, they were all research fodder, as was evidenced by the cages full of primates that were scattered around the lab. At present, she had six subjects, all rhesus monkeys. Two of them had been taken out of their cages and strapped down to a monkey-sized operating table. Both had IVs going into them. Neither one seemed coherent.

"Very interesting. Looks like Dr. Rose's experiments were successful. Did he send you?" asked Dr. Hanley.

"I sent myself. I am Sun Wukong, the Monkey King."

"Yes, I'm sure you are. This is truly amazing. You'll have to tell Dr. Rose I'm very impressed by his work."

As Dr. Hanley was not quite getting the point Sun was wishing to make, he grabbed her with both hands and wall-slammed her twice, knocking the air out of her. Hanley's eyes now began to open a little bit wider. The first cringes of fear creeping into her system. It was then that Rumbles came in the door. Seeing the clown the doctor exclaimed, "Oh, it's just a circus trick."

"This ain't no circus trick. All of you belong in a freak show," spat Sun, truly disgusted.

Ignoring the Monkey King, Dr. Hanley turned to Rumbles and said, "That is some very impressive ventriloquism, but you had better call your beast off of me before I call security."

"I only see one beast here and it ain't me," said Sun. "What in the hells are you doing here?" Sun slammed the lady scientist against the wall again. "I asked you a question."

"We are testing out truth serums and mind control drugs" said Dr. Hanley.

"Pretty harmless stuff," said the lab assistant.

"You really are talking. You're an amazing piece of work," said Dr. Hanley.

"So are you," said Sun.

"Dr. Rose did the surgical modifications on you, didn't he? I have to give your creator my compliments and tell him he's gone a little bit far for a practical joke. Tell him he can make it up to me by letting me dissect you."

Disgusted, Sun threw Dr. Hanley down into a chair. She jumped up. "Hey wait a minute. . . ."

Sun, realizing it was next to useless to give the woman orders, reached out with one of his fingers and gently touched her solar plexus. Dr. Hanley screeched and doubled over in pain, whimpering softly.

"Impressive," said Rumbles. "I forget sometimes that you're a martial arts master."

"I've only been practicing a few thousand years. My favorite is cloud dancing," said Sun. He then turned his attention toward the lab assistant. "What's your name, boy?"

"Harold."

"Well, Harold, what you're going to do is unhook the monkeys from the IVs immediately," said Sun.

"But. . ."

Sun took a step closer to Harold with a threatening posture. Harold was much easier to intimidate then the doctor was.

"Okay, I'll do whatever you want." Harold put on a pair of white latex gloves and removed the IVs from the monkeys who were not in the cages.

"Now release the rest of my people," ordered Sun, pointing to the cages.

Harold didn't need any further prompting as he unlocked the cages. The monkeys inside ran out, confused and overjoyed by their sudden freedom. Although they had never met, somehow they recognized the Monkey King and stood quietly in front of him, their heads bowed. Sun returned the bow and the monkey formalities were over. The monkeys who had been removed from the IV drips were slowly coming to. Harold undid the restraint straps that held them down. Sun, and even Rumbles, were disgusted by the appearance of the lab monkeys. Their fur was matted and unkempt and the heads of two were shaved where tiny electrodes had been placed through the skulls to the primates' brains. In the language of the monkeys, Sun spoke to them. All at first, then one at a time, they spoke back. Explaining to him what had been happening Sun's anger grew even hotter. Harold watched in amazement.

"You can talk to them?" Harold asked.

"Of course. Only humans need to make up their own language. The rest of the higher species are born knowing it. Okay Harold, you're going to tie that woman down to the same table she tied my people down to. Then you're going to put the same IV in her veins and see how she likes it."

Harold was too afraid to argue, Rumbles wasn't.

"Sun, are you sure about this?"

Sun turned his red eyes on Rumbles, "Oh yes, I'm sure. Don't worry, it won't kill her, but maybe it will teach her some compassion. Think of your reaction if you found another species experimenting on your people. Would you just walk away?"

"No," said Rumbles.

Sun lifted Dr. Hanley off the chair where she was still doubled over in pain and carried her to the examination table where Harold strapped her down. Sun watched carefully as he put the IV into the doctor's vein. The pain prevented Dr. Hanley from doing any more than whimpering as she stared at the needle going into her arm.

"Enjoy doctor. Now Harold, if you'd be so kind as to climb onto the other table, it's your turn," said Sun.

"Me? Why me? I did what you said," said Harold trembling.

"I thought you said it was pretty harmless stuff. What's the problem?" asked Sun.

"You can't do this to me. I was just following orders," stammered Harold.

"That excuse has been used by men without conviction for centuries. It doesn't hold any water with me. Maybe this will help you grow some backbone. Get on the table Harold," ordered Sun.

Harold, without any more protest, climbed on and Sun strapped him down. From Sun's earlier observation, he had learned enough to be able to insert the IV needle into the lab assistant's arm. Within moments his eyes and the doctor's were glassy. Over at another examining table, the monkeys began to scream and jump frantically around the still-unconscious body of a young female monkey. It was at that moment that her heart stopped beating. The drugs had just been too much for her.

"No!" screamed Sun, being so close he was able to feel the start of her dying begin, "No!"

"What?" asked Rumbles.

"She just died," said Sun rushing to the young monkey's side. He picked her up and cradled her in his arms.

"Rumbles, do you know CPR?" asked Sun.

"Yes," said Rumbles, taking off his gloves.

"Good, you take compressions, I'll do the breaths," said Sun.

"I don't know how to do it on a monkey," said Rumbles, not letting that stop him from trying.

"Use the same CPR you would use for a child. The physiology and anatomy is very similar."

Working frantically, the clown and the Monkey King were able to keep air and blood flowing through the young monkey's body, but none of their efforts were able to allow the little one to breathe or have her heart pump on its own.

"It's not working," said Rumbles.

Sun lifted his mouth breaking the seal that he had made with the young monkey, "I know, stand back, I'm going to try to jolt her heart back."

"But you don't have any paddles."

"Don't need any. Clear," said Sun as he put his two index fingers on the young monkey's chest. Magical sparks flew from his fingertips into her chest, jolting her entire body into spasm. A second later she gasped.

"It worked. You did it! She's alive," said Rumbles.

Sun did a quick examination of the young one, using his sight to see inside of her.

"She's alive, but she won't stay that way for long. The damn drugs have weakened her heart too much. I'm keeping her alive by sharing my life force with her. The problem is she'll never be able to survive apart from me. When it comes to healing, I'm only an amateur, so it's time to go to the master," said Sun picking up the small monkey in his arms. He said something to the other monkeys in their tongue and then turned to Rumbles and said, "Let's go see Hermes."

Sun took off running; five monkeys and Rumbles trailing behind. Sun ran through the corridors, down the stairs and out the door past the guards. They saw Sun coming and tried to stop him. It was a foolish mistake.

"Excuse me sir, you're not authorized to take those animals out."

Sun ignore the pair of sentries completely so they tried to block his path. He tore through them, knocking them down like a linebacker would a pair of toddlers. The other monkeys ran over the stunned guards. One of them got to his feet and went for his sidearm. Rumbles got to it before he did and a second later removed the sidearm from the second guard.

"I wouldn't do that if I were you. At least not if you value your health," said Rumbles.

The sentry looked back up at him, confused at being lectured to by a man dressed as a clown. Rumbles decided it wasn't worth arguing about and tapped a vertebra on the back of each of the guards' necks, rendering them unconscious.

Using his expertise in cloud dancing, Sun leapt the length of the entire base, landing on the road outside in one bound. He was still holding the dying she-monkey in his arms.

"Hermes!" Sun screamed into the sky. There was no answer. "Hermes!" Sun screamed again. "Get your butt down here." Still nothing. "Please Hermes."

That did it. Hermes' gray trench coat flapped in the wind, as he descended from the sky, red winged sneakers first.

"Sun, we're supposed to be doing this on the Q.T.," scolded Hermes, hovering five feet above the Monkey King's head.

"She's dying. She needs your help," said Sun. Hermes drifted the rest of the way to the ground and took the monkey in his arms to evaluate her. Sun could not have brought her to a better healer.

"There are holes in her mitral valve along with some prolapse. She needs surgery," said Hermes. At this point, Rumbles and the other five escaped monkeys finally caught up.

"Can you save her?" asked Sun.

"I think so. I just won't be able to watch for Mab while I do it. Rumbles, you're on watch duty," said Hermes.

"Me!?" said Rumbles. "But I can't even see Fairies."

"Well, you're going to have to try," said Hermes. "Don't worry. I doubt Mab is going to waste the energy on a cloaking spell."

Sun said something in the monkey tongue to the five monkeys. "They'll help you. They'll be able to tell when Mab and her army come, spell or no spell."

The monkeys ran off in different directions to keep watch. Rumbles stood nearby, keeping his eyes on the woods. Hermes got to work. Hermes waved something under the she-monkey's nose to assure she would feel no pain. Out of the folds of his trench coat, he pulled out a white cloth and put it on the ground. He lay the female monkey atop it, then took a small satchel out of another pocket and unzipped the goatskin case. He pulled out a glowing scalpel. With it, he made an incision in the young monkey's chest, cutting through skin and bone just as a warm knife would go through butter. He then separated her rib cage to expose her still-beating heart. Working deftly, Hermes went into the heart, closed up the holes and fixed the problem with the valve so the blood flowed easily again. With another finger he touched the heart, forming a glowing barrier for the blood to pass through. The now glowing blood flowed through all the arteries, capillaries and veins, healing much of the damage the researchers' drugs had done. He then wove the rib cage back together, stimulating the bones to grow back together. With a wave of his hand, Hermes closed her up, his energies speeding the growth of the skin and muscle cells to replace the damaged ones. The surgery didn't even leave a scar.

"She'll be fine," said Hermes, patting Sun on the back. The Monkey King wept a tear from each eye.

"Thank you. I owe you," said Sun.

"Don't worry, I'll send you a bill," said Hermes with a wink. "I better get back on watch."

"I don't think you have to bother with that," said Rumbles pointing to the woods. The monkeys were running back toward them, frantically leaping and chattering. Dozens of human-looking folk started pouring out of the woods, most of them dressed in what could be best described as medieval looking fatigues. Most of the soldiers could pass for human, although many sported pointy ears, wings, or blue or green skin. The ground started to shake in rhythmic jolts not unlike every dinosaur movie made in the last ten years. If there was a glass of water or puddle lying around, little circles would start to radiate outward. The tops of the trees parted, pushed aside by gargantuan hands. The entire forest was parting like the Red Sea. Through the divide walked a giant, easily twenty-five feet tall. "I'd say they're here," said Rumbles.

The element of surprise is crucial to any campaign.
-Mab, Faerie Warrior Queen

The attack on the base was swift and precise. The front-line foot soldiers each held what looked like a bazooka, molded out of a silver metal. They pointed the weapons at various locations of the base and fired. The projectiles soared straight through the air, each a tiny glass globe filled with an orange gas. The globes shattered on impact, releasing the vapors and in seconds the entire base was covered in an orange fog. Men and women began to drop like flies. Around the garbage dumpsters, flies were dropping like people. The only ones prepared were our group, each of whom managed to get their gas masks on in time, although the pair in the showers got them on just barely.

I exaggerated when I said our people were the only ones. There was one other, the Air Force captain who in Hex's future had managed to track Mab back to Faerie. That was when this was now, and this was actually when now was now, or something like that. If I start to make sense, feel free to stop me.

The captain moved around the base, inspecting his fellow servicemen who had fallen to the gas. He checked the first few for pulses. After leaning down over the fourth person, satisfied that everyone was still alive, he started to stand with the intention of investigating what had happened. He looked up to see Hex and me standing over him, with gas masks in place.

"Thank God, I'm not the only one. Do you have any idea what's going on?" the captain asked, muffled by his breathing apparatus.

"Yes, the base is being invaded," said Hex.

"By who?" asked the captain. Hex whipped out a hand and snatched the gas mask off the captain's head before he even knew it was happening.

"Sorry, Gravedigger, but this time that's something you're never going to find out," said Hex. "The you I know would thank me."

The captain grabbed his throat in an attempt to hold his breath, but it didn't do him any good. His gasp of surprise when the mask was ripped from his face had allowed just enough of the gas into his lungs to take effect. He dropped to one knee, then the other and whispered, "Why?"

He looked fully betrayed and dejected as he fell unconscious to the floor. Without him to guide them, the U.S. military would never find the entrance to Faerie and would never launch nuclear missiles. By falling victim to Mab's gas, the captain may very well have saved the future.

The reason the smart gods load the dice when playing with the universe is because the universe cheats.

> *-Hermes, Greco-Roman god of trickery, thieves, medicine and travelers*

The orange mist hadn't escape notice in the Command Center, where Loki, Paddy and Kyna were waiting.

"What happened to our advanced warning? Hermes fall asleep on the job?" yelled Loki.

"I'm sure there's a very good reason," said Kyna, defending her father.

"That doesn't do us a whole lot of good, does it?" spat Loki.

"Easy. What's done is done. We deal with the cards we have now. We'd better head out and see what's happening. It's possible Mab may somehow have even captured Hermes, in which case the element of surprise is also gone," said Paddy. Hex and I crossed paths with the three of them halfway to the gate.

"You two better come with us," said Paddy.

"In a minute. I have an idea. Let me speak to Loki for a minute first," said Hex. "I think it might be best if you didn't confront Mab directly."

"I'm not one to run from a battle," said Loki indignantly.

"Who said anything about running? I just have a sneakier, better way," said Hex. Loki smiled. "Besides, you don't want Mab to see you and realize who you are. Knowledge is power and if she knows you're here, she'll have no qualms blackmailing you or Paddy with the threat of telling the big O."

"The lad's got a point," said Paddy. "What's your plan, Hex?"

Hex whispered something to Loki and he smiled. He then whispered it to Paddy, who joined the other two in a grin. I was left without a smile to call my own.

"I like it. Take care of it," said Paddy. Hex ran off with Loki.

"What's going on boss?" I asked.

"For the moment, Murph, it's better you and Kyna don't know. Some of my people can read surface thoughts. What you don't know, you can't tell," said Paddy.

By the time Paddy, Kyna, and I caught up with Rumbles and Sun, Mab's army was advancing on the base. The lot of them were swaggering with the confidence that they'd be unopposed. Hermes dropped from the sky to hover a hundred feet in front and fifty feet above Mab.

"Hi, honey. Miss me?" asked Hermes.

Fighting rarely solves anything. However, losing a fight solves even less.
-Rumbles, professional clown, former Golden Gloves boxer

Mab saw her former lover floating there in front of her and her facial expressions ran the gamut from pleasantly surprised to shocked to angry. Amazingly, after that run, her face was not even tired.

"What are you doing here?" demanded Mab with authority. She was dressed in golden armor, a breast plate of which was molded in such a way as to give no doubt to the fact that she was a woman. A red cloak was attached to two shoulder pad armaments and she wore a golden helmet, open faced except for a nose piece that dipped down between the eyes and the sides of which had white wings welded on. A huge war blade jutted up from her back through the top of her cloak.

"I heard you were throwing a party. Didn't think you'd mind if I crashed," said Hermes, shifting his weight as if he was leaning casually against a wall, instead of thin air. The local atmosphere had been dieting.

"Well, you're not welcome. Besides I thought you and your ilk would be too busy with your Fools' Day celebration."

"Mab, you wound me. I always willing to make time for you. Pity you couldn't say the same. Pity your daughter couldn't say the same."

"Leave Kyna out of this," ordered Mab.

"I hardly have to leave her out. After all, she's here. I'm sure she'll want to talk with her mother," said Hermes. Mab scanned the surrounding terrain and noticed the rest of us across the way.

"Either get out of the way or I'll take you out of the way," said Mab.

"Wow, can I take tough lessons from you?" said Hermes.

"Blow him out of the sky," said Mab. She had with her a mixture of infantry who carried everything from spears and crossbows to guns and other high tech weapons. At her command, they all fired at Hermes. Hermes danced through all the projectiles with no more difficulty than if he was walking around a group of parked cars. If they were cars, he was moving so fast Hermes could have ticketed each of them and still had time for a donut. Instead of writing citations, Hermes caught some of them and dropped the combination of spears, arrows, projectiles, and bullets at Mab's feet.

"Not bad. Let's try it again, but this time just to make it interesting, I'll blindfold myself," said Hermes, taking a handkerchief out of his pocket.

"This is pointless. What is it you want?" said Mab.

"We want to stop you from getting the missile."

"Out of the question. Is Moran with you?" asked Mab.

"Of course."

"You barflies always travel in packs."

"Actually, it's wolves that travel in packs. I think barflies travel in flocks or 1930 Caddys," said Hermes. Mab was unmoved by his sense of humor.

"That damn car of Moran's. Tell him I'll meet with him in the center of the field in five minutes."

"Will do," said Hermes, speeding to Paddy's side. Paddy had already found out the reason why we had lost our advanced warning, but he wasn't upset. Saving a life was probably the only excuse that would have held whiskey. Hex had returned to the group, followed by a soaking and dripping Coyote and Pan.

"What happened to you guys?" I asked.

"You could say we hit the showers," said Pan. I could see him smiling even through the gas mask.

"What took so long?" I asked.

"We were occupied and didn't notice what was happening at first," said Coyote.

"My keen observation skills saved us," bragged Pan.

"Great skills there, Pan. Women were passing out all around him, and he still didn't notice until I bit him on the butt," said Coyote. "Twice."

"I thought you were one of the women at first. Besides I wasn't done yet," said Pan.

"You didn't know the woman had fallen unconscious?" asked Coyote.

"I couldn't exactly see her face. I thought she had gone limp to not put out her back or pull a muscle. It was weird. Women collapsing from exhaustion afterwards happens to me lots, but it never happened during the festivities before," said Pan.

Hermes relayed Mab's message.

"Fine. Let's go talk to the warrior queen," said Paddy. So the lot of us walked forth and met Mab at the field's halfway point.

"Well, Mab," said Paddy. "Fancy meeting ye here."

Kyna was fidgeting nervously. She obviously was uncomfortable.

"Hello, mother," said Kyna.

"Hello, daughter," said Mab. "You look well."

"Thank you, so do you," said Kyna. Mab nodded. I had seen warmer snow during a blizzard. The reunion over, Mab turned her attention back to Paddy.

"Let's dispense with the niceties. Hermes tells me you want to stop me from taking the missile. That's not an option," said Mab.

"Sorry to hear that, because we're gonna stop you, like it or not," said Paddy.

"We're a long way from your bar, little man. Your threats don't carry much weight here."

"That may be so, but I didn't come alone," said Paddy. Mab laughed.

"Moran, I have an army of thousands at my back. From where I stand you have an assembly of clowns to aid you," said Mab.

"Hey, I resemble that remark," said Rumbles. Everyone just loved stealing my line today.

"So Mab, do you think I am a clown?" said Hex in a soft, raspy voice that got Mab's attention.

"I don't know you, but if you're with this crowd, I'd have to say yes."

"Well then allow me to introduce myself. My name is Mr. Hex." Mab did a double take. "And I stand with Paddy Moran. You might want to go back and get tens of thousands to be at your back."

Hex had an exalted opinion of himself, and apparently Mab considered him a threat, because her manner changed, although not enough for her to even consider backing down.

"Sorry to hear that you've allied yourself with the losing side, Mr. Hex, but I doubt even you can stand against this army. I even have a giant with me," she said pointing to the sky. It was an impressive thing to have someone the size of a building looking down on you, knowing full well that with a single step he could crush you to an unrecognizable blob on the bottom of his boot. Coyote stepped up to the negotiations.

"Ah, yes, Tairde," said Coyote.

Mab looked down at him. "You know him?"

"Oh, yes. He and I tangled a few centuries back. I beat him," said Coyote, licking the top of his left front paw in a bored fashion.

"I doubt that," said Mab. Coyote took it as a challenge.

"Hello, Tairde," shouted Coyote to the sky. A booming noise answered back.

"Hello, Coyote. How are you?" asked the giant in a good natured tone. No fe-fi-fo-fumming here.

"Very well, and how is your leg?" asked Coyote.

"Much better, thank you," said the giant, in a tone only slightly softer than a firecracker.

"Let's see, the last time we tangled it was broken so bad that he couldn't walk on it. If you're putting Tairde on board as a chess piece, I'll just simply say check and mate to you," said Coyote, with a condescending nod of his head.

Later, Coyote explained to us that he hadn't broken the giant's leg with brute force, but instead through trickery. Coyote broke his own leg and mended it and then convinced the giant that he could and would do the same for him. The giant broke his own leg, but Coyote didn't mend it.

"My army still has the numbers. If you insist on fighting, we will triumph," said Mab.

"If numbers are all you're worried about, then I think I can help even the odds a bit. Allow me to introduce myself, in case you've forgotten me. I am Sun Wukong, the Monkey King."

"I know who you are, banana breath," said Mab. "Why should I be afraid of a monkey?"

"Action speaks so much louder than words, don't you think? Allow me to demonstrate," said Sun, as he pulled a small tuft of his fur out and threw the hairs in his mouth. Through the fine art of mastication, he reduced the hairs to one-cell components and then spit the lot of them out onto the ground.

"The humans have been so excited lately over their ability to clone. It's no big deal. I've been doing it for centuries," said the Monkey King as each cell shifted and morphed into an identical version of Sun. There were two hundred plus Monkey Kings surrounding us.

"I could make a million of those if I chose to," said Sun.

"Maybe so, but each of them is weaponless. My warriors will cut them down like summer wheat," said Mab.

"Ah, if it's weapons you want, that I can supply." Sun reached behind his right ear and removed the only piece of jewelry that he wore, a small silver toothpick-like band.

"You're going to defeat an army with a toothpick?"

"It's not a toothpick," Sun said as the metal in his hand grew until it was eight feet long and four inches in diameter. With a simple twist and a pop, the staff duplicated itself so that all two hundred Suns now had one.

"So they have staffs, big deal," said Mab, nervous, but unwilling to give an inch. Sun simply raised his eyebrows, pointed his staff at a tree a hundred feet away and thrust the point straight ahead. The staff grew and telescoped, shot forward, shattered the tree trunk then retracted back to its previous size.

"I think my toothpicks can do a little bit more than clean teeth, so if it's just numbers we're talking about, I believe we have a stalemate," said Sun.

"We'll still fight and people on both sides will die. Is that what you want, Moran?" asked Mab. She knew Paddy well enough to know he would avoid the loss of life at any reasonable cost.

"Well, Mab, I don't want anyone to have to die, so I propose a contest. Your champion versus our champion, one on one, winner take all. If ye win, we stand aside and ye get the missile. If we win, you'll go home missileless and give me your word you'll never try a stunt like this again," said Paddy.

"I'll agree to it if I can pick your champion," said Mab.

"You can pick anyone, except for Murphy," said Paddy.

"Hey," I said indignantly. Paddy turned to face me.

"Murphy, she's probably going to pick the giant to be her champion. Do you want to fight him?"

"Not even with a slingshot," I said.

"Then shut up. Okay, Mab, you have a deal," said Paddy. They shook on it.

"I'd gladly take him on again," said Coyote.

"I'll do it," said Sun.

"Actually, I was thinking more along the lines of the clown," said Mab, with a smile.

"His name is Rumbles," said Paddy.

"Me? Wait a second," said Rumbles nervously.

"Don't worry, Rumbles. You'll do fine," said Paddy, patting the clown on his shoulder. Although this was meant to be a comforting act, it didn't work. "Then I'm assuming you choose Tairde as your champion."

"Of course," said Mab.

"Paddy, are you sure about this?" asked Rumbles.

"Yes."

"Are a giant's anatomy and nerve centers the same as a human's?" asked Rumbles.

"Almost exactly," said Paddy. "Just a lot bigger."

The deal was relayed to the other side and the field between cleared. Rumbles walked out to meet the giant, reached up his hand to shake his opponent's. The giant stuck out his pinky, which was almost as large as Rumbles. "Good luck," said the giant.

"Thanks, you too," said Rumbles taking ten paces back before bowing and beginning the fight.

98

Bright light my eye. I love sunlight. I can touch water without making babies pop out of my skin; I need a man for younguns. And as far as after midnight snacks go — I love 'em. Except for what they do to my girlish figure.
-Bubba Sue, Southern Gremlin

"I'm not going to use an anal probe on you," Fred assured the naked and spread eagled General.

"Yes, you are," argued Swanson.

"No, I'm not," promised Fred.

"Yes, you are," responded Swanson. "You're just trying to lull me into a false sense of security."

"You must have me confused with my father," said Fred.

"I won't talk," said Swanson.

"Good, I can use the peace and quiet," said Fred.

"Nothing you can do can change that," said Swanson.

"I'm beginning to see that. Now look, you said you wouldn't talk."

"No, I said you couldn't make me talk."

"Can I make you shut up?" asked Fred.

"I know my rights under the Geneva Convention," said Swanson.

"Is that the one where all the men wear little fezzes and ride around on the go-carts?" asked Fred.

"No, it outlines the treatment of prisoners of war," said Swanson.

"You work for the United States, right?" asked Fred.

"Yes."

"Is the United States at war with anyone?"

"No," answered Swanson.

"Then how can you be a prisoner of war? You are so stupid. I'm sick of listening to you," said Fred. Walking over to the bar, he picked up a bar rag and stuffed it the General's mouth. Swanson muttered a few things, but the level of noise he could put out dropped dramatically. "That's better."

The doggie door that led to the garage flipped open, as a two-foot-tall gremlin tumbled through into the barroom.

"Ta da!" announced the little lady. She was dressed in a white t-shirt and kid-sized blue overalls. Her skin was battleship gray, and her head managed to be both round and triangular simultaneously. She changed her hair color often, but today it was neon blue. When she realized the bar was empty except for Fred and Swanson, she asked in a thick southern drawl, "Where's everyone?"

"Hey, Bubba Sue," said Fred. Bubba Sue is a good ole girl—or rather, good ole gremlin—born and raised in a factory in Atlanta, Georgia. As for the name, all of her family has the first name of Bubba, even the women. "Everyone is in Arkansas."

"Really? Give me a beer and tell me why," said Bubba Sue, kissing the satyr on his cheek. Fred explained it all.

"Hex has outdone himself this time," said Bubba Sue.

"You think Hex was pulling a fast one?" asked Fred.

"Of course. It's Fools' Day. I remember when I first met Hex. He was a kid then and I was messing with his father's TV. I was in stealth mood and he still managed to see me. Wasn't mad at me for messing with his Dad's set. Apparently they didn't exactly have the closest relationship. Together we rigged up all the appliances in the house so they only worked for him and his mother. Anytime his father touched anything it would go haywire. After that we had some fun with his car. Then we went to work on a few neighbors and other assorted authority figures. The kid was a blast. I didn't even find out until much later he was a Magi. Imagine my surprise," said Bubba Sue. "I was just happy I was on his good side."

"I don't think Hex was fooling. He gave his word," said Fred.

"His word? That's a different story. Hex's word is one of the few things in this world I'd say was unbreakable," said Bubba Sue.

"I'd have to second that," said a deep voice from the door. A large man, with a farmer's build and thick arms, stood in a dark gray trenchcoat. Despite himself, the sight gave Fred a start. It was the eyes that did it. They were deep, sorrowful and somehow managed to look right through someone, at if they could see through to the soul. The reason for that was simple: they could.

"Wisp!" shouted Bubba Sue, as she leapt into the air, landing with her arms wrapped around Wisp's neck. She planted a wet one on his mouth. "How the heck are you?"

"Good," said Wisp. Actually he went by Jack Wisp these days, combining the two names he is best known by: Will-O'-The-Wisp and Jack-O'-Lantern. Wisp's an Immortal. Actually he's an Eternal. There's a subtle difference. Most of the gods are Immortals, but Immortals can be killed if the injury is severe enough. For the gods, the injury can be something as simple as a lack of belief. For human Immortals, usually it's a physical injury, like losing a heart or head.

An Eternal is just that, eternal. They can't be killed. Most can't even be injured. The ones that can be hurt simply grow back whatever is lost, be it a finger or liver. Joseph, the Wandering Jew is an Eternal, at least until the Second Coming. Sun's an Eternal, but because he later obtained godhood, he can pass into afterlife realms if he chooses to. Wisp is an Eternal from now to the end of forever. He'll be around long after Earth has turned to so much cosmic dust.

The details on how and why are a little sketchy, since Wisp doesn't usually talk much about the subject. As the story goes, Wisp was a farmer, way back when. He was a proud man, bragging about a few of his talents, going so far as to say not even the Devil could beat him. Apparently, Old Scratch took offense at this and told Wisp to put his soul where his mouth was. Wisp wasn't stupid enough to bet his soul, but a wager was made and Wisp won. The Devil tried to get out of the bet, but Wisp tricked and/or trapped him and got himself the gift of Soulfire. Or maybe curse would be a better way to describe it.

The major plot line happens after Wisp dies. His shade made its way to Hell, but the Devil wouldn't let him in. Hell didn't have enough of a claim on his soul. Wisp apparently wasn't bad enough for damnation. Wisp hadn't been forgotten by Old Scratch. Without a mortal form to keep it in check, the Devil was able to let loose the full power of the Soulfire. It set his spirit ablaze, transforming Wisp into a metaphysical fireball.

Having been rejected by Hell, Wisp made his way to Heaven. He had some problems with the doorman. Seems that, while he wasn't evil, he wasn't good enough for Heaven. The incident where he bet with the Devil and won the Soulfire had tainted him. Wisp believed he knew what was right and just better than Heaven. He wouldn't acknowledge Heaven's superiority, so they wouldn't let him in. Problem was, for the most part, Wisp had followed Heaven's rules and lead a good life. By way of compensation, the angels gave him a new body to keep the Soulfire in check. In some of the legends this is a lantern to keep coals that the Devil gave him in and light his way in the world.

So Wisp has wandered the world, looking out for the good of mankind, ready to step in if either Heaven or Hell is trying too hard to impose their rule on humanity. In short, he is a Graywalker.

The Soulfire can do amazing things. When he unleashes it on someone, which he refers to as branding, it burns away at their soul. The branded person relives everything they ever did to another person. They experience every pain they ever caused and every joy they ever made happen.

For instance, if a man saved a child's life, during branding he would feel not only the child's joy but that of the parents and family, and even that of the children's children. On the other hand, if a man kills a man, he feels the pain of not only his victim, but that of the victim's loved ones. Usually, the Soulfire leaves the body unharmed, but the mind is another thing. Seeing all the damage that they've begotten has caused more than one person to end up on the other side of insane, a candidate for a rubber padded cell at Ringvue, the asylum of choice for this crowd. Unlike the better known Bellevue, Ringvue can handle the more mystically unusual.

The only time I've heard that the Soulfire actually burned someone was at the end of World War II. The literal end. Wisp had managed to track Hitler to his bunker and let him have it. Normally, the branding lasts a few seconds to several minutes. Hitler burned for hours, until nothing was left of him but ashes.

The Soulfire has other properties, not the least of which was the ability to engulf Wisp's head in a fiery halo as flames shoot out of his eyes. Not the friendliest sight to see on a dark night.

Most of the time Wisp, runs The Eternity Club: a place for Immortals to hang out, relax, network, that sort of thing. It's in Philadelphia. The minimum drinking age is 150 years, although they can make exceptions for some junior members.

"Bring me up to speed," said Wisp and Fred did as he was told. "We need to go to Arkansas."

"No, you need to go to the Ukraine," said Mosie, as he staggered drunkenly through the door.

"How do you guys know when to enter to get in on just the right part of the conversation?" asked Fred. In most cases, the answer was probably luck, but not in Mosie's. Mosie, simply put, is the most powerful psychic that has ever lived, bar none. His visions are so strong that they put him in a waking coma unless he remains drunk at all times. The alcohol keeps his sanity, but must play havoc on his liver.

"Fred, this is no time for joking. Paddy and his crew will handle Mab. It's Puck I'm worried about," said Mosie.

Don't make an ass out of yourself. I'll do it for you.
-Robin Goodfellow, aka Puck

The Ukraine had fallen on hard times. No one had realized just how much of a stabilizing influence the Soviet Union had been until it was gone. Sure, the Ukrainians wanted freedom, but no one had realized had hard it would be to enjoy without food in your belly or toilet paper for those hard to reach places. Sure, leaves and catalogs did the job, but it just wasn't the same.

Dimitri Gorkofsky was disillusioned with freedom, but what he wanted was money. Money to live decently in his backwater province. Money to feed his twelve children. Money to buy his wife the nice things she deserved, like bread and a good coat. Unfortunately, Dimitri had just been laid off again and he had no job prospects. Things were getting dark, but Dimitri had a candle to light to way to a better place. A great big nuclear candle.

Years ago, long before the fall of the USSR, Dimitri had worked in the factory that made Scaleboards: road-based nuclear missiles. He was good at his job and he liked it, at least in retrospect. One night he heard an old Johnny Cash song, translated into Russian. In the song, Mr. Cash had stolen a Cadillac, "one piece at a time and it didn't cost him a ruble." The song gave Dimitri an idea and a new hobby. Over several years, Dimitri built an entire nuclear missile with parts stolen a piece at a time. He even managed to get the uranium out undetected. The twelve-meter-long missile, hidden in the basement of his old barn, was Dimitri's pride and joy. It was as good as any he had built at the factory and better than most. He kept it a secret all these years, known only to him, his wife, and kids. Last week, in desperation, he went out to the hills—the same hills his grandfather claimed the fairy folk lived in—and cried out that he would sell his beloved nuclear missile to feed his family.

The next day, Mr. Goodfellow showed up wearing a suit that cost more than Dimitri made in a year. It was the kind, without collars, named after the Chinese. Manchurian, that was it. He had on a pair of Italian sunglasses that made him look like a movie star or a hitman, maybe both. Mr. Goodfellow had driven up in his fancy red car made of plastic. The engine was even made of aluminum, like the Gremlin his neighbor Ivan drove. Mr. Goodfellow's ride was nothing like Ivan's. It had more in common with a decadent German-style sports car, but Dimitri had never heard of the make, "Puck 2000". Mr. Goodfellow said it was custom made. It had one of the quietest engines he had ever heard. Despite having been looking out on the dirt road that led to his family's rural home, he hadn't noticed the car until it was practically at his front of his door.

Mr. Goodfellow said he had an offer to make Dimitri. The little man spoke in perfect Ukrainian, without a trace of a foreign accent.

"An offer I can't refuse?" laughed Dimitri at the obvious American movie reference.

"Do I look like Marlon Brando?" asked Puck, raising his eyebrows.

"No. I thought, because of your name, it might be funny."

"My name?"

"Goodfellow, like the American gangster movie, *Goodfellas,*" said Dimitri.

"The Brando line is from *The Godfather.*"

"Oh. Sorry."

"Nothing to be sorry about," said Puck, with a smile that could convince a drowning man to sell his life jacket in exchange for an anvil. "I understand you have been having some financial difficulties. It has also come to my attention that you have sometime of value you are willing to sell to end those difficulties."

Dimitri looked at Puck suspiciously. In his world, any offer too good to be true was a setup for prison or worse.

"I don't know what you mean," said Dimitri with his best smile of innocence, which did nothing but make him look sick to his stomach.

"I heard you are interested in unloading a Scaleboard."

Dimitri froze. His first thought was the same as it would have been a lifetime ago: was Goodfellow KGB? It took him a moment to remember the KGB was no more. Those that once served it had moved on to control local governments and organized crime. If they wanted his missile, they wouldn't ask for it. They would just take it.

"Where did you hear that?" asked Dimitri.

"From you. Or rather one of my agents," said Puck.

"Agents?" asked Dimitri, taking a step back, visibly shaken.

Puck put his arm around Dimitri with all the sincerity of a used car salesman moving in for the kill. As if reading Dimitri's mind, Goodfellow said, "Don't worry. I don't work for the government. Not your government anyway."

"Whose government?"

"That's on a need to know basis. Let me just say, I am in His and Her Majesty's Service."

"Great Britain? Like James Bond?"

"In a way, but the kingdom I work for predates the British Empire. That's all I can tell you. I can share with you that I knew your grandfather, Piotr. We had done some business."

"But you are so young. How could you know my grandfather? He vanished years ago," said Dimitri, remembering the strange disappearance of his grandfather. Fear had kept the family from speaking too loud of their suspicions; that he had crossed the KGB and had been sent to Siberia or worse.

"I'm older than I look."

"What business?" asked Dimitri.

"A last, great adventure. But that was then, this is now. Can we do business?" asked Puck.

"What are you offering?"

"Step over here to my car," said Puck, opening up the red trunk, revealing over a hundred bars of gold.

"Oh my," said Dimitri, his eyes wide.

"All that can be yours if you sell," promised Puck. "What do you say?"

Dimitri stared at the gold, but unlike many that Puck had done business with in the past, he looked with the eyes of a husband and father, not with eyes of greed.

"No, not for this. It is too much," said Dimitri.

"Too much?" asked Puck, shocked to hear those words from a mortal. "What you have cost many millions of rubles to build."

"Yes, but it cost me nothing. This gold is too much. I could never explain how I got it. It would make me a target. Mobsters would steal it from me or government officials would take it away."

"What could I offer you instead?"

"I don't need to be rich. What I need is a way to support my family, not just for now but for always. Can you give me that?"

"Let me think about it for a minute," said Puck. "I could set you up in another land."

"No, thank you. This is my home. I want to stay here."

"Then you tell me what you need. What would you pay for? Chances are if you want it, so would your neighbors," said Puck.

"What I need? Where do I begin? We need everything. We don't even have decent toilet paper," said Dimitri.

"That's it then," said Puck, snapping his fingers.

"What?" said Dimitri.

"I'll trade you this for the missile," said Puck, handing Dimitri a brown cardboard box he seemed to pull from the very air.

Dimitri reached into the box and pulled out a white fluffy roll.

"Toilet paper?"

"Yes."

"You expect me to trade a nuclear missile for a box of toilet paper?" asked Dimitri, raising his voice.

"Yes," replied Puck.

"I'm poor, not insane," shouted Dimitri.

"Obviously. This is not just an ordinary box. How many rolls do you think that box holds?"

"Maybe sixteen."

"Okay, start taking out rolls," said Puck. Dimitri did, one at a time, until the stack they made reached his knees. He kept pulling. "That's sixteen. That's twenty." Dimitri keep unloading the box and the toilet paper showed no signs of stopping. "That's forty five."

Dimitri looked at the white paper all around him then held the box up to his eyes.

"There is no way all that could have fit in here," said Dimitri.

"But it did. Your own eyes saw it," said Goodfellow, leaning against the trunk of his car.

"But how?"

"Magic. What you hold, to my knowledge, is the world's only endless box of toilet paper. No matter how many you take out, there will always be more," said Puck. "And feel how soft and fluffy that paper is. Like a cloud."

Dimitri felt it with his hands, but Puck corrected him and rubbed a piece of the paper on his cheek. It was easily the softest thing Dimitri had ever felt, softer than silk or satin or even a newborn's bottom.

"This is a wondrous thing, but a box of toilet paper is not worth a nuclear missile," said Dimitri.

"Isn't it?" asked Puck. "You said you wanted a way to support your family. This is it."

"So we won't have to buy toilet paper. How will that help us?"

"You won't have to, but your neighbors and countrymen will," explained Puck and a light finally went off over Dimitri's head.

"They'll buy mine. And since it is so much softer than the rough paper they are buying now, they'll pay even more."

"Exactly," said Puck. "Using this toilet paper will make going to the bathroom an experience people look forward to, instead of dread. And once their bottoms have been caressed and cleaned by this, they will never be able to accept anything less. They will be obsessed with your toilet paper. They won't want to live without it. They'll take laxatives just as an excuse to use your toilet paper. Why, the merest touch of this paper will even cure hemorrhoids."

Dimitri's face lit up. He had an obvious personal interest now. "You are kidding?"

"No, I'm not. Do we have a deal?" asked Puck, putting out his hand.

"Will this box work for anyone else but me?"

"Not if you don't want it to."

"You realize this may be the last Scaleboard missile in the world?" said Dimitri.

"Really? Why is that?" asked Puck.

"The rest were destroyed back in 1987 by the INF Treaty. I also don't have the launcher vehicle. They were made at another factory."

"Launch will not be a problem."

"Can you assure me this missile will never be used against me or my family?"

"I can give you my word," promised Puck.

"Then you have a deal," said Dimitri, shaking Puck's hand.

"You made the right choice," said Puck, knowing full well that the type of fairy gold he was planning to use would have turned to dirt in a week's time.

"Will you be bringing in a truck to get the missile out?" asked Dimitri.

"No. I'll take it out myself," said Puck, as the pair walked into the barn where the missile was kept.

"Yourself? I don't think that car of yours has enough horsepower to pull the missile."

"I didn't mean the car. I meant me," said Puck.

"Mr. Goodfellow, you are such a kidder. The missile weighs many tons."

Puck took a spray bottle out of his inside jacket pocket and spritzed the missile. In less than the blink of an eye, it shrunk to the size of a child's toy.

"It did. Would you do me a favor and please put that in here?" asked Puck, holding out an open bronze box. Stunned, Dimitri bent down and did as he was asked. Puck closed the box tightly. "Thank you. I have a problem touching iron. Best of luck to you, Dimitri."

Puck walked out of the barn, bronze box in hand and after opening his car door, climbed in.

"You are welcome, Mr. Goodfellow," said Dimitri, as he looked down at the piles of toilet paper. "And thank you," he said, but the red car and driver had already vanished.

You don't want to know. Trust me.
  -Mosie, drunken psychic

"It's too late. The missile is already on its way to Faerie," said Mosie.

"What do you mean it's too late?" asked Wisp. "Did Paddy and the rest fail?"

"No, not yet. I don't mean Mab's missile. I mean the one that Puck got for Oberon and Titania," said Mosie.

"Hex never mentioned that one," said Fred.

"That's because the bombing of Faerie will start before anyone learns about it. But if Paddy prevents Mab from taking the missile, Oberon will lord it over her and it will get launched at Mab in retaliation for an attack she makes on his kingdom. The other Faerie kingdoms, in a panic, invade Earth and steal more missiles to use against Titania and Oberon. The US won't have to destroy Faerie; Faerie will destroy itself in a round of mushroom clouds. The Nuclear Magic will seep onto Earth and the Mystacaust starts only two months later than in the future Hex's world."

"What can we do to stop it?" asked Bubba.

"First," said Mosie, "Paddy needs to let Mab win and take the missile with her into Faerie. Then the three of you need to go into Faerie, to Oberon and Titania's kingdom. . . ."

The bigger they are, the harder they hit.
-Rumbles, professional clown, former Golden Gloves boxer

I was amazed. Much like a matador with a bull, Rumbles was winning. He was more than winning, he was kicking the giant's butt. Literally. Rumbles tripped Tairde onto his knees and landed a roundhouse kick in the giant's gluteus region, knocking him flat out in the mud on his face. Quick to press his advantage, Rumbles ran up his spine, leapt so he grabbed Tairde's left ear as he landed and twisted. The giant screamed in pain, same as any kid whose mother had pulled that self-same move on them.

Tairde struggled to roll over onto his back, but Rumbles held him down, increasing the pressure on his ear every time he tried to move. With one foot planted firmly in the mud, Rumbles stuck his other foot in the front of Tairde's neck, into the giant's carotid artery. Rumbles had explained to me that the carotid had two receptors, both of which had shut-off valves. One monitored blood chemistry. This was what made you pass out if you held your breath too long, so you couldn't really turn blue and die. The second monitored blood pressure. If it senses a sudden drop or increase in the pressure, it makes the person pass out. Helps prevent strokes, heart attacks and the like.

The trick to making this knowledge work for a fighter, is knowing exactly where it is and how to press on it. Done right, it tricks the body into thinking its blood pressure just shot through the roof. The end result is an unconscious, but living opponent. In the average man the move takes about seven to ten seconds. Rumbles had been holding his foot on the giant's neck for going on twenty seconds, all the while avoiding Tairde's attempts to hit and crush him. So far, Rumbles had been both fast enough and lucky enough to dodge the blows, the end result of which meant the giant was hitting himself in the head.

If the giant didn't pass out, sooner or later one of those couch-sized fists was bound to connect with the battle clown.

While this battle raged, Paddy's cell phone rang on vibrate mode. The boss answered it.

"Hello? Mosie? What? Wisp, Bubba and Fred have gone where? To do what? We have to let Mab what? Do ye have any idea what we've done to stop her? Well, I guess ye do know. Rumbles is about to win. I'm not going to tell him to lose. The giant's eyes are rolling back in his head. Are ye sure? Fine, then ye tell Rumbles," Paddy said into the phone. He waved Hermes down. "Mosie says we have to let Mab take the missile back with her."

"You're kidding?" said Hermes, already knowing the answer. Mosie is never wrong.

"No. Rumbles has to lose."

Hermes looked out at the battle. "But he's about to win."

"I know," answered Paddy.

"Who's going to tell Rumbles?" asked Hermes. Paddy handed him the flip top phone.

"Mosie is," said Paddy.

Hermes flew over the battlefield built for two and hovered above Rumbles and the giant's head. Tairde's hands were barely leaving the ground now.

"Excuse me, I hate to interrupt," said Hermes.

"Then don't. I'm a little busy here," growled Rumbles.

"I understand, but Paddy says you have to talk to Mosie."

"Can't it wait?"

"No," said Hermes.

"I. . . don't. . . mind," muttered the barely conscious giant.

"Shut up," said Rumbles, as Hermes extend the phone to him. "Maybe you didn't notice, but I sort of have my hands full. Think you could hold it for me?"

"I suppose," said Hermes, holding the phone to the clown's ear.

"Hey, Mosie. What's so important that. . . I will not. I may have lost, but I've never thrown a fight in my life and I'm not about to start now. You're kidding? Are you sure? If I don't, everything we're trying to stop happens anyway? Damn it. Fine," Rumbles said, taking his foot off the giant's throat and letting go of his ear. As he did, Tairde's eyes shut hard, fast and promised to stay that way for a while. "Oh no. I can't believe I'm doing this."

Rumble walked down to Tairde's limp left hand and lifted it up, as if he was about to wrestle with it. As he moved, Rumbles lost his footing and fell on his back, pinned by the huge hand. He stayed pinned, even though the clown had to move the fingers some more so they covered him.

"I win!" shouted Mab triumphantly. "The Trident is mine!"

"Paddy, what the heck just happened?" demanded Pan.

"Rumbles had Tairde beat," said Sun.

"Why'd he throw the fight?" asked Coyote. From across the battlefield, Hex looked at Paddy and nodded. Somehow, he had figured out what was going on. I just hoped they were going to tell me soon.

"I'll explain when I can, but the gist is we have a new game plan, quarterbacked by Mosie. Just follow my lead," said Paddy, walking over to Mab's section of the field. Somehow, her troops had assembled a table and chairs for the meeting. Paddy took his seat.

"Well, Moran, it looks like the best won," said Mab.

"To a blind man," muttered Paddy, under his breath.

"What!?" demanded Mab.

"'Tis a good race ye ran," covered Paddy.

"And you know what that means," said Mab.

"You get to keep us as your prisoners," said Paddy happily.

"Exactly. I get to keep you as my. . . what?" exclaimed Mab.

"We lost. You get to take us prisoner," said Paddy.

"What's the deal? I don't trust you, Moran," said Mab.

"Which is why ye should kept us close, so you can keep an eye on us."

"I don't want prisoners. You have no tactical use," said Mab.

"I wouldn't say that. We agreed to let ye take the missile. We never agreed to let you keep it," said Paddy. Hex was whispering to one of the hundreds of Sun Wukongs, who nodded his head.

"What's your point, Moran?" demanded Mab.

"If we are left to our own devices, we would undoubtedly cause ye no end of inconvenience. It would be wiser to kept us out of trouble. You don't have to keep us long term, say two days or so," said Paddy.

"Why two days?" Mab asked suspiciously.

Paddy leaned in to whisper. Mab bent over to give him her ear.

"You know of our Fools' Day tradition," said Paddy.

"Yes."

"At present, I have the best practical joke going. If my competition was tied up and unable to contend. . ."

"You would win," said Mab.

"Exactly," said Paddy, clapping his hands.

"So if I do this, you will owe me?" said Mab, already scheming.

"Rather it would be one less than you owe me. Not to mention it would get you a chance to spend time with your daughter, something ye have neglected for far too long," said Paddy.

"Moran, you know as well as I the condition my people were living under. They were slaves while Thandu ruled them. I had to come back. I had responsibilities," said Mab.

"Ye had a responsibility to your daughter as well," countered Paddy.

"I couldn't very well take her with me. We both know she was safer and better off with her father and you. Besides, you chose to ignore the fight," said Mab.

"Not true and ye know it. Who supplied you with the things ye needed?" said Paddy.

"You could have gotten me better weapons," said Mab.

"I could not be a party to things that would take life and ye refused the weapons I did offer," said Paddy.

"Thandu was a butcher and a murderer. The toys you offered meant the troops we fought today would be alive to fight us again tomorrow. A bad strategy," said Mab.

"A matter of opinion. As long as there is life, there is the chance for redemption."

"Or betrayal."

"True. I prefer to err on the side of hope," said Paddy.

"I can't afford to err at all," said Mab.

"Why are you taking this route? Oberon and Titania have never been conquerors. They act more like petty children. What do you have to fear from them?"

Mab raised an eyebrow. "Interesting. You knew I was taking the Trident and my plans for it. How?"

"Ye know better than to ask that. Besides, ye haven't answered me question yet," said Paddy.

"Oberon and Titana were powerful enough that Thandu could not conquer them, yet they never helped the resistance."

"They are more concerned with their own pleasure than fighting," said Paddy.

"What if that changes? They could become the next Thandu. They believe in slavery, I don't. I agree with the human state that has the motto 'Live Free or Die.'"

"I don't like slavery any more than you, but a nuclear missile would kill the slaves as well as the masters."

"They are too much of a danger."

"Our kind are bound by rules. If you get a gilded promise, they cannot break it, even if they want to," said Paddy.

"Your point?" asked Mab.

"Unlike mortals, if those two signed a peace treaty, it would be a gilded promise, unbreakable. There could be no aggression. If would be more effective that a threat."

"True, but with the missile I can force them to sign whatever I want," said Mab.

"A gilded promise cannot be made under threat or coercion. They could break that promise any time they wanted."

"Also true," conceded Mab.

"If I can get such a treaty signed, will you turn the missile back over to me and give me a gilded promise never to acquire a missile again?"

Mab thought it over. She was no madwoman bent on destruction. Paddy's solution made sense.

"Yes," said Mab.

Paddy spit in his hand and extended it. Mab did the same. By shaking and mingling fluids, they had a binding contract. From what I've been told, this method originated among the Gentry and was adapted centuries back by humans who had contract with the Good, and not-so-good, People. A contract was breakable, unlike a gilded promise. Both parties had to extend trust.

"Please send word to Oberon to attend the peace conference. We will schedule it for tonight," said Paddy.

Mab took out a piece of parchment and wrote on it. "I have a better idea. Why don't you do it? Unless there is some reason you need Hermes to be a prisoner. He will after all, be busy and unable to try to one-up you," said Mab.

Paddy nodded. Mab hadn't believed his story completely, but was willing to play along. Problem was, there was bad blood between Mab and Hermes, which could muck the whole thing up. This would help avoid any spats between the ex-lovers.

Paddy nodded. He called Hermes over and explained the plan. Mab handed Hermes the parchment, rolled into a scroll.

"You never write me letters anymore," said Hermes.

"Sometimes I forget you can read," shot back Mab.

"The memory is the second thing to go. The first is. . . ."

Paddy cut Hermes off with a nod. Hermes turned and leapt, his winged red high tops carrying him into the sky. He didn't need to use the portal to go into Faerie. As the former messenger of the Greco-Roman pantheon, he can slide between realities easier that most of us can fall out of bed.

"I'll go get Kyna," said Paddy.

Mab froze up, her apprehension obvious.

"Think of it as a battle to win your daughter's friendship," said Paddy. Mab caught herself and regained her composure. Battle was something she could relate to.

Mab nodded, the closest she usually got to a thank you.

"Are we still going with the prisoner deal?" she asked.

"If you don't mind," said Paddy.

"I don't see why, since you already have what you want, but all right," said Mab, giving her troops the order to take us prisoner. Paddy joined the rest of us as the troops moved in.

"Are you sure about this, Moran?" asked Pan, not thrilled with the number of weapons being pointed his way. The troops were forcing the tricksters to march toward the portal to Faerie.

"Sure enough to be doing it."

"Why is Mab going along with it?" asked Coyote.

"I told her my prank was in the lead and I would win if the rest of you were out of commission for the duration of the contest," said Paddy.

"But you haven't even had a chance to pull your prank yet," I said.

"Mab doesn't know that and she didn't buy it entirely, but she is going along with it. Mosie says we need to be on the inside to do what needs to be done and this is the best way to get there," said Paddy.

"Yes, but what can we do from the inside of a prison?" asked Pan.

"Who said we would be inside for long?" said Paddy, with a wink.

More fun than a barrel of monkeys? What's that supposed to mean? What's fun about a barrel of monkeys?
-Sun WuKong, the Monkey King

Rumbles had already climbed out from under Tairde's hand, but the giant was still unconscious. Mab ordered her troops to bring the body. Over a hundred of her troops, trolls, ogres and goblins among them, pulled on Tairde's boot straps, dragging the behemoth at a painfully slow rate. Four of Sun Wukong's doubles shooed them aside and, using only one hand each, lifted the giant up and carried him with ease.

Even Mab's jaw dropped at that one. Another Sun Wukong walked up behind her. This was the original, as near as I can figure, because he was still carrying the healing she-monkey.

"I may have banana breath, but if you try to hurt any of my friends while they are in your custody, I will tear your kingdom down around your ears," said that Sun with a smile.

"Are you threatening me, monkey?" growled Mab.

"Oh yes, definitely. I thought that was obvious. Next time, I'll speak slower," said Sun.

"Listen. . ."

"I'd rather not," said Sun.

"I will not be mocked in front of my troops," said Mab.

"Oh, I'm sorry. We can do this in private next time then," said Sun.

"I don't appreciate this, Wukong," said Mab.

"Fine," said Sun. At that moment the four doubles that were carrying the giant dropped him. "Then I won't be doing you any favors. Time to come home, boys."

At that, the two hundred plus doubles turned and rushed toward Sun. He put the little she-monkey down. Frightened, the warrior queen stepped back and pulled her sword. In waves the Monkey Kings leapt into the sky, high enough that they became little specks. As they descended, it was for all intents and purposes raining monkeys. They became larger, only to shrink down to their original one-cell size a foot above Sun's open mouth. The Monkey King swallowed each wave until there was only the original. The Monkey King let out a huge belch when it was done.

"Excuse me," said Sun, covering his mouth.

The little she-monkey looked confused and moved toward Mab, who still had her sword drawn.

"Get away from me," Mab said, swinging at the she monkey with the flat of her blade. The blow would have hurt the she-monkey, but not done serious harm if it had connected. It didn't.

Using his back to shield his actions from Mab's troops, Sun caught the blade between his right thumb and index finger, plucking it out of Mab's hand as if it was an apple from a tree. I was impressed. Mab is no pushover. From the stories I've heard, her skill as a warrior is supposed to be in the league of Hercules, meaning she possibly could have taken the base without an army.

Mab ruled by the sword, by being the best warrior. Sun had disarmed her with less than a thought. Had her troops witnessed the act, she would have lost face and her leadership ability might have been brought into question. By shielding his actions, the Monkey King had put the Warrior Queen in his debt.

The little rhesus monkey bounded over to Sun and leapt into his arms. Sun handed the sword back to Mab hilt first.

"That goes for all my friends, big and small. Am I understood?" Sun whispered. Mab nodded. "Good. Now I believe I have to go be taken prisoner with the others."

The flock of monkeys followed Sun. Kyna joined Mab.

The taking of the tricksters was far from an orderly process.

Hex was leading Rumbles and me in a mock military march, with cries of "Left, left," but making sure we didn't move in the same directions for more than three steps at a time. The troops assigned to us kept jumping out of our way. They had seen Rumbles fight and apparently knew Hex by his reputation. They scurried from me only because of the company I kept.

One brave soldier decide to put a stop to it and stood in front of Hex with a bronze colored sword drawn.

"Stop this or I will cut you down where you stand," the soldier, who was named Yuron, said. I stopped short, while Rumbles dropped back into a defensive stance. Hex smiled.

"*Rubber*," Hex whispered. The blade began to shimmy and wiggle. Hex lashed out, smashing his forearm on the blade. The no-longer-bronze sword bent, wrapping itself around Hex's arm. Hex pulled, yanking the rubbery weapon out of the Yuron's hand.

"We are going with you because we want to, not because of any intimidation factor," said Hex. "You threatened us. Don't do it again. This is your only warning."

Hex has a weird way of dealing with bad guys. He gives them a warning before taking drastic action. Claims if they ignore the warning and do the evil deed, they choose what happened to them and it absolves him from guilt or blame. According to him, it keeps his soul clean. I suggested a good detergent.

"Gentlemen, I think a good pantsing is in order," said Hex.

Yuron was still amazed by what had happened to his sword and hadn't taken his eyes off Hex. I walked up behind him and got on all fours. Rumbles pushed him down over me, grabbing his pants as he fell and pulling them off over his boots. Rumbles tossed them to Hex, who tied them on the rubber sword, then waved it like a flag while he marched in circles.

Sun was leading the rhesus monkeys through the formations, all of them hopping on heads and soldiers, taking the occasional helmet and tossing it on the ground.

A troll by the name of Gonk, took offense, but Sun taught him the error of his ways with a painful nerve pinch.

Pan was flirting with the female soldiers, distracting some from remaining in formation.

We started walking through the portal and the world around us changed. There were trees that weren't exactly trees, more like plants gone wild. The air was cleaner and crisper, the sky a different shade of blue, bordering on purple. Rumbles and I moved closer to Paddy.

"Make sure you stay on the path," Paddy said to us.

"Why?" asked Rumbles.

"Because traveling in Faerie is different than traveling on Earth. A short path can take you hundreds of miles, even if it is only a few feet long. The paths fold time and space," said Paddy.

"Quantum geography," I quipped.

"Pretty much. If you step off, you could end up anywhere or anywhen. Odds are you will never find a way to get back on the path," said Paddy.

"How will we get back out?" I asked.

"There is a path that will take us to the parking garage under the bar. That's the route Mab expects us to take, because the time we spend here will roughly correspond to the time that passes outside. I figure we'll take this path back. We'll end up back in Arkansas a few minutes after we left, regardless of how long this takes."

"Aren't Faerie paths hard to find?" I asked.

"Extremely," said Paddy.

"So you can find it again?" I asked.

"Probably not, but Coyote has things covered," said Paddy.

"Don't I always have to take care of you two-leggers?" said Coyote. He was stopping every few feet and lifting his rear leg up. He was marking the path in his own way.

"The path is short enough so Mab and her troops could just walk to Earth. Pretty convenient," I said.

"Not really. See the woman leading the troops?" said Paddy, indicating a woman with maroon hair and blue skin. She looked like she was in her teens, but with the Gentry looks didn't mean much.

I nodded.

"Her name is Tralla."

"She can find the paths?"

"No, she's not a Path Finder. Tralla is a Path Maker. It's a rare talent, but she can create paths between any two points in Faerie. Since she joined Mab's cause, troop movements have become much easier. Tralla can even make temporary paths that fade with time. It helps keep the clutter down. She can also cloak them or limit access. Tralla may be one of the most powerful of the Gentry."

"Do her powers work outside of Faerie?"

"Some, but not as well," said Paddy. "I assume both of you know enough not to eat or drink anything while you're here?"

Rumbles nodded.

"Demeter's drilled that into my head enough times," I said. Demeter has never really gotten over the food incident between her daughter and Hades, and makes sure everyone else knows enough never to fall for it.

The little she-monkey jumped from Sun to land on my shoulder.

"Hey there," I said holding out my hand for her to smell. It was what I was taught to do with dogs. Apparently, she didn't care to sniff. Instead she grabbed my index finger and held on.

"Hey Murphy, I think she likes you," said Rumbles.

"There's no accounting for taste," said Paddy.

"Maybe you should introduce yourself," suggested Rumbles. He had a point.

"Me Murphy. You Jane."

Jane seemed to understand and reached out to mess up my hair. She kept playing with my 'do'.

"Maybe she's grooming you," said Rumbles.

"I think that means you're engaged," said Hex.

Pan reached out his hand, trying to get Jane to jump onto his arm. Jane ran to my opposite shoulder.

"I guess not every woman is swayed by your charms, Pan," said Hex.

"I suppose it's about time something female showed an interest in Murphy. The law of averages demanded that it was going to happen eventually," said Pan, who seemed to be insulted.

"You're just saying that because you don't handle rejection well," I said. Jane was back playing with my hair. I still had one more question for the boss. "Anything I should know about Mab's prison?"

""Nothing you won't find out soon enough," said Paddy with a smile.

A lot of people besides me call Mab mother. Of course, with everyone else, that's only the first half of the name.
-Kyna, Demigod, Demifairy

"You look well," said Mab formally. The estranged mother and daughter walked on the path, close behind Tralla. The troops and supposed prisoners walked behind them. Mab did her best to ignore the commotion, in hopes that it might stop. There was no worry of that.

"You already mentioned that," said Kyna.

"I suppose I did. How have you been?" asked Mab.

"Good," Kyna said.

"You no longer live above Moran's bar?" asked Mab.

"Moved out on my own years ago. I thought you knew that," said Kyna.

"I did. I'm not much good at small talk."

"There's a lot you're not good at."

"I am aware of my shortcomings, especially where you are concerned."

"That's comforting to know," said Kyna, unable and unwilling to hide the bitterly sarcastic tone in her voice.

"Look, I'm trying," said Mab.

"Why?"

"You are my daughter," said Mab, as if the answer should be obvious.

"Is that the only reason?"

"Leaving you behind left a hole in my heart that has never healed," said Mab.

"I've heard that before," said Kyna.

"It was as true then as it is now," said Mab.

"After you left, I never heard from you," Kyna said.

"I couldn't exactly drop a letter in a mailbox. Crossing between the realms is very difficult. Moran and his ilk only make it look easy," said Mab.

"You didn't seem to have a problem managing it when you needed a hostage," said Kyna. "Or a missile."

"I have begged your forgiveness for what I had to do. I made sure you would be safe and my actions saved ten thousand lives," justified Mab.

"You made sure I'd be safe!? I practically died," said Kyna.

"But you didn't."

"No thanks to you," spat Kyna, turning and walking farther back in the procession.

"Where are you going?" demanded Mab.

"To be with my real family," said Kyna, falling in step beside Paddy, who was one of the few prisoners that wasn't causing some sort of trouble. Actually, Kyna's mood had a sobering effect on the tricksters. They fell into line behind Kyna and started behaving, other than singing "Working On the Chain Gang".

From my position behind Paddy, I could see a spilt second vision of Mab's left eye, under her helm. A single tear had flowed down to her cheek. Mab turned forward, hiding her face in an act of faked indifference.

You don't want to light my fire.
  -The Wisp, aka Will-O'-The-Wisp and Jack-O'-Lantern

Sole, the gate guard, was having quite a depressing evening, despite being in the center of a wild party. Titania and Oberon had thrown the soiree to celebrate Puck's successful mission in the mortal country known as the Ukraine. The revelry was unmatched since, well, the last party. The bronze box, with the missile inside, was laid on the table between Oberon and Titania's respective thrones.

Titania was currently feeding Oberon grapes and washing them down with wine. The king was in his glory. He and the queen had been quarreling on and off for ages, ever since he used the love spell to make her fall in love with a man who had a donkey for a head. Titania was not quite as forgiving as Shakespeare made her out to be. It seemed after this latest plan of Oberon's, the marriage might finally be on the mend for real, as opposed to the pretend emotions that they had been going through for so long.

It's therefore understandable why Sole, standing in front of the thrones, was doing his best to appear invisible, hoping that Oberon would notice him before he had to interrupt. Sole was prepared to wait all night. He figured if he remained as still as possible, it might just work. Under normal circumstances, it might have. But in the midst of a party, one who stands still, staring forward for any length of time without falling over drunk, tends to attract more attention than three dancing girls cavorting nakedly on a table. Case in point, Oberon noticed Sole, but ignored the girls.

"What is it?" said Oberon as he closed his lips around another grape. Titania delicately dabbed at the corners of his mouth where some grape juice had dribbled down. She had never been this attentive.

"Sorry to bother you, My Lord. There are people at the gate who demand to see you," said Sole. Oberon, a manipulative king who loved to revel in decadence, had no problem inviting anyone and everyone to his parties, but had a problem with anyone demanding anything of him.

"Is that so? Tell them to go away and don't bother me with this again," ordered Oberon. Sole bowed his head and groveled, walking out backwards. The party continued. The table the three dancing girls were atop collapsed when a fourth girl, who appeared to be even smaller than them, climbed atop it. It was only her glamour that made her appear thin and frail, when in reality her bulk exceeded that of a walrus.

The fashions worn were as timeless as they were dated. The robes and gowns would both pass and be out of place in any period from the Roman Empire to the Renaissance to the 1960s. The variety of colors in the clothes made it look as though a rainbow had thrown up, scattering colors indiscriminately around the room. Titania, having run out of grapes, decided to join Oberon on his throne and straddled him, so she sat atop his lap while facing him. She kissed him with passion and with caring. She hadn't shared a kiss of this type with him any time in recent memory. Oberon matched her lip lock with a passion of his own. Seeing this as he walked back into the room, Sole became even more depressed because he knew he had no choice but to interrupt, and that punishment would follow this interruption.

"My Lord," whispered Sole tentatively. There was no response from either the king or the queen. "My Lord and my Lady. I am sorry to interrupt." Oberon broke his wife's embrace and turned furiously on the guard.

"If you're sorry to interrupt, then why bother at all?" growled Oberon.

"I would not bother my lieges with anything if it was not important. The party at the gate includes a man and a satyr. The man claims he is the Wisp and he wishes an audience with you."

"The Wisp? It must be some sort of joke. What would the Wisp be doing here? It must be an impostor," said Oberon turning to nibble on Titania's pretty pale blue neck.

"But my Lord, to accentuate his point his head burst into flames which did not consume him and he said that if you do not see him, he will burn down the gates," whined Sole.

"Burn down the gates! Utter nonsense. Tell him to go away and if he does not, you have my leave to kill him. So, what are you waiting for?" asked Oberon.

"Yes, My Lord," said Sole, intimately aware he was in a no-win situation. If he did not obey his king, Oberon would punish him. But he still feared what the Wisp might do. Sole left and the people partied on; the revelry, though, became slightly less rambunctious as the sound of a great WHOOSH filled the air. It was a sound of something going up in flames very quickly. A great light now lit up the night outside, but only from the gate-side windows. The throng ran to the windows to witness the inferno.

Moments later, with his clothes charbroiled and smoke rising from his hair, Sole walked back into the party and stood before the thrones. This time he did not have to wait to be noticed.

"What happened?" asked Oberon.

"I asked him to leave. He didn't."

"So, did you kill him?"

"We tried twice, but nothing we could do could hurt him. Our weapons shattered on his skin, then he waved his hand and a fireball flew to the gates. In less than a second they were aflame."

"So what did you do with him?"

"I brought him inside with me," said Sole, gesturing behind him. Out of the doorway walked Wisp and Fred. Bubba Sue had promised to find her own way in. Wisp walked in and checked out the place.

"I'm so glad you could fit me into your busy schedule. Love what you've done with the place. Stone walls and forests, indoor plumbing by way of natural streams. A lot like what Frank Lloyd Wright might have done," said Wisp. Titania climbed off of Oberon's lap and stood behind his throne, resting one hand atop his back.

"Allow me to introduce myself. I am Wisp and my traveling companion is Fred, son of Pan," said Wisp. At this, Titania's eyebrows raised, then a twinkle came to her eye as she tried to suppress a smile.

"How dare you invade my kingdom like some savage," said Oberon.

"Invade? Nonsense. I asked very politely twice and you refused to see me. I have urgent business to discuss with you, and it won't wait."

"What business could you possibly have with me?" asked Oberon, regally ignoring the fact that his guests had stopped the party to listen to this conversation.

"I wish to discuss the Russian missile that you just acquired. I would like to acquire it back from you," said Wisp.

"Well, as you can understand, I have gone through a great deal of effort to acquire this object, so I am not planning to give it up any time soon. Perhaps you would like to talk over some wine and some food," said Oberon, gesturing Wisp and Fred to a table.

"Certainly," said Wisp having a seat, Fred beside him. Serving girls with blue hair and green skin brought trays of delectables. Fred seemed unsure, but Wisp loaded up both their plates then poured large glasses of wine for each of them. Wisp cut a piece of roast meat, put it on his fork and lifted it to his lips. Oberon smiled, amazed that it could be this simple. Wisp caught the expression on his face.

"Ah, you think that if I eat your food, I'll be bound to your kingdom and then my desires will be as meaningless as a swim on a rainy night?" asked Wisp. Oberon's expression became stern.

"Let me show you a little trick I picked up a long time ago," said Wisp lifting his plate and Fred's. Soulfire flowed from his fingers, enveloping the food in a fiery nimbus. "That burns away all traces of your kingdom's magic, making the food safe for anyone to eat. There is no worry of being trapped here," said Wisp picking up their wine goblets and burning away the magic again.

"I must thank you for your hospitality. This food is very good, even though I had to barbecue it myself," said Wisp.

"I won't give you the missile," said Oberon simply.

"I could simply take it from you," said Wisp, sniffing the wine before taking a large sip.

"I'd like to see you try," said Oberon.

"I hope it doesn't have to come to that. Since you're not willing to simply give up the missile, I'd like to extend an invitation to you to meet Mab at the bargaining table."

"Mab would never sit down at the bargaining table," said Oberon. Just then another guard came into the throne room, bowed before Oberon and announced a messenger.

Oberon sighed. "Show him in."

Hermes appeared at the foot of the thrones in the blink of an eye, moving so fast he seemed to appear out of nowhere. Hermes handed Oberon the scroll. The Faerie King, trying to remain unimpressed, unraveled it and read its contents.

"How very interesting. It's an invitation to a peace summit in Mab's kingdom. How utterly convenient. So you're working for Mab," Oberon asked Wisp darkly. Hermes raised an eyebrow, but kept silent.

"Hardly. If you check, you'll find the summit is being given by another for whom I do not work, but I am proud to call a friend," said Wisp.

"Ah, Padriac Moran. I should've known. I suppose my attendance is mandatory," asked Oberon.

"No, of course not. It's purely voluntary. But if you choose not to go, I will be taking advantage of your hospitality on an indefinite basis."

Hermes moved and sat on Oberon's throne. Oberon turned and exploded in anger.

"For a messenger, you overstep your place," yelled Oberon.

As if Oberon had never spoken, Hermes said, "Hi, Wisp. Hi, Fred."

"I am speaking to you," growled Oberon. Hermes was still turning a deaf ear.

"You actually have to sit here? Couldn't you make it more comfortable?" asked Hermes, wiggling his bottom, trying to get cozy and comfortable.

Oberon moved as if to strike Hermes, but was stopped short by the sound of Wisp's voice.

"Your highness, allow me to introduce Padriac Moran's messenger, Hermes," said Wisp.

"The Olympian?" said Oberon, the twinges of respect forming in his voice.

"Formerly. I'm a New Yorker now."

Wheels began to turn in the Faerie King's head. "Is it true Zeus has left Olympus?" asked Oberon.

"My father's whereabouts are his business," said Hermes. Apparently,

Zeus had left both the mortal and godly planes for points unknown. "But Olympus is still occupied," Hermes added as an afterthought, sensing that Oberon might be contemplating acquiring some real estate.

At this point, a human boy walked over with a tray of pastries and offering them to Wisp.

"You still use human slaves?" said Wisp, his halo bursting into flame.

"The lad marched in and partook of our food and one of our maidens. What other choice did I have?" asked Oberon.

"What other choice besides making him a slave? Hundreds, I'd imagine. I demand he be set free this instant," said Wisp. Oberon, still not taking well to demands being made at him, threw a snit fit.

"You demand of me? By what power do you plan to enforce these demands?" In the background, Fred had followed Wisp's instructions of keeping quiet and letting him do all the talking. At this Fred took a step back and muttered, "Oh boy." Oberon seemed to be growing in size until he dwarfed Wisp, standing easily ten feet tall. Wisp wasn't impressed and stood to his full five foot ten height.

"I plan to impose my demands with this," said Wisp, holding his left hand out in front of him, where a fiery nimbus appeared above his open palm. "I am sure you heard of the Soulfire. If I choose to use it on you, you will experience everything you have ever done to another, both good and ill. There is often enough evil in men's souls to drive them quite mad."

"I am not a man," said Oberon, standing and taking a step back.

"That won't make a difference to the Soulfire. One of the Gentry can become just as mad as a man, perhaps even more so," said Hermes, standing up and moving away from the throne. It gave the impression that even an Olympian feared Soulfire.

"That's true. After I brand you, I will proceed to burn your kingdom down around your ears and make sure, should you ever recover from madness, that you will not have the power to enslave another. So, the ball is in your court. The question is, do you want to dance?"

The fiery nimbus had spread, engulfing Wisp's entire body. The king had indeed heard of Soulfire. Oberon looked ready to make a run for it, but the eyes of his subjects gave him strength to stand his ground.

"To avoid my wrath, you need only do two things. End slavery in your kingdom and go to this summit."

Oberon laughed.

"You amuse me. Therefore, I will agree to your. . . requests." Turning to the teenage boy, he said, "Miguel, you're free. Do what you will. No unnecessary burdens shall be placed on you."

"Thank you, my lord," said Miguel on both knees bowing and groveling before the king. Apparently he had been here so long he didn't quite understand the concept of freedom. Wisp grabbed his arm and pulled him to his feet and sat him down at the feast at the place next to his.

Oberon snapped his fingers and the party resumed as if it had never stopped. "I guess I must pack and be off for the summit. Please stay here as my guest," said Oberon.

"I plan to," said Wisp. Oberon walked out. Titania came over to the table and, ignoring Wisp, extended her hand to Fred, who shook it.

"A pleasure, a great pleasure," said Titania before leaving to follow Oberon out.

It's always better to be the one setting a trap than to be the one caught in it.

-Coyote, Native American Trickster god

The monkeys, even Jane, wouldn't leave the forest, so we left them there. I counted an extra, so I figured one of Sun's other selves had morphed into a rhesus monkey to keep an eye on them.

Paddy and Kyna had been given rooms in the castle proper, while the rest of us were sent to the depths of Mab's fortress. It wasn't made entirely of stone, like a traditional castle. Actually, it looked little like a traditional castle. Mab had updated the design. It was made mostly from metals of different colors, looking almost like a five story mini-high-rise, minus the windows. It deferred to tradition by having an outer wall with battlements and one gate. There were mini-towers on each corner, each looking like something more out of a spy movie, with shielded swiveling turrets, with what looked like machine guns and mystic energy cannons. There were four total, one each of stone, silver, bronze and á blue metal I didn't recognize. Apparently there was some mystic significance for the four elements of earth, air, fire and water respectively. The castle itself also had four towers and four walls, one each of the same materials. The architecture was meant to be intimidating, sort of a gothic castle look with a slick skyscraper sensibility. I didn't want to think about what was meant to be on the pikes lined up along the outer walls. I was pretty sure it wasn't party lights.

The dungeon was still in the traditional underground location. It was made of the blue metal and the turquoise walls parted for the dungeon guard, like automatic doors at the mall. The lot of us went inside and the walls closed behind us. No worries about prisoners picking locks or slipping through windows. Iron bars might not a prison make, but a metal box might do the trick. I just hoped they had poked air holes somewhere.

I had never been in an actual dungeon before. The experience is highly overrated. It was dark, damp and musty. There were no bars like a traditional prison. We were surrounded by metallic blue walls, some of which were decorated with silver colored shackles, designed to hold prisoners suspended off the ground. Instead of rust, the manacles were tarnished. None of the soldiers had been daring enough to try to put any of the tricksters—or captured bartenders, for that matter—in chains.

The only light came from what Hex said were glow globes.

"Poor quality, too. Flickers like candle light," said Hex.

"And the blue stones will make poor pillows," said Pan, mocking out Hex.

"Luckily, I brought my own," said Rumbles. He took off one of his over-sized, padded boxing gloves, put it against the wall, and sat, leaning against it. Pan ignored him. The walls were shimmering and glowing in the glow-globe light, giving the illusion that we were surrounded by water.

"When do we get out of here?" grumbled Pan.

The Monkey King sat in cross legged position, like some Zen sage. "When it's time," he said.

"When will that be?" demanded Pan.

"When it's time," repeated Sun.

"What are we supposed to be doing?" said Pan.

"Providing a distraction," said Hex.

"We're doing a great job. I doubt anyone in the fortress can concentrate on anything but us," said Pan.

"We haven't started yet," said Coyote, cleaning his hind leg with his tongue.

"Duh. Why are we providing this distraction?" asked Pan.

"Because Paddy will need one," said Hex.

"When?" asked Pan.

Hex motioned to Rumbles to toss his other glove. The clown complied and Hex made himself comfortable next to Rumbles. "I'll let Sun field that one," said Hex with a smile.

"When. . ."

"It's time. I get it," grumbled Pan. "I want out now."

"You are welcome to leave any time you want," said Coyote, who turned himself three times in a circle before lying down.

"How?" asked Pan. "I couldn't get out of here if I wanted to. Could you, fleabag?"

Coyote laid his snout on his front paws. "Maybe, but I'm willing to wait."

Hex smiled. "I could."

"Prove it," said Pan.

"I don't have anything to prove," said Hex.

"Yeah, right. So how are we going to know it's time?" grumbled Pan.

"I'll know," said Hex.

"So will I," said Sun.

"And if you're real good, maybe we'll tell you, too," said Hex.

Rumbles was shaking his head and rolling his eyes back. "What's wrong? You want out with the amazing goat legs here?"

"I can't believe I threw a fight," said Rumbles. "Mosie better be right about this."

"Mosie's always right," said Hex.

"How come you didn't know about the missile Puck acquired?" I asked.

Paddy hadn't had a chance to give us details. Luckily, Mosie had informed Rumbles of the basics and he told us, after Hex assured him nobody was listening in.

"From when I came from, the second missile never came into play. I'm not in Mosie's class when it comes to second sight, so I didn't know until the scene at the base played itself out," said Hex.

Rumbles was still moping. Sun got up and sat next to the clown, putting a hand on his shoulder.

"You did very well," said Sun.

"Thanks, Sun. From you, that means a lot," said Rumbles.

"You would have won," said Sun.

"Rumbles did win. He had to throw Tairde's hand on himself to lose," I said.

"Don't remind me," said Rumbles, covering his face with his own hands.

"You expended too much energy, running and jumping like that. I still liked my way better," said Coyote.

"You think you could have tricked Tairde into breaking his own leg again?" said Sun dubiously. "Even giants aren't that dumb."

"Maybe an arm," mused Coyote.

"Maybe not," countered Sun.

"Why don't we just grab the missiles and leave?" asked Pan.

"Because Mab and Oberon will just get more and eventually the mortal two-leggers will catch on. Then Faerie goes boom," said Coyote.

"We need to get the treaty signed or this won't stop. I refuse to let that happen," said Hex.

"We'll stop them," I said to Hex.

"We?" asked Pan. "What are you going to do to help? You have no powers. Can you get out?"

"Don't know. I haven't tried," I said.

"Try," sneered Pan.

I walked over to where the door had been and raised my hands dramatically.

"Open sesame," I shouted in a voice any good Shakespearian actor would have cringed at. As quick as lightning, the wall did absolutely nothing. "Nope. I'm stuck."

"Bah, even for a human, you're pathetic. Rumbles at least can fight," said Pan.

"I've learned not to underestimate Murphy in the future," said Hex.

"Maybe in the future, but this is now. Murphy's useless," said Pan.

"I'm sure if we need to sleep our way out, you'll be a big help. Other than that, I don't see you being any more help than powerless old me," I shot back.

Pan pulled out his pipes, although I'm not sure from exactly where, and waved them at me. "I can do a little more than sleep."

"Did you even ask Fred if you could borrow them?" I said.

"Borrow? They're mine," countered Pan.

"Were yours, past tense. You lost them fair and square to Paddy, when he kicked your furry butt," I said. It was during a musical contest at the bar on a Halloween past. "Paddy gave them to Fred, something you had promised to do. Next time show some respect for your son and ask Fred first."

"I'll give them back," Pan grumbled.

"You'd better," I said.

"Really? And what are you going to do if I don't?" asked Pan.

"Simple. Tell Paddy," I said.

"I said I'd give them back," Pan said, annoyed that a lowly mortal would dare try to correct him.

"Why didn't you just make a new set?" asked Rumbles.

"I did, but the original was made from special reeds and I haven't been able to duplicate the effects," said Pan.

"That's because the reeds were taken from the body of a transformed nymph, a lady friend of yours I believe," said Hex.

"True. My new pipes work musically and for seduction, but they fall short in the offensive category," said Pan.

"Offensive?" I asked.

"Murph, you're a writer. Think about where the word panic came from," said Hex.

"From Pan?" I asked.

Pan smiled and I had my answer.

"Be afraid. Be very afraid," said Pan.

It's hard to shine living in someone's shadow.
-Fred, satyr, son of Pan, busboy at Bulfinche's Pub

Fred sat staring out the window. The room he had been given was lavish enough to make a suite in a five star hotel look poverty stricken by comparison. Fred couldn't care less. He was feeling quite useless. Bubba Sue was off tracking down the Soviet missile in stealth mode and Wisp had so intimidated the king and queen that he and Fred had been made honored guests. Fred was so oblivious to his surroundings that he didn't notice the tiny pixie that flew in through one of the keyholes. The pixie had green skin and fluorescent red hair with tiny yellow gossamer wings and looked like some bizarre Christmas decoration. She fluttered carefully around the room searching in the closets and under the beds to make sure that Fred was alone before she exited the same way she entered. A moment later there was a knock on the door. It took several more to get Fred's attention. He stood and walked to the door.

"Yes," asked Fred.

"Fred, it is I, Titania. May I come in?"

"Sure, I guess."

Slowly, the door opened, and in walked the queen wearing a gown, that while technically qualifying as clothing, was actually much more revealing than if the queen had walked in naked. Fred was struck dumb at the sight of the beautiful woman in his room. There are a few advantages fairy women have over their human sisters. For starters, many of them have the ability to cast glamours. Even the simplest glamour could put the work of the best Hollywood plastic surgeon to shame and there are no bandages to worry about. Titania, although able to cast powerful glamours, did not need them. Her skin was a pale blue, the kind that reminded you of a faraway frozen land. Her hair was constantly changing colors but tonight it was white; not the white of gray or yellow, but pure white like driven snow. Her body was the stuff of men's delirious dreams. She had an hourglass figure that was not to be believed, with amazing muscle tone and definition.

Titania knew how to move. It was evident from the way she strolled into the room that she had taken even the most basic act of walking and raised it to an art form. Fred could not have taken his eyes off her if he wanted to, which he didn't. The tiny Christmas-colored pixie fluttered in behind her. Titania gestured and a gust of wind blew the tiny fairy out the door and then the breeze shut the door behind her.

"Alone at last," said Titania with elegant sensuality.

"Titania, is there something I can help you with?" said Fred wondering what had brought the queen to his chambers, but still too naive to guess correctly.

"Yes, I'd say there is," said Titania, as she sauntered over to Fred's bed and sat down on the edge, making herself comfortable. She patted a spot to her right for Fred to sit and join her. Once they were side by side, Titania turned on the charm. Fred was caught like a deer in the headlights, double entendre intended.

"I knew your father," said Titania.

"My father and I are nothing alike," said Fred.

"I hope that's not true. Your father and I spent two days together that were not to be believed," said Titania.

A light flashed on somewhere in Fred's head and he realized what the queen's intentions were. "Your majesty, I'm flattered, but you're a married woman," said Fred. Titania laughed as if Fred had made a hilarious joke. When Fred did not join her in her revelry, she stopped and took a good look at Fred.

"You're a satyr. You can't be serious. What difference does a thing like marriage mean to you?"

"Marriage is a sacred bond between two people," said Fred, serious in both manner and tone.

"I don't believe it. Your time with Moran and his ilk has corrupted you."

"Maybe, maybe not, but marriage is supposed to be forever. I can't get in the way of that," said Fred shifting uncomfortably. It was obvious he was saying one thing, but parts of him were disagreeing vehemently. The disagreement was obvious enough for Titania to notice. She smiled.

"Oberon and I have been married for a very, very long time. Civilizations have risen and fallen since our wedding day. We married for many reasons, including love—or what we thought was love—and I do love him after all this time, but I need more. I need you."

"I'm very flattered. . . " said Fred scurrying down the bed away from Titania. The queen was no back-room floozy to go chasing after the satyr. It was not something she needed to do. She simply stood and displayed herself to her full advantage. Fred stopped and stared, somehow managing not to have his jaw drop and drool all over himself.

"Come here, young satyr," whispered Titania, extending her hand. Fred stood, walking to her, taking her hand in his. Titania bent and gingerly kissed the back of his hand and then caressed his hand with her cheek. Fred was in turmoil. He was torn physically, ethically, and by his heart. That which he had wanted for so long was being laid before him on a silver platter. The only problem with silver is that in the long run, it tarnishes.

"I have never. . ."

"You're the son of Pan. Of course you must have—" said Titania, halting in mid-sentence as Fred removed his hand from hers in embarrassment.

"You mean you're a. . ."

"Yes," said Fred, mortified.

"So I would be the first?"

Fred nodded. Titania's face lit up with excitement. With a hand she helped Fred stand on the bed, so they were almost equal heights. She rubbed her fingertips along his cheeks, forehead, then his lips. Fred closed his eyes with an audible moan. Titania leaned in and kissed Fred passionately, pulling him close in a tender embrace. Caught off guard, Fred went through shock then pleasure, but after a few moments of pleasure pulled back and turned his head away, his eyes downcast.

"I'm sorry."

"I'll be gentle, I promise," said Titania.

"It's not that."

"Then what is it? Is it the way I look? Does my form not please you?" said Titania, but with one look she was fully aware that this was not the case. "I can be anyone or anything you want me to be." Using her glamour, Titania suddenly became a gorgeous nymph similar to the kind who frolicked with the satyrs in Nysa, the land where Fred grew up. Seeing this had no more effect on the young satyr, she switched gears and became a she-satyr and then a beautiful human woman. None of the forms changed Fred's mood. Titania was troubled by this. She moved closer, putting her hands one on each side of Fred's head. "Let me see what it is that you most desire," she said looking into Fred's mind and plucking from it an image which she then became.

"Toni," said a startled Fred.

"So you know me by name. I can be this Toni for you. We can do anything you want to do," said Titania pulling the satyr close and kissing him again. Fred pushed away.

"No."

"Why do you pull away? I can see in your heart that this is what you want more than anything else," said Titania.

"Yes, but not like this," said Fred stepping down from the bed and walking to the window. There were tears in his eyes. Titania was thrown off guard by his reaction.

"Who is this Toni?"

"She's a waitress at Bulfinche's Pub, and I've fallen hopelessly horns over heels in love with her."

"Does she feel the same way about you?"

"I know she loves me, but I don't think she's in love with me yet. She's not ready to become seriously involved. She's a single mother and the most important thing in her life is her daughter, B.G."

"So you waste your time pining away for someone who doesn't want you?"

"I guess it's like that, but I know in my heart that someday we will be together, and as bizarre as this may sound, I was sort of saving myself for her," said Fred stopping and waiting for the mocking; the mocking similar to that he had received from his father when he told him his plans.

No mocking came.

"I can also see in your heart that you lust after me with a fire that you've never known before," said Titania.

"Yes, that's definitely true," admitted Fred.

"You have given no vow. There is no reason why you and I cannot share pleasure."

"You're absolutely right. There's a million reasons why we should and only one reason I can give why we can't. It just would feel wrong to me. I feel guilty just thinking about it." Fred was expecting her to tell him that it was ridiculous to think like that, but instead he looked up and noticed something in her eyes that he hadn't expected to see there: envy.

"How long do you plan to wait for her?"

"As long as it takes."

"It could take a very long time. She might never. . ."

"I know, but I want to give her every opportunity. She's only human after all. She only has another 70 years or so. I can wait that long."

"And if the day comes when you know she will never change her mind or the day you change yours, will you come back to visit me?"

"I'll be here in a heartbeat," said Fred grabbing her hand and holding it tight. Titania smiled. She sat down on the bed awkwardly, not knowing where to go from here.

"Do you have any plans for the evening?" asked Fred with a smile.

Titania looked at him and smiled back. "No, it seems what I had intended to do for the evening has fallen through."

"Would you like to go for a walk in your gardens?" asked Fred extending his arm as an escort at a ball would do to his lady.

"I would like that very much indeed," she said.

The two of them walked out of the room and into the gardens, and ended up spending the entire night talking and looking up into the stars of Faerie.

The warrior's way is not for the faint of heart or spirit.
-Mab, Faerie Warrior Queen

"Teach me how this thing works," demanded Mab of the two Shapelings that had infiltrated the missile silo control room.

"Well, first off, the warhead—"

"I'm not an idiot. I spent years on Earth and I took the time to study their weapons. I understand everything I need to know about how the missile and warhead work. I need to know how to operate the guidance system," said Mab.

"There will be some problems using the missile in Faerie. First, there are no magnetic fields. Second, there are no satellite tracking systems," said the male Shapeling.

"So are you telling me I can't aim it?" said Mab.

"Yes and no," said the female. "The missile can still be fired in a straight line. There are also ways to launch it magically."

"That's the problem. Magically, Oberon and Titania have us outgunned, which is why we need the missile to even the odds. I want this missile to be magic free. That way, there is enough steel and iron in it to ensure that they won't be able to stop it," said Mab.

"Permission to speak freely, my queen," said the male. Mab had watched a few too many military movies during her time on Earth. Mab had liked the military form of address so much that she had adopted it.

"Granted," said Mab.

"As I understand it, we wanted the missile as a deterrent, not to actually use. Its killing power is unparalleled," said the male.

"That's the point. If the missile isn't pointed and ready to go at a moment's notice, it's not much of a threat. Without that threat, the missile would actually have to be used," explained Mab.

"Would you actually use the missile?" asked the male.

"I would do everything in my power to prevent that eventuality," said Mab.

"What if events went beyond even your power? Would you use it then?" asked the male.

Mab looked away, but answered. "Yes."

"Do you think Padriac Moran's plan will work?" asked the male.

"I don't know," said Mab.

"Do you trust him?" asked the female.

"Moran has his own agenda. He always has, but if Moran gives his word, he will not break it," said Mab.

"What do you think his agenda is?" asked the female.

"He fed me some line about wanting to win a trickster contest, but he knows I didn't buy it. Moran places exceptional value on life. I believe that saving lives is his true motivation, and I have seen enough death in my time. Too much of it has been caused by me. If Moran can truly get a gilded promise from Oberon, I will no longer need the missile," said Mab.

"So you'll give him the missile then?" asked the male.

Mab sighed, thinking of all the time and effort that went into obtaining the Trident. "Yes."

"And if his plan fails?"

"We will have Oberon in our midst. He will not be allowed to leave. This is one time that Moran's failure would sadden me. Still, we must be prepared for that failure. Start teaching me how this works."

While the male Shapeling began explaining the missile's workings, the female casually turned her head toward the open door and nodded silently to Paddy Moran. He nodded back. Paddy left his hiding spot and returned to his room, sneaking again past the guards, who hadn't even realized he was gone.

One should always be accorded the respect due to one's rank.
-Oberon, Faerie King

Oberon arrived outside the gate of Mab's fortress. It was no surprise. Not only had the Faerie King been expected, he had been watched for the last leg of his journey. Oberon was aware of the spying eyes, but neither cared nor showed any signs of interest. In Faerie, there was very little he needed to fear or worry about, save the lout Wisp who he left back at his castle.

Oberon did not take being made a fool of lightly. Wisp had made an enemy who could, and would, hold a grudge for eons. Oberon would not allow his hand to be forced. Their own seer had divined what Mab had been up to, so the king had sent out Robin Goodfellow to make sure he was one up on the warrior queen.

He stood before the fortress gate. Mab had fortified her fortress with a moat, filled with a liquid far more deadly than water. Oberon would not lower himself to announce his arrival. They were aware he was here. Let them drop the drawbridge.

It didn't take long for Mab's guards to do just that. As the drawbridge touched down, a procession of armored warriors, in a military march formation, walked across the bridge. The group consisted of some of Mab's fiercest warriors and Daemor, running the gamut of the Faire races, from dwarf and elf to ogre and troll and several more in between.

It was a military show of power on Mab's part, to demonstrate the loyalty she inspired across the racial boundaries. In Faerie, Mab's mystic strength might not be the equal of Oberon or his wife, but without soldiers to fight for you, magic could only take you so far. Mab was doing her best to rub that in Oberon's face.

"Greetings, Oberon. We are your escort into the fortress," said Dawatt, the troll in command of the formation.

"You shouldn't have gone to the bother. I'm sure I could have found my way across a drawbridge," said Oberon. Before Dawatt could respond, Oberon walked through the center of the formation and out the other side. Dawatt called an about face, but Oberon was already halfway across before the company caught up with him.

He kept marching right up to where Mab stood waiting, one among her assembled troops. At least two thousand soldiers stood at attention in the large courtyard. It was meant to be an intimidating sight. It was.

Oberon merely raised an eyebrow.

"Welcome, Oberon," said Mab flatly.

Oberon nodded. "Mab."

"Hello, Oberon," said Paddy, offering his hand. He and Kyna were standing to Mab's left, Tralla to her right.

Oberon looked down disdainfully at Paddy. "Moran."

Paddy kept his hand out. "When a man puts out his hand, the polite thing to do is return the gesture."

"Neither of us is a man, although I suppose anything would be a step up for a leprechaun. I do not allow inferiors to touch me," said Oberon haughtily.

Paddy put his hand down. "Pity there is nothing with a pulse that is anything but superior to the likes of you. Saves me the trouble of disinfecting me hand," muttered Paddy under his breath. Oberon had good hearing.

"Excuse me?" said Oberon. The boss bit his tongue. He wasn't back at the bar, where he held all the power. He called the peace conference for a reason.

"Oberon, we should work at not falling into our old habits. We are here to make peace," said Paddy.

Oberon shrugged begrudging agreement.

Mab tried to hide a smile at the obvious discomfort Paddy and Oberon put each other in.

"Shall we adjourn to my great hall?" said Mab.

Visions of Mab sitting on her throne, lording it over Oberon danced in Paddy's head.

"I have a better idea. My quarters have a room with a table. That's all we need. Best to keep it simple," suggested Paddy.

"If we may put diplomacy aside for a moment, I can stand the smell, if you can," said Oberon, looking at Paddy.

"For a moment? Certainly, and I must add that ye wouldn't have to stand it, if ye would bathe more than once a century," shot back Paddy.

"You're a born diplomat, Moran. I'm learning so much from watching you in action," said Mab sarcastically.

"Glad to hear it," said Paddy.

Oberon smiled lecherously when he noticed Kyna in her blue jeans. "Who is this vision of beauty?"

It was Mab's turn to raise an eyebrow. "This is my daughter, Kyna."

"Daughter? How delightful. I hope to get to know you much better, dear Kyna," Oberon said, stepping forward and reaching for Kyna's hand in an obvious attempt to kiss it.

Kyna pulled her hand away as if it had touched a hot stove. The action shocked Oberon. Rarely had his attentions been rejected.

"Not a chance. And don't touch me. Since diplomacy is still shoved aside for the moment–Paddy, can I borrow some of that disinfectant?" asked Kyna.

"Absolutely," said Paddy.

Kyna leaned over and kissed Paddy on the cheek and gave him a big hug. "Paddy's such a cutie, isn't he?" Kyna asked Oberon. The king didn't answer, but his eyes grew colder and his blue skin more flushed. Her mother looked on, envious of Paddy's relationship with Kyna, and her loyalty to him. Mab knew how to inspire that loyalty in her troops, but not in her own daughter. Part of her was thankful that the chances of Paddy ever coming back to Faerie and raising an army or kingdom of his own were minimal.

"If all of you are done with your little games, please follow me," said Mab, leading the way around a corner. "Tairde, would you get the door, please?"

Oberon had been paying little attention to his surroundings, not deeming them interesting enough to rate the bother. The king hadn't noticed the giant, as he was standing around the corner by the stone tower. When the giant's hand reached down to open the door, the sight of those huge fingers caused Oberon to jump.

"Thank you, Tairde," said Mab.

"My pleasure, my Queen," boomed the giant's voice.

"Interesting doorman," said Oberon.

"He was the soldier closest to the door," said Mab.

"Of course he was," said Oberon. As Paddy passed the female Shapeling, who was in formation, he looked at his watch, then held five fingers at his side. The Shapeling blinked, indicating she had seen the signal. She slipped away quietly.

No more words were said until they arrived at Paddy's quarters in the stone tower. Paddy waved Mab and Oberon to opposite ends of the table, with Kyna and himself taking up seats on the remaining sides.

"I do not appreciate how I came to be here," said Oberon.

"I don't appreciate what you've been doing," said Paddy. Mab smirked. "Either of you." Mab lost the smirk.

"What exactly is the purpose of this so called peace conference?" asked Oberon, in a bored tone.

Before Paddy could answer Mab said, "Your kingdom is a loose cannon. You did nothing to stop Thandu."

"Nor did we aid him," said Oberon.

"You are too powerful not to be kept in check," said Mab.

"So you have done something that manages that task," said Oberon.

"Exactly," said Mab.

"And you believe your nuclear missile will suffice?" said Oberon. It was Mab's turn to be surprised.

"You know?"

"Not only does he know, but he sent Puck out to get one for him," said Paddy.

"You have a nuclear missile?!" asked Mab.

"Of course. It looks lovely in our throne room," said Oberon.

"And you knew, Moran?"

"Yes," admitted Paddy. "Now ye can understand the importance of this meeting. With both of you having missiles, too many may die. We have to put an end to this nonsense."

Outside, there was an explosion.

"What was that?" asked Mab.

Paddy looked at his watch. It had been almost seven minutes. They were late.

Iron bars and walls do not a prison make. Unless, of course, a pissed-off Buddha drops a mountain on top of them. That does a prison make.
            -Sun Wukong, The Monkey King

The Monkey King was in a lotus position, eyes closed and concentrating intently on his breathing. He was sweating profusely, not a pleasant experience for someone covered in fur. Or those downwind.

"Sun, you okay?" I asked.

"Yeah. No. Kinda," Sun said, opening his eyes. There was fear taking up residence there and it looked like it had paid three months' rent in advance. "I'm claustrophobic. Being buried alive for five hundred years will do that to you. I'm having flashbacks. Luckily, it won't be a problem for long."

"Why's that?" asked Pan, who was lounging on his back, drawing lazy circles with his hooves in the air.

The entry wall opened and the she-Shapeling stood facing us.

"I've come for you," she said ominously.

"Shapeling!" Pan yelled, and rushed at the Shapeling, leaping up into the air in a flying kick. The Shapeling waited until the last second and dropped to the floor. Pan flew over her head and landed on his furry butt. The Shapeling made no aggressive moves.

She leaned over and gave Pan a hand up. He grudgingly took it.

"Pan, it's time," she said, before morphing into a second Sun.

"What the?" said Pan.

Hex stood. "I figured replacing the Shapelings with shifters of our own was fair play. The real Shapelings are still in a locker on the base."

"So Loki is the male Shapeling?" I said. I already had figured he had shifted into someone in Mab's army.

"Yep. He refused to be the female. He got in too much trouble the last time he impersonated a woman. Not to mention he didn't want to risk it with goat legs around," said the second Sun, looking at the original. He ran all out, leapt into the air, flipping as he shrunk to the size of a breath mint. He landed in the first Sun's mouth and disappeared.

"That's pretty disgusting," I said.

"Think of it as recycling," said Sun.

"Plus, doesn't leave anything to be used in a spell against you," said the ever-paranoid Hex. Apparently hair, fingernail clippings and such can be used in magic spells to control people, a la voodoo and the like.

"Paddy needs for all of Mab's troops to be kept busy while he takes care of business. Mab has already set plans in motion for her soldiers to take Oberon prisoner if things go poorly," said Sun.

"And what are we supposed to do?" said Pan.

"Cut loose. Run wild. Cause chaos. In other words, be ourselves," said Hex with a smile.

"What about the missile? Shouldn't someone take care of it first?" asked Coyote.

"If Paddy gets the treaty signed, we get Mab's missile, and hopefully Oberon's as well. If not, we'll have to take them," said Sun.

"Which means they'll take more," said Hex.

"Which means we'll have to get those," said Rumbles.

"Which means we all have a new full-time job. We don't want that, because sooner or later, my future will become your present. What Paddy's doing is our best bet. Besides, it was Mosie's idea. He's never wrong," said Hex.

I'm good, but not infallible. There was a time or four when I knew ev-erything. . . and I never want to be that sober again.
-Mosie, drunken psychic

"Uh-oh," said Mosie, still keeping watch at the bar. "I didn't see that coming."

The best times in life are the ones where you find that special someone,
or someones, that you can make beautiful music with. The louder the better.
   -Pan, Lord of the Satyrs

It looked as if Chaos R Us was having a blowout sale at Mab's fortress. Hex started things out with a bang.

As soon as we had all cleared out of the cell, Hex turned around and said, *"Boom."*

The blue walls exploded, shaking the entire fortress.

"That's one cell that will never hold another prisoner," said Hex. With a wink and a smile he added, "By the way, Pan, I meant it when I said I could leave any time I wanted."

"Yeah, yeah. Show off," Pan muttered under his breath.

The male Shapeling arrived at that moment.

"Loki?" asked Pan, not wanting to be made a fool by a Shapeshifter twice in the same half hour.

"Why? You miss me?" said Loki, briefly shifting the Shapeling's face back to his own.

"You guys can kiss later. There's work to be done. We'll do maximum damage if we spilt up," said Hex. "I have a plan."

Hex shared it with the rest of us.

"What do you think?" Hex asked.

"Works for me," said Sun.

"Me too," said Loki.

"I'm not totally thrilled. I'm a coyote, not a fox," said Coyote.

"What? Don't think you can handle it?" asked Sun sarcastically.

"I can handle it," said Coyote, licking his right front paw. "I just hate exercise."

No one else had any objections. We returned to the surface, passing dozens of unconscious guards that Sun and Loki had laid out on their way in. The bulk of Mab's troops still stood at parade rest in the courtyard. If the treaty was signed, it would be a show of power to the leaving Oberon. If it wasn't signed, they stood ready to capture the visiting king. We stood inside a doorway that opened on the courtyard, just out of their sight.

"Okay, then. Pan, you're up," said Hex, passing out ear plugs he had just conjured to the rest of us.

Pan took out his—or rather, Fred's—pipes, lifted them to his lips, and began to play.

The music's effect was frightening, although not to us, thanks to the earplugs. The troops were another matter. They were being taught a lesson in terror firsthand. It seems that even Faerie folk had a fight or flight mechanism, and Pan's music was putting it on overdrive. The formation was falling apart, as the shakes and cold sweats broke out in the crowd. Since there was no one to fight, the lot of them had a burning desire to flee into the hills. Only Mab's military training keep them in place.

Nobody in the crowd was able to focus past the fear, which was fortunate in one respect. When Loki shifted into Mab's form and appeared before the crowd, those who would normally have questioned why she left the conference didn't. Those who could have seen through his disguise where too distracted to make the attempt.

The appearance of their leader eased some of the tension in the soldiers. Most didn't even notice Coyote strolling out into the courtyard.

"One of the prisoners is escaping. Capture him!" ordered Loki a la Mab.

With an outlet to turn their fear upon finally appearing, the troops leapt after Coyote. Fortunately, he was already at the gate and traveling at a good pace before the hordes got moving. Coyote's lead widened as the soldiers bottlenecked at the gate.

Hex casually strolled into the masses and pulled Tralla out. The Path Maker resisted at first.

"*Relax*," intoned Hex. Pan's music no longer agitated Tralla, and she could think clearly again.

"Hex, what's going on?" she asked. Hex and she had become friends with her during the time he'd spent in Faerie, and he was counting on that friendship.

"Do you trust me?" Hex asked.

"You worry me when you ask me questions like that, but yes, I do," Tralla said with a small smile.

"Then don't go with the troops," said Hex.

"Why?"

"I can't tell you," said Hex, knowing full well that with Tralla in the pack, the troops had a better than even chance of catching Coyote.

"What can you tell me?"

"If you do what I ask, you'll be saving lives. That, and I've missed you," said Hex.

"Sweet talker. Okay, but you don't leave my sight, deal?" said Tralla.

"Fair enough."

With most of the troops chasing through the woods after Coyote, Pan put his pipes down. I was stuck with old goat legs. Our job was to get to the missile and safeguard it. If luck was with us, all the troops would be otherwise occupied, and we could get to the castle tower the missile was in without any trouble.

As we rounded the second corridor corner, we spied a dozen guards standing at attention. Lady Luck apparently had decided we weren't the type of people she wanted to be seen with. She's the same way when I go to Atlantic City, pretending not to know me and refusing to even stop by to say hi.

These warriors had been too deep inside the castle to hear the pipe playing, and so were still at their posts. I recognized them from our march in. They wore the raven head on a silver circle insignia of the Daemor, Mab's elite special forces. As an item of note, the Daemor are all women.

Pan smiled.

"This is too easy," he said.

"Pan, it may not be as easy as you think," I said.

"Murphy, if I want excrement out of you, I'll squeeze your head. Hex put me in charge."

"Hex isn't that stupid. Listen, Pan. . ."

"No, Murphy, you listen. I will handle the Daemor. I don't need your help or advice. Like I said before, you are quite useless here."

"I'm amazed Fred turned out so well," I said. Fred may have been clueless at times, but he was a good guy. If Pan wasn't Dionysus' adopted brother and Hermes' son, I wondered if Paddy would actually tolerate him.

"Not my fault. It was his mother's influence. Now one of us has work to do, and it's not you. Maybe if you're nice, I'll let you hold the ladies' armor while I get to know them better. Wait, I have a better idea. When we get thirsty, you can bring us drinks. I know you can handle that," said Pan.

I raised my eyebrows and tried not to smile. I didn't need a comeback. Pan was about to hang himself and I was not about to hold back any rope.

"Knock yourself out," I said, extending my arm toward the corner.

"I will," said Pan. Old goat legs ran his finger through his hair and paused for a moment to check out his reflection in a shiny shield hanging on the wall. Confidently, he turned the corner and strode toward the women warriors. I hid in an alcove behind a woven tapestry of some battle that featured a well-muscled woman with pink hair and wings.

"Good afternoon, ladies. It's your lucky day," said Pan, certain of what was going to happen next.

The ranking Daemor turned toward Pan, but instead of getting naked, she got down to business.

"Seize him!" she said. I had never actually heard anyone order anyone seized in real life. This wasn't the type of grabbing Pan had been expecting, and he was caught off guard. Dodging, he spun in an attempt to put more of his musk into the air. The Daemor didn't slow down. Instead, they pulled their weapons: a combination of handguns, rifles, swords, and pikes.

Confused, he took off running. Six Daemor chased after him. These ladies were professionals. They weren't about to leave their post unguarded to chase an intruder. This would make getting in harder, which was good. Hex told us to make it harder for anyone to get to the missile. This should do the job. I could stay hidden in my cubbyhole, ready to back up the Daemor. How I would do that was still a mystery to me.

I peeked out a corner just in time to see Pan fleeing down the corridor we had just come from, with the women warriors in hot pursuit. He wasn't even thinking straight enough to pull out his pipes and try to play on the run. I wasn't about to suggest it.

I chuckled silently to myself that my deductions had proven correct. What I had tried to point out to Pan was that Mab had given all her troops filtering nose plugs for the raid on the Air Force base. Mab had not given an order to remove the plugs, so I figured there were good odds that some of her troops, especially the Daemor, were still wearing them. If the nose plugs could filter out the knockout gas, they could do the same to pheromones. Without pheromones, Pan was just an obnoxious little man.

An obnoxious little man who was getting what was coming to him. All that running was going to make him thirsty. Pity he wouldn't be able to stop long enough to have someone give him a drink.

Yeah, my name is Robin. No, I don't hang out with Batman.
-Robin Goodfellow, aka Puck

Bubba Sue had gotten into Oberon's castle even before Wisp and Fred had arrived. Gremlins had a gift for remaining unseen. A Gremlin's other major gift of playing havoc with mechanical things was limited in a place where magic was used in place of machinery.

Bubba Sue remained hidden until the party ended. Going after the missile while folk with the mystic ability of Oberon and Titania were nearby was too risky, so she bided her time. Mosie had told them that Wisp would be best off handling the king, while she would be better off disabling the missile. Mosie smiled when Fred had asked what his mission would be, and told him he would know when it happened.

The throne room was finally empty. Guards had been posted outside, but Bubba Sue was already inside, so the point was rather moot. She dropped down from her hiding place near the ceiling and walked over to the bronze box which held the Russian missile. Opening it, Bubba Sue took out the toy sized nuclear weapon to examine it.

"Anything I can help you with?" asked a voice behind her. Bubba Sue didn't even turn her head to look at Puck, still dressed in his suit, tie, and sunglasses.

"Sure. You have a metric wrench set? I hate not having the right tools," said Bubba Sue, turning the missile over.

"You realize that was sarcasm, right?" said Puck.

"I didn't just fall off the turnip truck, Goodfellow," said Bubba Sue.

"You've heard of me?" he said.

"I've read Shakespeare."

"At least he got it partially right. An impressive accomplishment, considering Willy was drunk the whole time he was here."

"I'm surprised your King didn't try to feed him in order to trap him here," said Bubba Sue.

"Ah, you saw what happened earlier. Actually, Oberon tried, but Will kept throwing up, so he didn't have much of an appetite. When he puked on the King's shoes, Oberon had me show him the way back home."

"Forcefully, I'd imagine."

"A bit, but I went with him, for a while anyway. Earth is an interesting place. I visit it often. But enough about me. What do you think you're doing?" asked Puck, making a grab for the tiny missile. Bubba Sue pulled it away before Goodfellow could get it.

"I'm disarming your missile."

"What makes you think I'll let you?" asked Puck.

Bubba Sue actually looked up at that one. "Let me? I doubt you could stop me if you tried."

"Is that a challenge?"

Bubba Sue bit her lip in order not to blurt out "yes." There was more at stake than defending her ego.

"Nope. Just a statement, probably of fact."

"Ballsy, especially for a Gremlin. I thought you folk tried to stay hidden and uninvolved."

"Just a stereotype."

"Be that as it may, you'd best hand it over."

"Not a chance. Too many people will die if I do," said Bubba Sue.

"Nobody is going to die. The missile is a toy for Oberon to taunt Mab with. It will never be used."

"Is that what Oberon told you?" asked Bubba Sue.

"Yes."

"And your king never lies to you?"

"Well. . ."

"He not only has plans to use it, he has readied the means," said Bubba Sue.

"What are you talking about?" demanded Puck.

"Look here," said Bubba Sue, holding the missile up. For those able to view the magic spectrum, there were three separate glow spots on the missile. One was the shrinking charm Puck had put on it. There were now two additional latent spells attached. One was an enlarging spell. The second was a guidance charm which would transport the missile to a target by levitating all the non-iron bearing parts. Both were armed and ready to go.

Robin Goodfellow's face went dark.

"I will not be a party to genocide. Oberon is not going to get away with this," said Goodfellow.

"Glad to hear it. I can take care of the missile, but the charms are a bit out of my league. Can you disarm them?"

"Yes. Oberon relies on power more than skill. I've had to do the opposite. Give me the missile."

"But. . ."

"The missile has failsafes against exploding. The charms can go off at any time. Give it to me."

"How do I know I can trust you?" asked Bubba Sue.

"You don't," said Puck, holding out his hand. Bubba Sue debated for a moment, then handed the mini-missile over.

Magical energies started flowing out of Puck's hands. His brows knit in concentration and sweat began to pour down his face.

"This may take a while."

"Don't worry about it. I'll wait. I've got nothing better to do," said Bubba Sue.

150

Yeah, I've chased my tail. You want to hear about the time it got away?
-Coyote, Native American trickster god

The forest wildlife was fleeing in terror as the ground trembled from the pounding of thousands of feet. The underbrush and some small trees were being trampled as Mab's troops hunted for Coyote. The effects of Pan's music were gradually wearing off, which meant wits were returning and the search pattern was becoming more organized.

"Damn two-leggers," whispered Coyote. He had managed to stay ahead of his pursuers, but it was getting increasingly harder.

"They're not all bad."

Coyote looked up, caught off-guard. It wasn't a feeling he enjoyed. Coyote hadn't been expecting anyone to answer. A rhesus monkey was looking down on him.

"Oh, it's you. Figures you would take their side. Two-leggers stick together," Coyote said to the Sun self. This Sun was still in the shape of a rhesus monkey, instead of his normal, more humanoid form. "How are the little ones doing?"

"Learning to survive on their own."

"Glad to hear it. Everything going well back at the castle?" asked Coyote. Sun and all his selves knew what all his other selves knew and vice versa. The selves weren't separate beings. Sun's mind was able to control all the bodies, although the concentration factor involved exhausted him.

"As far as I know. Rumbles and I are making sure no one else gets into the game or the castle," said Sun.

"Any idea how much longer I need to be leading this goose chase?" asked Coyote.

"Another hour should do it," said Sun.

"Joy," said Coyote, shaking his head.

Just then the little she-monkey who had been ill, bounded through the tree branches, ending up by Sun's side.

"Sun. . . soldiers come," said the she-monkey.

"She talks?" asked Coyote.

"Faerie magic helps evolve the intelligence and ability of ordinary animals," said Sun.

"I know, but I've never seen it happen so fast before. You've been speeding up the process?" asked Coyote.

"Guilty."

"She is looking well," said Coyote.

"She has name," said the insulted she-monkey, in broken Frankensteinian style English. "Me Jane."

"Jane?"

"Blame Murphy. On the march, he was joking with her and she remembered enough of the conversation to choose that as her name. He was also joking with one of the males who was chattering up at Jane. I barely talked that one out of picking Tarzan," said Sun.

"Bad soldiers come," said Jane, pointing beyond the next tree.

"Gotta run," said Coyote.

"No need to hurry. The other monkeys have things in hand," said Sun. Coyote turned and saw the soldiers running away from the little rhesus monkeys, who were throwing things down from their perches in the trees. It took Coyote a moment to realize what the brown and mushy projectiles actually were.

"They're not. . ." said Coyote.

"You know what they say. You can take the monkey out of the zoo, but you can't take the zoo out of the monkey," said Sun.

"At least I'll be able to smell them coming," said Coyote. "See you back at the castle."

It's good to be King.
　　-Oberon, Faerie King

"This is becoming pointless," said Oberon.

"That's the first thing we've agreed on all day," said Mab.

"If ye both weren't as stubborn as stone, we might be able to find some common ground," said Paddy, shaking his head.

Mab stood up to leave. Paddy had managed to convince her not to investigate the explosion, with the help of Loki, who had shifted into a Daemor named Tama. Loki promised to find out what was happening and instead made his way out to help with the prison break. After he impersonated Mab for the troops, Loki morphed back into the Daemor. He reported to Mab that there had been a small explosion in the armory, but it was nothing to worry about.

Mab asked the morphed Loki to stay, figuring that the presence of the female warrior would only help her negotiating position. To her surprise, Paddy didn't object.

Paddy did object to her leaving.

"Mab, where do ye think you're going?" Paddy asked.

"This conference is done. There is no middle ground to be found. There is no point to this, Moran," said Mab.

"Mother. . ." said Kyna. Mab ignored her daughter, much as she had most of Kyna's life.

"There are more lives at stake than you can imagine. I can't allow you to leave until this matter is resolved," said Paddy.

"Can't allow me? We're not at your swill house. This is my place of power, not yours. I rule here. I have tolerated you in the hope that you might succeed. That's not going to happen, so my indulgence of you is at its end. You can join your friends in the dungeon. Tama, take Moran into custody," Mab ordered, still not realizing that her Daemor was Loki.

"I'll leave you two to your squabble," said Oberon, as he got up to leave.

"You won't get very far. My castle has charms that prevent teleportation in or out, and my troops won't let you out that door," said Mab.

"A double cross. I can say I am not surprised. What else would be expected of a mud queen," said Oberon.

"I may have been born a commoner, but that means I earned my position. Can you say the same?" asked Mab. Oberon yawned.

Seeing that Tama had not moved any closer to Paddy, Mab said, "Tama, I gave you an order."

"What's your point?" asked Loki. Paddy smiled.

"You're not Tama," said Mab.

"What was your first clue?" asked Loki.

"Wukong?"

"Hardly," said Loki, not revealing his identity. At this point, Mab would almost assuredly tell Woden.

"For the moment, Mab my dear, ye don't rule your fortress. I do. Your troops have fled and scattered. What few remain have been disabled," said Paddy.

Mab rushed into the bedroom, which had a window, and looked out. Her troops no longer lined the courtyard.

"How?" asked Mab.

"How is not important."

"You couldn't hold the castle. I'll retake it," promised Mab.

"Maybe, maybe not," said Paddy.

"You don't have the numbers," countered Mab.

"You mean like an army? With a handful of friends I have beat your army. If you want me to gather one of my own, I assure you I could call on more friends," said Paddy.

"Leprechauns? That is funny. There is no standing leprechaun army," said Oberon.

"That's because we don't need one. No one is stupid enough to mess with us, but I wasn't referring to me relations. I could easily call on Orun Rere," said Paddy.

"Oh yes. The city of those dark skinned mortals who fled their rightful owners. I believe we have you to thank for bringing them here, Moran. We have much to fear from mortals. I am shivering even thinking about it," Oberon said dryly. Paddy and Bulfinche used to be engineers on the Underground Railroad, helping runaway slaves. Not all of them went North. Some settled in Faerie. Coyote even pitched in, and eventually the Underground Railroad expanded to help save Indian refugees. This is the stuff you don't read about in the history books. Oberon had a problem because Orun Rere had given refuge to some of his escaped slaves over the years.

Paddy and Bulfinche helped build Orun Rere, which was the name of the good heaven in one African language. Apparently there was a bad one. The boss and his late wife even lived there for a while before they opened the bar.

"Mortals can be more frightening than you give them credit for. Either of those missiles could destroy you, Oberon," said Paddy.

"I have my doubts," said the King.

"Plus, Hex could call on the forces of Sherwood," said Paddy.

"More mortals. They live among the trees," said Oberon. That also needs some explaining. It seems Robin Hood, Marian, and many of their merry band didn't die. There was a gateway to Faerie in Sherwood, which they used to their advantage in the good fight. Eventually, when their battle was won, they settled in Faerie and have lived here ever since. Robin became a King in his own right. Hex apparently learned fighting and strategy from Robin Hood himself. He also claims he learned the finer points of archery and has offered to prove it, usually by handing me an apple and asking me to put it on my head. I have yet to take him up on it.

"Not to mention my people, including Hermes and Hercules. Oh, and lest I forget, Wisp," Paddy added. Oberon had nothing to add, but his eyes glowed with anger. "Mab, I will return control of your castle to you once this matter is resolved." Paddy was careful that his wording contained no threat which would invalidate a gilded promise.

Oberon moved toward the door. Loki, still looking like the Daemor, stepped between the King and the exit. Oberon let loose a mystic bolt that made lightning look like a spark coming off a wool sweater. Oberon expected to be facing a pile of ashes. Loki's form wasn't even singed.

"You want to play? I'm game," said Loki, as he raised his hand and returned the favor. His fire bolt knocked Oberon into the wall, burying him in rubble. Oberon had the power levels of a god, but Loki had power that even other gods feared.

Paddy shot Loki a look.

"Don't worry. Strictly non-lethal," promised Loki. "I don't buy the 'turn the other cheek' philosophy."

Oberon was twitching.

"Fair enough," conceded Paddy.

"Mother, if you don't sign, you and I never need talk again," said Kyna. "Kyna—"

"Don't Kyna me. If you don't, people will die, including those you have sworn to protect. Can you live with that?"

Mab started pacing the room.

"Fine. I will sign what Paddy has written out, if Oberon does," said Mab.

"Now we are getting somewhere," said Paddy.

"No, we are not. I will not sign this paper. I will see the lot of you dead first," said Oberon, with a glowing red globe suddenly appearing in the air above his open palm.

"No!" shouted Mab.

"Oh, yes. I see you recognize what I have here," said Oberon.

"What is it?" said Kyna.

"The equivalent of a deadman's switch. It's to activate a spell, which I'm assuming will launch the missile," said Paddy.

"Very good, Moran. I will be leaving now," said Oberon.

"No. You stay. You won't use it if you'll be caught in the blast," said

Paddy.

"Are you sure?" said Oberon.

"Yes," Paddy said, calling his bluff.

"Then I'll just have to make sure I'm not here," said Oberon. Again he lashed out with a mystic bolt, only this time he aimed it at the already weakened stone wall. There was now a window to the outside. The King leapt outside and hovered. He turned and smiled, then tossed the deadman's globe into Paddy's chambers. It landed at Kyna's feet and started blinking.

"It's going to blow!" Mab screamed and, like a selfless hero in an army movie throwing himself on a live hand grenade, dived on the globe.

It exploded. Mab, thanks greatly to her body armor, deflected the brunt of the blast, but the magic fallout was enough to knock everyone in the room unconscious. Worse, Oberon's missile was activated.

I hate working under pressure.
-Bubba Sue, Southern Gremlin

"What's taking so long?" demanded Bubba Sue.

"Too much damn iron. I almost have the guidance charm," said Puck.

There was a flash of light and the missile began to grow, rapidly returning to its original size.

"You were supposed to disarm the thing, not set it off," yelled Bubba Sue.

"I didn't. Oberon must have done it," said Puck, as the expanding Scaleboard missile flew out of Puck's hand and toward the door, smashing it open.

"Oh crap," said Bubba Sue, chasing after it, but she wasn't going to be fast enough to catch it. Puck was hot on her heels.

"What can I do?" he shouted.

"Can you fly?"

"Not far or fast enough to catch that. But I can get you up there," said Puck.

"Do it," ordered Bubba Sue.

Puck used his magic to levitate the Gremlin up to the almost-full-grown missile.

"How are you going to get down?"

"I'll worry about that when I have to," she said, grabbing hold of the side of the missile, just in time to be swept off into the sky. Puck heard a rebel yell, as Bubba Sue climbed on and straddled the Scaleboard like it was a bucking bronco in the rodeo.

"That's going to be a bugger to catch up to," said Puck, giving chase.

The best way to rule is with an iron fist.
    -Oberon, Faerie King

Rumbles was busy playing sentinel, walking around inside the castle courtyard and open areas. So far, all had been quiet. That changed with the pounding of a pair of hooves, followed quickly by six pairs of running feet.

Rumbles decided to duck out of the way until he could figure out what was happening. He ducked behind the foot of a large statue just in time to see Pan running by and screaming, while being chased by six warrior women.

"What the. . . ?" muttered Rumbles as the mini-parade rushed by. "There's something you don't see every day. Too bad Roy's not here. He would love to see this."

Rumbles moved out from behind the foot, when the foot moved, practically trembling. Rumbles looked up.

"Tairde?" he said. The giant was huddled in the corner of the courtyard, between an outside wall and a tower. "What's wrong, big guy?"

"Afraid," stammered the giant, sounding like a cross between a frightened toddler and a jet engine.

Pan's pipe music seemed to have more of an effect on Tairde, maybe because a giant's hearing is supposed to be more sensitive than that of someone normal size.

"Everything is going to be okay," said Rumbles, trying to be consoling while at the same time realizing that a terrified giant would fit better into the overall plan.

"Really?"

"Really. You hang tough. In a little while I'll come back and help you out," said Rumbles.

"Promise?" asked the trembling giant.

"Promise."

The clown turned to go.

"Rumbles, wait," asked Tairde. "I know what you did back there on Earth. Thanks. A giant who can get beat by a mortal isn't worth much in an army."

"It's happened before. Ask David or Jack."

"Who?"

"Never mind."

"I just really appreciate it."

"Don't mention it. Ever. Really," said Rumbles. "I have to go."

Before the clown could move on, the sky exploded and it started raining stone and mortar.

"And me without my umbrella," said Rumbles, pressing himself flat against the wall. The rubble bounced harmlessly off Tairde. The giant barely noticed. Rumbles looked up in time to see Oberon floating out from the hole he had blown in Paddy's room.

"And what have we here?" whispered Rumbles, as the king hovered twenty feet above the ground. "Looks like the king has left the building."

Oberon, knowing that death and destruction was winging its way toward Mab's castle, wanted out fast. Knowing full well that he would lie in Mab's position, Oberon assumed the warrior queen was lying about the charms preventing teleportation. If there was one, he couldn't sense it. The King was so confident that he assumed that was beyond Mab's abilities, so he decided to do a vanishing act.

Mab may not have been in Oberon's weight class, magically speaking, but she was no slouch, and she wasn't in the habit of bluffing. She rarely needed to.

The result was not pleasant for Oberon. Had he been outside trying to get in, the spell would have failed and he would have been able to disperse the backlash harmlessly. Mab's castle was her place of power, not his. It dampened any magic that wasn't allied with Mab. Inside its walls, Oberon couldn't disperse the backlash, and it hit him full force. Using his own power to shield himself from injury had the effect of draining off much of his mystic energy. In a ball of mystic fire, Oberon plummeted to the ground like an action figure a demented child had taken lighter fluid and match to. The fallen king laid in the crater, weakened and dazed. It was a new experience for him.

Struggling, Oberon pulled himself to his feet. He began to race for the drawbridge and the woods beyond and the path that would take him far from the fallout of the coming mushroom cloud. Before he could reach the gate, he found Rumbles blocking his path.

"Out of my way, mortal clown," ordered Oberon.

"Was that supposed to be an insult?" asked Rumbles.

"I said move," ordered Oberon.

"No, you said out of my way. Pretty sad when a king can't even remember what he said last."

"Regardless of my words, my meaning was clear. If you continue to block my path, I will strike you down where you stand."

In the world outside Bulfinche's Pub, when a person of power repeats a command three times, something is wrong. Rumbles was willing to gamble he knew the reason.

"If you could have blasted me, you would have already. I'm taking you back inside," said Rumbles, going nose to nose with the king.

"You are taking me? I don't think so." A fierce glow was gathering around Oberon's hands as Rumbles realized he had gambled and lost. "I choose not to waste my power needlessly. I suggest you make peace with whatever gods you worship."

Rumbles fumbled in his pocket for his souvenir from his run-in back in the subway and slipped the steel knuckles on his right hand, under cover of his huge red glove. With a look of surprise, he snapped his head to the area behind the king's right shoulder and said, "Wisp!"

Oberon turned his head just as quickly, realizing even as he did so that it was a trick. Realization came too late, as Rumbles dropped his glove and sucker-punched Oberon in the jaw with the steel knuckles. He struck full force knowing, from sparring with the likes of Hercules and Mista the Valkyrie, that mystic folk were made of sterner stuff than the mortal variety.

Oberon had just enough time for his eyes to go glassy before he hit the ground.

"I wasn't about to lose a second fight today," said Rumbles, slipping the knuckles back in his pocket.

Rumbles threw the unconscious monarch over his shoulder and marched up to Paddy's quarters.

The only thing worse than coming to a party late is passing out before it's over.
        -Hex, cursed magí

The explosion of Oberon's deadman's globe caused Hex and Tralla to come running. Hex threw open the door to Paddy's quarters and the magí was greeted with the sight of four bodies. No one was moving.

"No! It happened anyway," gasped Hex, running first to Paddy, then Kyna.

"Mab!" screamed Tralla, running to her queen's side. "She's dead. They all are."

Hex had taken a reading on the room and knew not only what happened, but everyone's condition.

"They're not dead yet, but they will be soon. Oberon launched his missile."

"Oberon had a missile?" asked Tralla.

"Yes. It'll be here in ten minutes," said Hex.

"Can you stop it?" asked Tralla.

"Yes, but then I won't have enough power left to save them," said Hex. Hex was lying. Tralla didn't know about his curse. Not many people did. That knowledge would put Hex at risk from the numerous enemies he had made over the years. He had a plan and knew what it would do to him, so he had to concoct a cover story. "I owe Paddy too much to let him die and I can't bear to let the Reaper get Kyna while I watch helplessly. I'm going to save them."

"Hex, I love Mab as much as you do Paddy, but what about everybody else the explosion will kill? Including them."

"They'll be able to stop the missile."

"And if they can't?"

"It's been nice knowing you, Tralla. To save them, I need to share my life force, so the spell will knock me out for a while," Hex lied, but it was a good explanation for why he would pass out. Beat explaining the curse.

"It'll be up to you to bring them up to speed. Have Kyna find Sun. He can probably intercept it," said Hex.

"And if the Monkey King can't?"

"Make a path to someplace far away and save as many people as you can. Contact Coyote and have him run down it. Most of Mab's troops will follow. Shut it behind you."

"Okay," promised Tralla, as she kissed Hex on the cheek.

Hex turned to the unconscious and dying forms of Paddy, Kyna, the disguised Loki and Mab.

"*Live*," he ordered simply. The amount of power required to bring back four people from the rim of the Valley of Death gave Hex more pain that he could bear and remain conscious. He collapsed into a padded chair he had made sure was behind him.

Paddy and the rest began to stir.

Tralla helped each of them up, bringing everyone up to speed.

"Kyna, go find Coyote and have him lead my troops back here now. Tralla will set up the path inside the front gate. If we can't stop it, we will save as many as we can," said Mab.

"But Tralla said Hex wanted me to get Sun," said Kyna.

"Kyna, we have minutes. I am evacuating. If Wukong fails to stop it, I don't want anyone here caught in the blast. Your father might have time to do both, but you won't. My way saves the most lives. For once in your life, listen to me without question," said Mab. "Please."

"Okay, mother," said Kyna, her winged black boots lifting her up and carrying her out the hole Oberon had made.

"You go after the missile. I'll find Sun and send him after you as back up," Paddy said to Loki. The Norse trickster nodded, shifted into a hawk and flew out the window.

"Wait," cried Mab, but Loki ignored her and flew out the hole. "Moran, a Shapeling is not going to be able to stop a missile."

"He's more than a Shapeling. Trust me," said Paddy.

"I did. That's how this mess started," said Mab.

"No, your trouble started when ye decided ye needed a nuclear arsenal. I've been trying to make things better," said Paddy.

"Kids, play nice or I'm going to have to separate you two," said Rumbles, walking in, with Oberon still unconscious over his shoulder. The clown dumped the king unceremoniously on the floor at Paddy's feet.

"Sparky here was making a run for it back to his kingdom. I stopped him," said Rumbles. Paddy nodded, suitably impressed. Rumbles looked at the chair. "Is Hex okay?"

"He will be. You did good work, Rumbles, but we've got bigger problems," said Paddy. "Oberon launched his missile and it's on its way here now."

"Oh crap," said Rumbles, as his painted white face became even paler.

"You needn't have bothered. He would be in the same predicament back at his castle that he is here," said Mab.

"What are ye saying, Mab?" demanded Paddy.

"I have a sensor spell built into the Trident launch system. I suspected Oberon might eventually get a missile of his own, so I took precautions against a first strike by him."

"Meaning?" said Paddy.

"Once that missile reaches the halfway point, my Trident automatically launches," said Mab.

"Stop it," ordered Paddy.

"I would if I could, but I can't. The spell is set up with a failsafe. Nobody, not even me, can stop it from being launched," said Mab.

"Well, you're damned well going to try," said Paddy.

Mab nodded, biting her tongue. "Tralla, get the path ready. Start evacuation the moment it's done."

"I will," said Tralla.

"Take Hex with you," said Paddy.

"I was planning on it," said Tralla, picking up Hex in a reversal of the traditional carrying over the threshold routine.

"Rumbles, you go with her and get out," said Paddy. "I'll find Sun."

"Tairde is paralyzed with fear on the side of this tower. He'll stay there unless I go get him," said Rumbles.

"Tairde?" asked Mab.

"Pan played a little song to get your troops riled up. It hit Tairde harder than most," said Rumbles.

"Go! We'll have time for explanations later," said Paddy, running and jumping out the window. He couldn't fly, but a long fall wasn't going to hurt him much. . . nowhere near as much as nuclear fallout would, at least.

No one ever notices the bartender unless they're thirsty.
-John Murphy, Bartender at Bulfinche's Pub

I was still trapped behind the tapestry. Trapped may not have been entirely accurate. I could leave at any time, provided I didn't mind dealing with the Daemor who had taken up a sentry post on the wall opposite the tapestry. I could claim I didn't like the idea of hitting a woman, which is true, but I was more concerned with getting my butt kicked. Drunks I can handle. Trained warrior women are a bit out of my league.

My bladder was urging me on, like an ever expanding water balloon in my gut. I would have been in real trouble if I hadn't made a pit stop before we left the bar. Nature's call had helped me realize what my hiding spot was. I was standing next to a chamber pot, the medieval version of the toilet. It seemed archaic, especially since there were modern-style bathrooms elsewhere in the castle, but this was where guards on duty went. Kept them from leaving their post unguarded, plus not being able to sit down literally kept them on their toes. They could also arrange the curtain for both privacy and a good view of the corridor.

I was hoping the Daemor hadn't had a lot to drink before she went on duty, or things were going to get awkward and probably painful.

On the plus side, as far as I could tell, nobody had gotten past the Daemor to the missile.

That was about to change. Mab came charging down the corridor.

"My queen. . ." said the Daemor opposite my hiding spot.

"Tama?" said Mab, shaking her head, remembering that the Daemor had been here the entire time, while the impostor stood by her side. "Never mind. Get that door open. Oberon has launched a missile at us, so the Trident will launch in retaliation if it gets close enough. We have to stop it," said Mab.

"But if we are being attacked—"

"Moran and his companions are going to try to stop Oberon's missile."

"What if they fail? We should destroy those who would destroy us," grumbled the Daemor, as she fumbled with the key to the door.

"We will not be destroyed. We are evacuating. Oberon's missile will not make it here," said Mab.

"Do you trust Moran that much?" she asked, throwing open the door.

"Yes. That mortal wife he took changed him. He would die to save an innocent life, and somehow that rubs off on his companions. They will stop it, so if the Trident launches, it will not be an act of vengeance, but of mass extermination. That is not the legacy I wish to leave," said Mab. "If we disable the thrusters, the missile will not be able to lift off."

"Should I call the Shapeling technicians?" asked the Daemor.

"No time," said Mab, drawing her sword. "All of you head for Tralla's escape path near the front gate. I'll take care of this myself."

The Daemor obediently trotted off.

Mab lifted her blade high above her head in a two-handed grip, intending to bring it down, slicing the lower half of the missile. Enchanted Faerie swords can cut though most things like a knife through butter, except without the gooey mess.

Before she could bring down the sword, however, the thrusters fired, and the force threw Mab back like a fisherman would a small fish.

"I'm too late," said Mab, climbing up from the floor. Her sword lay several feet away. When Tama the Daemor moved from her post, I had come out from my hiding spot. Actually, I had first made use of the chamber pot. The thing was enchanted. The moment I finished using it, it glowed and was empty again. Not only that, but it had a springtime fresh scent. No wonder they didn't have indoor plumbing. They didn't need it.

I made a mental note to try and convince Paddy to get a couple of these, instead of the porta-potties he keeps in the garage for the homeless to use. Our models are not self-cleaning, which means, more often than not, Mama Murphy's favorite bartender gets stuck cleaning them. Paddy could give the magic chamber pots dispensation to work and my life would become much easier and better smelling.

I moved to a position outside the door, barely daring to look in. I saw Mab knocked down and the missile fired up. Hex's stories of the future ran through my mind. All the dead and the devastation.

I'm no hero. I know plenty of real heroes, so you'll have to trust me on this. I wasn't thinking: I was going on adrenaline alone. I ran into the room, picked up Mab's sword and ran at the missile. I lifted it above my head like I had seen Mab do and sprinted up a ramp attached to the scaffolding. The missile was lifting off. I leapt off the ramp and stabbed down at the missile.

The sword went into the metal hull like a dart into a dart board. It also stayed there like a dart, and I was still holding onto the hilt. Before I realized what was happening, the missile had cleared the scaffolding and the stone tower.

I held on for dear life as the missile went higher and higher. Problem was, the missile began to accelerate and my fingers weren't up to holding the rest of me suspended on a missile a couple of hundred feet above the ground.

Like the strands of a rope above a burning candle in a melodramatic movie, I felt my fingers give one by one, until I could not hold on any longer.

I fell.

Sometimes the hardest part of an act is knowing the right time to make your exit.

-Rumbles, professional clown, former Golden Gloves boxer

"Tairde, you have to go," said Rumbles.

"I don't wanna," said the giant. Instead of getting better, his fearful state seemed to be getting worse. As he became more afraid, Tairde was becoming more childlike. He had curled up in a fetal position and was rocking himself back and forth.

"You have to. Otherwise, you might die," said Rumbles.

That got the giant's attention, and he sat up. "I don't want to die."

"Then come with me. Tralla's made a new path to take us away from here," explained Rumbles.

"But I'm scared," whined Tairde.

"Of what?"

"I don't know," said Tairde, frustrated.

"Are you scared of me?" asked Rumbles.

"A little," admitted the giant.

"Then get your sorry butt up and moving, now!" yelled Rumbles in his best imitation of a drill sergeant.

It had the desired effect. Tairde's eyes got wide and he jumped to his feet, causing the ground to shake.

"Now get moving toward the main gate!" screamed Rumbles. Tairde was in tears and trembling.

"Okay," he whispered meekly.

"I don't believe this. I feel like a bully," whispered Rumbles, looking up at the giant in disbelief.

The ground started to shake again. At first, Rumbles though the giant had fallen, but Tairde was just as startled as the clown. Worse even, because the giant had started to turn tail and run back toward his corner.

"Oh no, you don't. We are not going through that again. Keep moving!" ordered Rumbles.

"Yes sir," said Tairde, moving in double time.

The missile then cleared the tower.

"Oh sh. . ." said Rumbles, looking up. He saw a body hanging onto the side of the missile by way of a sword. He saw that body fall. "Murphy!?"

I've never been afraid to fall flat on my face. After all, it wouldn't be the first or the last time.
       -*John Murphy, bartender at Bulfinche's Pub*

I couldn't see Rumbles, although I probably could have made out Tairde if my concentration wasn't completely focused on the rapidly approaching ground.

They say that in the moment before you die, your entire life flashes before your eyes. If that's true, I was so frightened that I missed the show. I was too busy accepting the fact that my life was ending. Surprisingly, my thoughts were not sad ones. First and foremost in my mind was that I was going to see my dearly departed wife Elsie again. That one helped take the edge off the fear. The only other thought was that I was going to hit the ground below with such force that I was going to dig my own grave, although technically it would be more of a crater.

I said a silent prayer, closed my eyes and hoped heaven was in need of a bartender.

My prayer was answered. I stopped falling. I opened my eyes and was greeted by the sight of a huge leathery palm. Not a palm tree, but that of a hand, or maybe a paw. A monkey paw, and a giant one at that.

"Sun!?" I said, looking up to where I imagined his face would be.

"You were expecting Coyote?" he said.

Thankyouthankyouthankyou," I said, showing my gratitude. I was truly happy to still be alive.

"Murphy, it's okay. You can stop kissing my hand," Sun said.

"You're huge! Bigger than Tairde. I didn't know you could do that," I said.

"Murph, I don't advertise everything I can do. Hard to keep up the element of surprise that way," said Sun.

"You look like King Kong," I said.

"That's always been a sore point with me. They ripped me off and changed the name around enough that I don't get any credit."

"King Kong ripped you off?" I asked.

"Say my title and last name together," said Sun.

"King Wukong. King Wu Kong. King Kong," I said.

"Bingo. You have a choice. I can drop you off and you can run for an escape path near the front gate. . ."

"Or?" I asked.

"You can come with me. I'm going to try to stop that missile," Sun said.

"Do you need me? Or will I be in the way?" I asked.

"Honestly? You'd slow me down, no offense," said Sun.

"None taken. I already tried to stop it once and it didn't work out so well," I said.

"Yeah, what were you thinking?"

"I wasn't."

"That I can believe."

"I'll take the path then," I said.

"Okay," said Sun, as he shrunk down to his normal size, still holding me in his right paw. He gently put me on terra firma.

"Why didn't you stay super-sized?"

"Harder to cloud dance with all that mass. Run Murph, there isn't much time," said Sun, leaping up into the sky after the missile. A cloud seemed to form around his feet, something that happened with long distance cloud dancing, therefore the name.

As there were no cumulus bodies gathering around my feet, I sprinted for the front gate.

The problem with most people is they're in too much of a hurry. They should take time to smell the Roses. And the Michelles. And the Donnas. . . .
—Pan, Lord of the Satyrs

When I got to the front gate, people were already running down a path that seemed to go straight into a silver castle wall.

Rumbles was running behind Tairde, yelling, "Move! Move! Move!" like a drill instructor. The giant was running from him like a 1950s' TV housewife fleeing a mouse. The tactic worked, because both he and the giant made it onto the path and disappeared.

I looked to my left and noticed that Pan was running alongside of me.

"I think. . ." *wheeze* "that I finally lost those Daemor. . . ." *huff* "No thanks to you."

"I think they had somewhere more important to get to," I said.

Wheeze. "More important than chasing me? Surely, you jest," said Pan.

"I ain't jesting. And don't call me Shirley," I said. Pan never got the reference or the joke. "C'mon, we gotta get down that path."

Pan stopped short, right in front of the open front gate.

"I don't gotta do anything. I'm exhausted and I'm not moving from this spot," said Pan. I looked behind him, out the gate and decided not to argue. He'd change his mind soon enough.

As I began to pass Tralla, she reached out an arm to stop me.

"Would you please take Hex?" she said, pointing to Hex who was unconscious on the ground behind her.

"No problem," I said, bending down to lift the unconscious magí up and put him over my shoulders in a fireman's carry. I carried him down the path. There was a mild tingle as we vanished.

Meanwhile, Pan was hunched over in front of the gate and trying to catch his breath, which was proving to be an elusive quarry.

First in the gate was the Sun self that had stayed with the monkeys. He had shifted back so he looked like himself. He had monkeys under each arm and gripping onto his neck and back, as he made like a racehorse.

"Move it or lose it, goatlegs," said the Sun self.

"I ain't going anywhere," said Pan.

"Suit yourself," Sun said, leaving Pan in the dust as his he and his charges disappeared down the path.

Next in—or rather over—the gate, was Kyna flying to the path.

"Pan, there's no time to lose. Get on the path," said Kyna.

"No, I'm tired. I'm staying put," said Pan.

"Whatever," said Kyna, before flying through the vanishing point.

Then Coyote came through the gate.

"Pan, better ease on down the road," said Coyote, moving at top speed.

"Listen, Toto, what is it with this stinking path? Nobody is moving me from this spot until I'm good and ready. An army couldn't get me to budge," said Pan.

"You're about to be able to put that statement to the test," said Coyote, as he breezed by the Lord of the Satyrs.

"What are you talking about?"

"Look behind me," said Coyote, almost to the vanishing point.

Pan did as Coyote suggested and saw thousands of Mab's troops bearing down on the gate, weapons drawn. Although the effects of his pipe playing had diminished, it hadn't gone away yet. The troops were still in fight or flight mode, and it seems like the majority had decided to go with fight.

"By Aphrodite's breasts and Athena's ass!" said Pan, now in a panic himself as he turned and sprinted toward the path himself.

Mab's troops couldn't all fit in the gate at once, so they started to storm and scale their own walls. Several were at risk for falling into the deadly moat. Mab arrived in time to make sure her own troops didn't injure themselves.

"Atten-hut!" she bellowed. Every last soldier snapped to attention. "Assume formations now and triple time it inside and down the path Tralla has ready."

"But you said get the coyote, my Queen," said Yuron, none the worse for wear after his earlier pantsing.

Mab decided it would be quicker not to explain the imposter just now.

"And now I'm giving you new orders. Any problem with that, soldier?" asked Mab. She knew each of her troops by name, but knew sometimes other terms struck home faster.

"No, my Queen," shouted Yuron.

The troops did as they were told and in less than two minutes were through the gate and on the path. The only ones who hadn't left yet were Mab, Tralla, and Paddy, who had the unconscious and bound Oberon over his shoulder. Paddy wouldn't even leave behind a guy who tried to kill him. You gotta love the boss.

"Is that everyone?" asked Paddy.

"I hope so," said Tralla.

"I'll do a finder spell to locate any stragglers," said Mab.

"I'll wait just in case," said Paddy.

"No, you'll go now," said Mab. Paddy started to open his mouth, but Mab cut him off. "Moran, this is not the time to argue with me. The longer you do, the longer it'll be before I can work the spell and the less time Tralla and I'll have to get any stragglers out," said Mab.

"Okay, but hurry," said Paddy.

"Moran, I didn't know you cared," said Mab. Paddy remained silent and left.

Mab closed her eyes and worked her spell.

"It's clear. Let's go," she said, turning down the vanishing point herself, with Tralla taking up the rear and erasing the path behind them.

It's hard to soar like an eagle when you hang out with turkeys.
-Bubba Sue, Southern Gremlin

Bits and pieces of the Scaleboard's shell flew off as Bubba Sue burrowed deeper into the missile.

The gremlin had no idea on how to disarm a nuclear missile. It wasn't something she had any experience with. It was one strike against her. In her favor was an uncanny ability to sense how anything mechanical worked, and how it could be made better or broken. Bubba Sue's abilities didn't just border on the supernatural, they crossed the border, and then invaded supernatural territory before taking up permanent residence there.

Normally, a gremlin has the power to invade any piece of machinery, no matter what the size, so subtly that their presence went undetected. Bubba Sue wasn't bothering with subtlety. She had neither the time nor the energy. The nuclear payload was armed and ready. Any sizeable impact—with the ground or a mountain, for instance—could set off the explosives that triggered the nuclear explosion.

Surprisingly, once she got to the right part of the missile, it took Bubba Sue less than thirty seconds to render the entire thing useless. It took another twenty seconds to remove the nuclear payload from its housing, before she went back out the way she came in.

The real problem came when she reached the outer shell of the missile. Her abilities made sure she wouldn't fall off, but that was only a solution in the short term. Gremlins have something in common with rocks. When left to their own devices thousands of feet above the ground, they both end up doing the same thing: plunging downward.

Where they differ is that gremlins can problem-solve. Bubba Sue was about to try to build a rocket sled out of the missile to get her safely to the ground. The only question was if she could do it before her ride crashed into the ground. The missile would still blow, but the explosion would be of the more mundane variety. It wouldn't make much difference to Bubba Sue. She'd still be dead.

As she was about to start piecing together the rocket sled, a hawk with a twenty-five-foot wing span dropped out of the sky at her. Bubba Sue tossed a metal tile at the beast bird.

The bird caught the two inch thick steel plate in its beak and snapped it in half.

Bubba Sue ripped a bar out of the housing frame and held it in front of her like a bo staff.

The giant hawk chuckled, then became a man, who dropped out of the sky to land beside the gremlin on the flying missile.

"Loki!?" said Bubba Sue.

"You got the thing disarmed?" asked Loki.

"Was there ever any doubt?" she asked. "I was just trying to figure out a way off."

"Can I offer you a ride?"

"Never look a gift hawk in the mouth, I always say," said Bubba Sue.

"Want me to take care of that?" asked Loki, pointing to the nuclear payload.

"Sure," said Bubba Sue, handing it over. Loki waved a hand over the payload and it shrunk to the size of a pack of gum. He put it into his pocket before morphing back into the hawk.

"Wait. Let me make sure this will crash harmlessly in a field," said Bubba Sue.

"No, leave it. I already computed the missile's trajectory. It will crash just outside Mab's castle. She should have evacuated everyone by now, so let it crash," said Loki, although the words came out of the hawk's beak high pitched and squeaky.

"Why?" asked Bubba Sue.

"Trust me," said Loki.

"That ain't going fly," said the gremlin.

"Neither are you. I'm your ride off," said Loki.

"You ain't going to leave me here," said Bubba Sue.

"How can you be so sure?" asked Loki.

"I've seen you change since Paddy's been busting you out. You've developed a conscience, even if it is a little one. So are you going to tell me?"

Loki the hawk let out a bird sigh and bent his neck down so the gremlin could climb on.

"Yes. Get on and I'll tell you on the way back," promised Loki. Bubba Sue took him at his word and jumped on the back of the hawk. Loki pushed off and started flapping.

In the distance, he spied the Trident rocketing toward them.

"Oh no," he said.

"What?" asked Bubba Sue.

"Look," said Loki.

"Another one!?" exclaimed Bubba Sue.

"Heading right toward Oberon and Titania's castle. You up for doing it again?" asked Loki.

"Twice in one day? That's more action than I've seen in a month of Sundays, but if I gotta, I gotta. Just get me there," said Bubba Sue.

Loki started pumping his wings harder to catch the Trident. Before he could reach it, Bubba Sue shouted, "Incoming!"

High above them, something was dropping out of the sky fast. It looked like it was going to land on the Trident.

"What is it?" Bubba Sue asked.

"Wukong," said Loki.

Sun had managed to catch up to the missile and he landed on the Trident without missing a beat. Unlike Bubba Sue, he didn't try to go inside the missile. He just started ripping sections of the missile off. While he didn't have a gremlin's natural ability with things mechanical, he had actually made a study of the basic design of a nuclear missile back when mankind had started using them, and had keep his reading current. He knew what he was looking for, and it didn't take him long to find it.

By this point, Loki had caught up and was perched like a giant canary on the missile. Bubba Sue jumped down. Sun may have been well read, but he knew enough to defer to expertise.

"Care to do the honors?" Sun asked.

"Make me happier than a pig in slop," said Bubba Sue, kissing Sun on the cheek before reaching out and pulling a few wires. "Thing couldn't go nuclear now if it wanted too."

"Good. Now let me knock this thing out of the sky," said Sun.

"Wait," said Loki, morphing to his normal form before explaining his plan.

"That's a good idea," admitted Sun.

"It might work," concurred Bubba Sue. "I may have to bring Goodfellow in on it to make sure it works."

"We'll worry about that when we have to." Loki reached in, removed the Trident's nuclear payload, and shrunk it down, putting it in his pocket next to the Scaleboard's. Loki returned to his hawk form and dug his talons into the sides of the missile. Flapping his wings he altered the missile's course slightly. Mab had apparently had better aim than Oberon. The new course would have it land so the impact explosion would take out Oberon's front gate instead of the castle proper.

"Now we just have to figure out how to find Paddy and the rest," said Loki, bowing his head so Bubba Sue could climb on.

"Just follow me," said Sun, jumping off the missile, onto a newly formed cloud.

"You got some sort of locator power?" asked Bubba Sue.

"Naw. Part of me is already there, so it's just a matter of finding myself," said Sun, taking off into the sky. Loki flew off after him.

"I guess that beats paying a shrink to help you do it," said Bubba Sue, as she grabbed a fistful of Loki's hawk feathers and held on tight.

174

Don't get mad; get even.
    -Hex, cursed magi

Mab and Tralla were the last ones off the path. Tralla shut things up tight behind them and went to check on Hex. Kyna was already looking after him. He had started to come around.

"Are you okay, Hex?" asked Tralla.

"I'm still breathing," said Hex.

"So am I, thanks to you," said Kyna, kissing Hex's cheek. "Thanks."

"My pleasure. We've known each other since we were kids. I wasn't going to let anything happen to you," said Hex.

"Let me add my thanks, Hex," said Paddy, careful not to use his given name outside of the bar. The boss shook Hex's hand. He had dumped the still-unconscious Oberon off with Tama and some other Daemor. The king wasn't going anywhere, especially since the chains that bound him had been made especially for him, for use in Mab's contingency plan.

"One of the reasons I came back was to save you, Paddy. I wasn't about to fail," said Hex.

"Came back?" asked Tralla.

"Long story, and let's leave it at that," said Hex.

"For now, but next time we meet you are going to owe me a lot of answers," said Tralla.

"I may not be the same man then that I am now," Hex said with a smile.

"Whoever you are better answer my questions," said Tralla, smiling back.

"Fair enough," replied Hex.

"What do we do now?" asked Kyna.

"We wait and hope," said Hex.

That's when the gods and the gremlin dropped out of the sky.

"Did you stop them?" asked Mab, a second before Paddy could ask the same question.

"No," said Sun, actually telling the truth. Mab asked if they did, not if they could. Sun bowed his head.

"By the eternal blade. . ." said Mab.

With fire in his glare, Hex angrily looked up and met Sun's, then Loki's, eyes. The dark cloud over his face gave way to a wide-eyed neutral expression, as his power kicked in, letting him know what happened. Paddy had no such insight.

"What do ye mean ye didn't stop them?" Paddy demanded. Oberon chose this moment to regain consciousness, and began to chuckle softly. Tama hit him hard with the hilt of her sword.

The king stopped laughing.

"I will remember that," he promised Tama. The Daemor hit him again.

"Good. Make sure you don't forget that one, either," she said. Meanwhile, the Monkey King was apologizing to the boss.

"We did our best, Paddy," said Sun.

"Well that just wasn't good enough, then, was it? Do you realize. . ." raved Paddy.

"No, Moran, it's my fault. I set these events in motion. It is my fault, not theirs," said Mab. "When will the missile hit my kingdom?"

"It should have hit several minutes ago," replied Sun.

"That's impossible. I am linked with my kingdom. I would know if it was destroyed. It hasn't been," said Mab. "Tralla, open up the path. I'm going back."

"But—" said Tralla.

"Do it. I have to see. Open it long enough for me to get through, then shut it. Open it again in fifteen minutes," said Mab. She had adapted military time for her people as well. Tralla nodded.

"I'll go with you," said Paddy.

"No, Moran. I am going alone," said Mab. Paddy began to argue, but then saw Sun's hands and became quiet. Many of us at the bar have become fluent in sign language, in order to understand one of our regulars, Judah Macabee. Judah's a golem, and mute, so the only way he can "speak" is via his hands.

Sun had signed "Don't" and "Trust me." Paddy did.

Tralla opened the path and Mab ran down it. As soon as she was down the path, Tralla closed it up.

It was a long fifteen minutes. There wasn't a lot of talking. Those in the know couldn't risk anyone else catching on.

When the time was up, a jubilant Mab came running off the re-opened path.

"It's incredible. The missile exploded, but didn't do much more damage than a strong explosion spell. There's no radiation, no mushroom cloud, and very little damage. It's wonderful, but I don't understand it," said Mab.

"That's impossible," said Oberon. Mab held up her hand for Tama to hold back the blow she was about to land.

"Maybe I can shed some light on it. The physical laws in Faerie are different than on Earth. The nuclear fission reaction must somehow be inhibited by Faerie's magic," said Hex.

"That makes sense. If you are right, the Trident will have been a dud as well," said Mab.

"Trident? You mean you launched your missile against my kingdom!?"

shouted an outraged Oberon.

"Actually, you did. By sending your missile against us, you activated an automatic launching system," said Mab.

"How dare you!" said Oberon.

Mab walked over and smacked him across the face with the back of her hand. Mab was stronger than Tama, and blood dripped from Oberon's mouth where she struck him.

"How dare I? You were the one who made the decision to slaughter thousands when you launched your missile," said Mab.

"But to have a spell to launch just because another does is diabolical," said Oberon.

"A little trick I picked up from the humans, and it makes brilliant tactical sense. A rational opponent would not attack if she knew the attack meant her own death. Pity, I wasn't dealing with a rational opponent," said Mab.

"A pity you didn't tell me about it," said Oberon.

"You would have learned about it if you hadn't tried to kill us," said Mab. "Which brings us to the point of deciding what to do with you."

"If you hold me, it will mean war," said Oberon. "My people will come for me."

"That's assuming that Mr. Hex's theory is right. My missile might have erased your kingdom from the face of the Faerie," said Mab.

"I'm guessing that the Trident was as much of a dud as the Scaleboard. Oberon would also sense his people's destruction, and he seems fairly calm. How fares your kingdom?" asked Hex.

"My kingdom lives on, so these toys must have been worthless," spat Oberon.

"So that proves that nuclear bombs and missiles are useless in Faerie," said Hex.

"But I thought. . ." started Pan, about to ruin the con and put us right back where we started. I kicked him in the shin and Rumbles tried to cover his mouth, but he kept talking. Kyna solved the problem quickly, although harshly, by bringing her knee up in Pan's groin. Pan's eyes began watering as he grabbed his crotch and doubled over in pain, fortunately unable to talk.

When everyone looked over to see what the commotion was, Kyna covered.

"You're disgusting. I'm your half-sister, pig," she said, then stormed away. Pan's reputation preceded him, and there were some knowing chuckles from the assembled.

"All that for a useless weapon," said Mab, able to see humor in the situation. "Live and learn."

"Regardless, I would like to see a peace treaty in effect between you two before I leave," said Paddy.

"Dream on, leprechaun. I would sooner have relations with a sheep than sign your treaty," said Oberon.

Pan, who had managed to get up to a sitting position muttered, "What's wrong with sheep?" He was generally ignored.

From the surrounding woods, eyes were watching the proceedings, confident that no one was watching him. Having enough confidence in something doesn't necessarily make it so.

"Enjoying the show, Goodfellow?" asked Hex, who had gotten behind Puck without being noticed.

Puck was a cool customer and did not give away his surprise.

"I'd enjoy it more if I had my fingers around Oberon's throat," Puck said, trying to be slick and move off to the side to get past Hex. He stopped short when he heard Coyote growl from where he had planned to place his next step.

He was going to flee upwards, but a glance up at the Monkey King in the tress above him quashed that idea.

"Killing an anointed King in Faerie would buy more trouble than even you could handle," said Hex, not adding that after this stunt, the land of Faerie might be rethinking its stand on Oberon. Faerie itself was a living entity and one of its anointed protectors had almost killed parts of it. Oberon would still be king, but he wouldn't have his anointed right to fall back on. Hex wondered how long he would hold onto his kingdom after that happened.

"True, but he used me, and almost made me a party to slaughter and genocide," Puck said.

"I would have thought you would be used to being used by this point," said Coyote.

"I've used him as much as he's used me. This is different," said Puck.

"Bubba Sue said he helped her out," said Sun.

"What if I gave you a chance to get even with Oberon, without having to kill him. Would you go for it?" asked Hex.

Robin Goodfellow smiled. "What do I need to do?"

"A few things. With your help, we might even get Paddy's treaty signed. I'll need to get Mab's okay on this, but it should fly. Here's what we're going to do," said Hex.

What fools these mortals be. And everyone else ain't too bright either.
-Robin Goodfellow, aka Puck

Most of Mab's people had already gone down the path that returned to her castle. What was left comprised a skeleton crew. Tama and several other Daemor surrounded Oberon. In the chains that bound him, his powers would be a mere fraction of his full strength. With him as weakened as he was, he couldn't conjure enough magic to do a card trick.

An explosion rang out from the woods near the opposite side of the clearing. Tama and the rest of the Daemor rushed off to investigate, leaving the fallen king alone and unguarded. He was so feeble that he couldn't even make an escape attempt.

That's when Puck crept out of the woods behind him.

"Don't worry your majesty, I'll have you free in moments," said Puck.

"Robin? My puck, I am so pleased to hear your voice," said Oberon, as Puck picked the lock charm on the chains. A moment later they clanged to the ground.

"Hurry, we don't have much time. It won't take them long to figure out that the explosion was merely a distraction," said Puck, helping the king to his feet. "Follow me. There's a path here that we can take."

Oberon followed. The getaway seemed clean. They quickly moved down the path, putting as much distance between themselves and Mab's troops as possible.

They paused a minute and looked back. There was no sign of pursuit. Oberon laughed.

"Thank you Robin Goodfellow, for your timely rescue," said Oberon.

"I wouldn't thank me just yet," said Puck.

"Why not?" asked the King.

"You almost made me a party to genocide," said Puck.

"Forget about it. The nuclear missiles are useless here in Faerie," said Oberon.

"But you didn't know that when you launched it. You promised me when I got you the Scaleboard that it was just a deterrent against Mab's missile. You promised me that it would never be used," said Goodfellow.

"My dear Puck, things changed. I had no choice," lied Oberon.

"Not only did you have a choice, you had everything ready to go. I can't let this go unpunished."

"Robin, you overstep your bounds. If there is any punishing to do, I will be the one doing it," said Oberon angrily.

"Wrong, my king," said Puck, with bile in his voice. Then he snapped his fingers. "Turn around."

Oberon did as he was told. The path in front of him was gone.

"This is not within your power," said Oberon, shocked, his back to Puck.

"Wrong again."

Actually, Oberon wasn't entirely wrong. He just couldn't see the crowd in the trees above him. Hex, Tralla, Sun, and even Coyote, who normally hated to climb anything. At Puck's snap, Tralla had ended the path.

One of the laws that governed Faerie mandated that a guest of Faerie could not be forced off a path in any way. They could be tricked, though.

Fortunately, this didn't apply to Oberon. He was a native. One of the laws that applied to natives and guests alike did not allow a path to be pulled out from under someone. A native could be pushed off, however, which is just what Puck did. He planted his boot in Oberon's butt and pushed for all he was worth. The weakened king tumbled forward and disappeared into Faerie oblivion.

When in doubt, fake it.
-John Murphy, Bartender at Bulfinche's Pub

Everything after that went so smoothly, I was waiting for something to go wrong in a big way.

Mab was still interested in signing the treaty. Puck arranged for an appointment with Titania. Apparently, if the King is not available, the Queen has full monarchical powers, meaning that if she signed with a gilded promise, Oberon and the rest of the kingdom would be bound by it.

Titania was also agreeable to the treaty. The missile had destroyed not only the front gate, but part of her prized garden.

Mab arrived with Tralla and an honor guard of Daemor, and was given a warm greeting in Titania's great hall. The signing table was set up simply. Paddy sat in the middle. To his right sat Mab, flanked by her honor guard. On the boss' left sat Titania. Puck stood behind her and to her right. Who she chose to sit at her side was a bit of a shock, especially to Pan. Fred reclined at that place of honor. I later found out that Fred had played a crucial role in convincing the Queen to sign.

Besides the pair of Queens, there was an entire pack of jokers. All the involved tricksters were present. I was standing next to Hex.

"So Ober—" I began.

"Don't say his name here in his place of power, especially as an outsider. We don't want to give him a beacon home," explained Hex.

"So he is lost in the wild lands of Faerie?" I asked.

"Exactly. Faerie is not set up like Earth. Reality folds in on itself in places, it's part of what lets the path magic work. Stepping off a path assures getting lost, but the territory could be anything. The wild lands are the creases in the reality folds. It's hard to find a way out. Magic also doesn't work the same, so he'll have to learn new ways to survive," said Hex.

"So do you think he'll make it back?"

"Eventually, but he'll have gone through a personal hell and hostile territory to do so. The experience will be torture for a spoiled king," said Hex.

"Works for me," I said.

The signing ended with a party, but none of the Bulfinche's crowd wanted to stay. We had a party of our own waiting for us back at the bar.

Paddy seemed overly pleased with himself, and I said so.

"Why wouldn't I be, Murphy? I just got a pair of gilded promises that will not only protect the two kingdoms, but us as well," said Paddy.

"Huh?" I said.

"I slipped in a few lines about no retaliation for any involved party, which includes all of us," said Paddy.

"Do we really need that?" I asked.

"Oh, yes, especially from Titania. Don't let her current demeanor fool you. She is one vindictive lady. Don't forget what she did to poor Corny," said Paddy.

Corny was one of the kids who hung out at the bar. His mom is human, his father Gentry. Corny's a half-breed with the powers of a Shapeling. Titania kidnapped him as an infant and kept him in Faerie for years Faerie time, then returned him minutes later Earth time. She convinced him that his mother's "real" child had died and he was replacing that child. We sorted the whole thing out when Titania sent Hunter for him, who also happened to be his real father. Soap operas have nothing on life at Bulfinche's.

"Still, all and all, she's better than her husband," Paddy said.

"You're right," I conceded.

It was time to say our goodbyes.

Hermes stood by his daughter's side as they bid goodbye to Mab.

"Mother, I didn't thank you for throwing yourself on that bomb. You saved my life. Thank you," said Kyna.

"There is no need for thanks," said Mab, uncomfortable. Hermes leaned forward and kissed her on the cheek.

"Yes, there is. Thank you for keeping our daughter safe," said Hermes.

"She is our daughter. I did what any mother would do. I do love her, I only wish she believed me," said Mab.

"I don't understand how you show it sometimes, but I know you love me. . . Mom," said Kyna.

"You know, that is the first time you've called me Mom since you were a little girl."

"Well, work hard at being a better mother and it may not be the last," Kyna said, embracing her mother.

"I will," promised Mab.

"I love you," said Kyna.

"I love you too," said Mab.

Hex was hugging Tralla goodbye. Pan had decided to hit on the queen. Titania, that is.

"Hey, Tity. How about a quick one for old times' sake," said Pan with a wink, while wrapping his arm around her waist and staring into her open and exposed cleavage.

Then it happened. Pan struck out. Titania took his arm off her like it was a two-week-old, rotten fish and dropped it at Pan's side. Titania wasn't even wearing nose filters.

"Why settle for second best? I shall wait for the best, and that isn't you, Pan. At least not anymore," she said, bending to kiss Fred on the lips. It wasn't exactly a get-a-room type kiss, but it wasn't platonic either. Pan's eyes went wide and his jaw dropped at the sight of his son beating him in getting to a woman. He walked away confused. Fred was beaming.

"May I come visit you at Moran's bar? I haven't been welcome there in the past. It would be strictly as a friend," said Titania.

"I'll run it by the boss. I'm sure he'll be okay with it," said Fred.

"I believe I'm actually going to miss you," said Titania.

"Ditto."

"Ditto?" asked Titania.

"It means 'Me too.'"

"Ah."

They hugged good bye. Titania nestled Fred's face in her ample, exposed cleavage and he stepped away with a mile-wide smile.

He bumped into Wisp, who was watching the former slave boy Miguel talk to Tralla. Wisp had arranged for him to go elsewhere, away from his former masters.

"Wisp, couldn't you just use your Soulfire to cleanse the Faerie magic out of him so he could go back to Earth?" asked Fred.

"Sure, but the experience might leave him as nothing more than a husk, depending on what he's done in his life," said Wisp.

"Oh," said Fred, walking away, disappointed that there wasn't a simpler solution.

There were three Sun Wukongs milling about. One was Loki in under-cover mode. Another was seeing off the rhesus monkeys: Jane and the others had decided to stay in Faerie.

"Are you sure about this?" asked Sun.

"Yes. If us go back to Earth, we lose smartness," said Jane, who was leading the monkey pack in speech.

"Intelligence isn't all it's cracked up to be," said Sun.

"We no care. We like it. Thank you, majesty, for saving us," said Jane.

"It was my pleasure," said Sun.

"Why you not stay with us?" asked Jane.

"My place is not here."

"Will we see majesty again?" asked Jane, saddened.

"I will visit," said Sun.

"Good. Jane have one thing to do left," said Jane, before she ran over and leapt into my arms.

"You're looking good, Jane," I said.

"Murphy looking good, too," Jane said. "I come to say bye bye. You nice, especially for a human."

"You are the sweetest monkey I've ever met," I said.

"Even more than majesty?"

"Sun? Definitely."

"Murphy, will you kiss Jane bye bye?"

Rumbles, Hex and Pan were standing nearby and started laughing. Jane heard them and thought they were making fun of her instead of me. She got a sad look on her face that almost broke my heart. I had not known a monkey could cry up until that point. Screw those guys. I could never refuse a lady once the tears started flowing.

"Ignore them, Jane. They are just a trio of idiots. I'd be happy to kiss you bye bye," I said, praying she didn't expect there to be tongue involved. She didn't. It was a quick peck on the lips.

"Bye bye, Murphy."

"Bye bye, Jane."

Jane ran over to the other monkeys, who went with that Sun self to talk to Tralla about where they were going. They were making friends with Miguel. Maybe they would travel together and help each other out.

I walked over to the idiot trio.

"Murphy's got a new girlfriend, and she needs a shave," said Pan.

"You should talk. I hope you guys are happy. You made Jane cry," I said.

Rumbles and Hex had the decency to look sheepish. Pan was a different story.

"Who cares what a monkey thinks?" he said. The other Sun self heard him and walked over beside me, leaning one arm on my shoulder.

"You care to repeat that?" Sun said. There was no humor in his voice or body language. Sun suddenly went from a fun guy to someone with a major intimidation factor.

"Um. . . ." stammered Pan.

"You made Jane cry. That makes me very unhappy. I suggest the three of you go over there and apologize. Now," said Sun, raising his voice.

The three of them spit out an okay, then ran over to Jane to say "I'm sorry." The scramble brought back Sun's good nature and he laughed.

"I've said it before and I'll say it again. Murphy, you're okay, for a human that is," he said.

"Thanks, I think," I said.

After his apology to Jane, Rumbles went over and shook Tairde's finger. The effects of Pan's music had worn off. Tairde hadn't been included in the honor guard, but had insisted on coming to say good bye to the clown. Even Mab didn't take saying no to a giant lightly, so Tairde's presence was allowed.

Across the way, Bubba Sue was saying her farewells to Puck. That seemed to do it, and the rest of us walked over to Tralla. Wisp, Fred, and Bubba Sue decided to leave with us, which meant they would lose a few hours, instead of minutes. Tralla did her thing and we ended up near the path we had come into Faerie on. Coyote was confident he could lead us out from there.

Winning isn't the only thing, but it sure beats losing.
-Loki, Norse god of Mischief

Coyote's confidence was well founded. We left with no problem, emerging near the base only a few minutes after we had left. The Air Force personnel were all still in dreamland.

"Hermes, the Shapelings are still inside lockers at the silo. Would you object to getting them?" asked Hex.

"No problem," said Hermes, moving so fast he seemed to vanish into thin air. Seconds later, he reappeared with a Shapeling in each hand.

"Go back to Mab," said Hex, looking each of them in the eyes.

"But we want to stay," said the she-Shapeling, thinking primarily of the fun she was having with the husband of the captain she was imitating.

"The life you're leading doesn't belong to you," said Hex.

"Is there any way we could stay?" asked the he-Shapeling.

"For my okay, you would have to get the permission of the captains you are impersonating. Mab is your problem," said Hex.

The Shapelings looked at each other, then back at Hex.

"We'll risk Mab," said the she-Shapeling.

"Then take me to where you left them and let's see what happens," said Hex. "I'll meet you back at the bar."

"Won't you need a ride?" I asked.

"Nope. I may even get back before you do," said Hex. Hermes dropped the Shapelings on the ground. They stood, brushed themselves off, then lead Hex back down the path into Faerie.

Loki dropped his disguise as Sun. Sun did a new variation on the swallowing of his other self. He morphed his head and neck into a giant furry serpentine shape. Distorting his jaw, he swallowed his other self. The whole thing looked like a snake swallowing a mouse. The effect was helped by the self screaming and yelling the whole way down.

"That's disgusting," said Kyna. Sun's eyebrows went up and down, then his mouth opened to reveal the head and shoulders of the swallowed Sun self.

"Isn't it though?" said the monkey in the mouth, smiling. The tongue morphed and wrapped itself around the Sun self like a pink boa constrictor, pulling him down the snakey Sun's gullet. "Gotta go." The jaws slammed shut. Sun went back to his natural form and let out a huge belch.

"Excuse me," he said.

"You are one twisted monkey," said Kyna.

"Thank you," said Sun.

Coyote was lying on the ground, grooming his paws.

"I give it a 4.5," said Coyote in a bored tone.

"I have only one thing to say to that," said Sun.

"What's that?" asked Coyote.

"Shotgun!" said the Monkey King, running down the road toward where Paddy had left Baby parked.

"Not if I get there first," shouted Pan, taking off after him. Not wanting to be left out, Coyote sprinted toward the car.

"If it's a race you want, you two leggers don't stand a chance," said Coyote, passing Pan and quickly closing the distance between him and Sun.

"You brought Baby?" said Bubba Sue excitedly. She was a car lover, and Baby was a mint conditioned, albeit modified, 1930 Caddy.

"Don't you touch her, understand?" scolded Paddy. Bubba Sue had been offering for years to do the maintenance on Baby, for free no less. Paddy paid Vulcan to do it. The boss is cheap, so for him to go with Vulcan was significant. Apparently, Paddy had witnessed Bubba Sue strip down a car on a bet in less than ninety seconds. The experience jaded him on the idea of Bubba Sue as mechanic, although he once made her day by letting her do a minor repair when Vulcan couldn't make it.

"Sorry, no speaka the English," said Bubba Sue. Paddy glared at her. "Okay, I won't do anything. Hey, Fred, Wisp, I'll race ya."

Fred was off and running. Wisp, who is normally all grim and reserved, surprised me by joining in.

"We'll met you back at the bar," said Hermes, floating up. Kyna levitated next to him and took her father's hand. They flew away so fast the air rushing in to the space they had occupied made a popping noise.

"Rumbles, you better go get a seat," said Paddy.

"Sure," said the clown. That left Paddy, Loki, and me. I was wondering why Paddy hadn't told me to go, too, but I had a good suspicion.

"Loki, you'll be taking the cycle back, right?" said Paddy. It was obvious. Loki had already fetched the motorcycle.

"Right," replied Loki, putting one leg over the seat. He seemed anxious to leave.

"Would ye mind terribly giving Murphy a lift? Baby's going to be a little crowded," said Paddy. I almost mentioned that since Hex was gone, Wisp was only taking up his spot. Fred and Bubba Sue were small enough to still be able to squeeze in, but for once I kept my mouth shut.

"Actually, there's not a lot of room," said Loki, somehow hoping Paddy would overlook the sidecar.

"I see," said Paddy, looking up into the sky. "By the way, your plan was brilliant. You managed to convince all of Faerie that nuclear missiles were worthless toys in the Sidhe. Even managed to destroy all the evidence. Thank you."

"It was nothing," said Loki.

"Don't be going all modest on me now. It seems the only thing left to figure out is what to do with the nuclear payloads," said Paddy. Loki's eyes went wide. "Those nuclear payloads almost brought about a twilight of man and Gentry. I'd hate to think they might now bring about a twilight of the gods."

"Yes. . . that would be a horrible thing," said Loki warily, stepping back into a posture I had seen Hercules use at the bar. It looked relaxed and casual, but enabled the stander to attack or defend with ease. Loki thought Paddy was going to try to take the nuclear payloads away from him, and he was prepared to fight.

Fortunately, violent confrontations aren't the boss' style.

"We best be getting back. Now about that ride for Murphy. If it would be too crowded on the bike, I'm sure we could squeeze him in Baby," said Paddy. Loki let out a small sigh.

"No, I'll take him," said Loki.

"Good. I better go check on the kids in my car and make sure they aren't wrecking anything. See ye at Bulfinche's," said Paddy, walking away.

"See you there," said Loki. He tossed me a helmet. "Get on Murphy."

I put the helmet on my head and my butt in the sidecar. He started it up and we started speeding across the field.

"Where you really planning on taking off?" I asked, holding onto his back. Each helmet had microphones and speakers, so we could talk to each other easily.

"I was thinking about it," Loki admitted. "These things could even hurt a god."

"Why didn't you?"

"What makes you think I'm not?" Loki asked. I had a vision of being thrown off the motorcycle between worlds, where my body might never be found.

"Call it a hunch," I said. Loki laughed.

"As much as I'm ashamed to admit it, you're right," said Loki.

"What changed your mind?"

Loki was silent for a moment.

"Remember when I said I didn't think one person's opinion of me was enough?"

"Yes," I replied.

"I was wrong. The idea of letting down Paddy made me more ashamed than going straight," said Loki.

"I gotta admit, I'm impressed," I said.

"Thanks, but I could still change my mind," said Loki. I let that one slide.

"Hey, I just thought of something. Won't the Air Force notice that a missile is missing?" I asked.

"Sure, but they'll never admit it," said Loki.

"Why not?"

"They'll be too ashamed," he said with a grin. "Everyone on that base is going to wake up and think they were derelict in their duty by falling asleep at their post. Nobody is going to be rushing to confess anything. They'll cover it up and make it look like it never happened."

Just then we lifted off into the sky.

"Since I am actually going back, do you mind if we take the long way home? I don't get out much," said Loki.

"No problem," I said. I should have known better.

Home is where the heart and the booze are.
        -Dionysus, Greco-Roman god of wine, women and song, bartender at Bulfinche's Pub

The long way home warped dimensions and space. Loki and I had a bit of an adventure that lasted the better part of several weeks, but that's a story for another day. We still made it back only a few minutes after Paddy and the rest.

Hermes and Kyna were the first ones back. Mosie was there waiting with the general, who was still tied naked to a table. The greatest psychic had made preparations against the returning tricksters and was prepared to stay.

"Hermes, you might want to put the general elsewhere," suggested Mosie.

"Why?"

"Because Paddy's about to tell you to put away your toys," said Mosie.

Of course, because he has a standing dispensation from the boss, Mosie's powers work in the bar. At least as much as the alcohol lets them. Paddy walked in the door that lead to the parking garage with the rest of the tricksters behind him. Bubba Sue was going on about what a sweet ride it was.

Paddy took one look at Swanson and said, "Hermes, put your toys away. We have guests coming."

Hermes grumbled, but did as Paddy asked. Swanson had regained some of his anger.

"I am not a toy. I am a man, dammit, and I expect to be treated as one," yelled Swanson.

"Okay. Men all get the anal probes. Sure you're a man?" asked Hermes.

"What do the women get?"

"Impregnated with our alien spawn."

"Can I get back to you?" asked Swanson. Hermes rolled the table behind the bar, opened that door and rolled the table upstairs, no mean feat.

Paddy was busy, and Dionysus was still out working on his stunt which left nobody behind the bar. As soon as I walked in the pub, Paddy told me to get to work.

I did as I was told.

Rumbles was first on line. He wanted a vanilla egg creme with a shot of rum. As I handed him his drink, he took a good look at me.

"Murphy, what's with the beard? You didn't have one when we left Arkansas," said Rumbles.

"A little detour, but a long story. I didn't have a razor. I was just thankful the motorcycle had a fully stocked fridge," I said.

I watched as Loki pulled Paddy aside and took out what looked like two packs of gum. Loki handed them to the boss. Paddy slapped him on the shoulder with a big smile. Loki was smiling, but part of it was from sadness.

More tricksters started to arrive over the next few hours. Too many of the boss' relations showed, but nowhere near the amount we see on St. Patrick's Day. As soon as the sun set, Legba arrived. He prefers the dark. More trickled in, many through the doggie door. First a hare, then a fox, and in rapid succession a crow, tortoise, raven, and spider. More animals followed. It was beginning to look like a petting zoo.

Hex showed up, later than expected. He stopped off at the bar.

"How'd it go?" I asked.

"Interestingly. The Shapelings were prepared to beg the captains for permission to live their lives. They had assumed the captains' forms and that's when the weirdness started. Seems the captains had been having an affair with each other. The Shapelings had altered their human forms to have statuesque proportions. The humans took one look at the improved versions of their partners and feel in lust. The Shapelings had become addicted to sex with humans and weren't choosy about with whom. They decided to run off together and rejoin Mab's army."

"What about their spouses?" I asked.

"Who knows?" said Hex.

The party was in full swing. The all-news channel was on in the background, and every so often someone would claim credit for a story. I had a bit of trouble buying the moth's tale. She said that she spent the morning in China flapping her wings and was claiming credit for a hurricane in the Caribbean. She said why should butterflies have all the fun.

However, in her favor was the fact that it wasn't hurricane season.

Coyote caught her in a net and put her in a jar, although Paddy let her out soon after. The tortoise was challenging the hare to a race. The tortoise was boasting, but shut up as the Centzon Totochtin started racing in the doggie door. The Centzon Totochin are Aztec deities. The name translates loosely as "Four Hundred Rabbits". I understood why Paddy had stocked up on carrot juice.

The Centzon make Pan look frigid. They spend most of their days having sex like, well, rabbits. They have an interesting life cycle. Their births and deaths match up exactly: the last one to die is the next one born through the art of incestuous reincarnation.

They didn't let the fact that there was an audience alter their bunny orgy plans. Paddy had sectioned off a corner of the bar with a sheet to give everyone else privacy. Pan and Mantis were perched on the floor, with the corner of the sheet raised up. The floor was actually vibrating with the thumping of the Centzon.

"Wow," said Pan in awe.

"What I don't understand is why the females don't eat the males afterwards," said Mantis. Pan gave her a frightened look and moved away quickly.

Speaking of odd sexual habits, Dionysus finally showed up and joined me behind the bar, which was a good thing because I was swamped.

"How'd your prank go?" I asked.

"Unexpectedly," said Dion.

"You going to tell me what you did?" I asked.

"I'm not even going to enter it, Murph," said Dion, putting out a bowl of sugar water for some bees.

At half past midnight, Paddy jumped up on the stage.

"Attention, Tricksters! The guild judges have voted, and for the first time in recent memory, it was unanimous. First runner up is Loki, for a prank which may have to remain unknown, except for the voting council," said Paddy. Fortunately the entire voting council this year had been involved in the events of the day.

Loki lifted up his tankard of ale and saluted the room.

"The winner's prank also falls into the remaining unknown category. The new Lord High Trickster is. . . Mr. Hex!" said Paddy.

Hex was hanging at a table in the corner with Kyna. At the mention of his name, his head shot up.

"Me?" said Hex, walking up to the stage.

"Who else, Hex? You changed an entire time line and saved innumerable lives," Paddy whispered into his ear. Hermes, as the previous Lord High Trickster, handed off the trophy to the reigning one. Not to mention the year's supply of earwax. It was in a sealed glass bucket.

The trophy had a platypus on it. I didn't get it.

"Now if the High Yuk will grace us with a few words," said Paddy.

Hex took the boss literally. His speech was short and sweet.

"Thank you. I'd like to thank the little people," he said, giving Paddy a wink. The boss didn't even bat an eyelash at the short joke.

The party broke up around dawn. Most folks had left. Fred took Pan to JFK to catch a flight. Wisp headed back to The Eternity Club in Philadelphia. Bubba Sue took off. The news announced that the space shuttle crew had finally come out. They blamed it on a door malfunction. Paddy keep finding pairs of Centzon rabbits. He hosed them down with a seltzer bottle to separate them, then tossed them out the door.

"Paddy, after all we've been through today, I can't believe you're wasting time splitting hares," I said.

Paddy turned the seltzer bottle on me, giving me a good soaking.

It was time for him to take Loki back. I felt bad for the guy. He came over to the bar before he left.

"See you on Halloween," he said, clasping my wrist. Loki wasn't a big one for words, but his gesture spoke volumes. Other than Paddy's, Loki had never shaken anyone's hand that I could remember. Spend a couple of months roaming the Otherworlds with a guy and he gets all mushy on you.

I wanted to say something like "be strong" or "be well", but I couldn't. Loki was willingly going back to endure more than six months of torture. I had revised my earlier opinion of the guy. If I were in his place, I would have taken off on the cycle.

"Bye," I said simply. He and Paddy dressed up in their camouflaging costumes and went down to the garage.

"I'm beat. I'm going to bed, too," said Dion.

"You're tired?" I said incredulously.

"Yep. Good night," said Dion, going through the door behind the bar and then upstairs.

"I'm going to head out, too, Murph," said Coyote.

"Where you headed?" I asked.

"Off to Washington to help a kid I met with some bullies," said Coyote.

"When you coming back this way?" I asked.

"Expect me when you see me," he said. "Later, banana breath."

"Bye, fleabag," said Sun.

Coyote went over to Kyna and she hugged him.

"Take care, sweetheart," said Coyote.

"You too," said Kyna. Coyote headed out the doggie door.

Kyna got up and hugged everyone goodbye. I was last.

"What are your plans?" I asked.

"I have to figure out a way to spend ten million dollars," said Kyna.

"You could always leave your bartender a large tip," I said, hopefully.

"But would money make you happy?" she asked with a smirk.

"It wouldn't make me sad," I said.

"What would you do with ten million, Murphy?" asked Hex.

"Before or after I got back from my world tour?"

"I'm serious," said Hex.

I thought about it a while.

"I don't know. The only money problems I ever had were back when I owed a loan shark." I had borrowed money to help pay for medical care for Elsie, my departed wife. "Paddy bailed me out and gave me a fresh start. I'm not rich, but I have everything I need. I guess I'd find a way to give other people that same chance. But it's not like I'll ever have that problem."

Kyna smiled and handed me her two briefcases. "Don't be so sure about that, Murphy."

"What's this?"

"Ten million."

"Kyna, I can't take this," I said.

"Sure you can. You're idea sounds as good to me as anything," said Kyna.

"But it's so much money."

"Murph, I have all the money I need," said Kyna.

"But. . ."

"Murph, take the money," said Hex.

"I don't know."

"I have four words that will change your mind. The Elsie Murphy Foundation," said Hex.

I thought of my late wife and a tear came to my eye. "A memorial to Elsie. I like that. Thanks Kyna," I said, hugging her and kissing her cheek.

"My pleasure. Talk to Dad and Paddy about setting it up," said Kyna.

"I will."

"I'm going to take off, too," said Sun.

"Sun, thanks again for saving my life," I said.

"What else could I do? You make the best banana daiquiris I've ever tasted."

"You have plans?" I asked.

"Naw. Figured I'd wander around and see where I ended up," said Sun.

Rumbles strolled over. "I have an idea. Since Kyna no longer has to worry about spending her money, why don't the two of you come back with me to the circus. I know Roy would love to see you both."

"A giant talking monkey at the circus?" said Sun.

"We might be able to work you into an act. Roy's part owner, since the accident," quipped Rumbles.

"Oh joy. What the heck," said Sun.

"I'd love to see that. I'm in," said Kyna.

The three of them exited together. That left Hex and me alone in the bar.

"You did it, Hex," I said.

"I did, didn't I?" he said with a sad smile.

"What's wrong?" I said.

"I'm thinking about time travel paradoxes. I'm going to have to leave soon," said Hex. What he was getting at started to sink in.

"So if you changed the future, what happens to you when you leave?" I said.

"Exactly. If my future no longer exists. . ."

"Where do you go?"

"Or did I cause a divergent time line?"

"In which case, you'll go back to your world just as you left it," I said.

"When I left, it wasn't good. We did a suicide run to get an amulet that would send me back. The spell was of such intensity that the backlash probably killed my body," said Hex.

"So for you, it really was a suicide run," I said.

"Yes."

"And you didn't tell anyone. Why?" I asked.

"It was easier this way."

"But nobody got to say goodbye."

"What do you say to a man who's about to die? I've been there too many times, and I wouldn't wish that on anyone."

"Why don't you just stay? It's your body, too," I said.

"It was, once upon a time. If I stay, the Hex of today dies. I can't do that to myself. I lived a long life and fought the good fight. If I have to die, that's my burden," said Hex.

"Why tell me?" I asked.

"Murphy, after Paddy died, hope seemed to die. Too many gods and angels followed suit. Then you fought your way back from Hades. You gathered a small guerilla force and you stood up to the new powers that be. What's more, you won battles. You risked yourself for others and showed people that hope wasn't dead, so long as good people refused to stand by and do nothing. You kept Paddy's ideals alive. What Paddy was to us, you became to the whole world. You led the fight against the dying of the light and managed to re-kindle the flame. You even managed to awaken King Arthur to lead our armies. Millions owed you their lives, including me. It was more than anyone else, mortal or divine, had managed to do."

"You make me sound like some kind of hero."

"You were." Hex saw my mouth start to open. "Don't give me that spiel about you not being a hero. You earned as much right to that title as anyone who ever lived. Paddy would have been proud. I know I was. There was no way we could properly thank you. That was now, this is then. Get me your laptop," Hex said.

I ran up to my room and got it. It was one of Paddy's old throwaways, but it was built by Vulcan, so it was light years ahead of anything available commercially.

I came back down and handed it over to Hex.

"Paddy never revoked my dispensation," Hex said with a wink, then sat down at the laptop. His fingers moved across the keyboard in a blur, working magic. Hex smiled and handed it back to me. "Here, a gift from me, your future-self and a few friends."

I looked at the screen. There was a new folder named Nuclear Magic, and it was full.

"What is it?" I asked.

"We found something called a Chronicler. It hooks up to the user's brain and warps time. It let the future-you mentally write a book in less than a minute. I downloaded the files into my mind before I came back. There are a few from some others, including me."

"There must be dozens of books here," I said.

"At least. Just before we pulled off the raid, hundreds of thousands were slaughtered and it looked like millions more would follow. It was something we couldn't fight, so you came up with the idea of going back in time. You knew Vulcan had managed time travel, but he had been killed. I found a mystic solution. The future-Murphy figured preventing our future would save the world, but he hated the idea of us ceasing to exist, with nobody to remember everything we did. He figured sending our stories back in time to you would let a part of us live on."

"I'm honored," I said.

"No, I'm honored to have known you, Murphy," said Hex. "I'm going to go now."

"Are you sure?" I asked.

"Makes no sense putting it off. Bring the me of today up to speed, will you?" said Hex.

"Sure," I said. "Hex. . ."

"What?"

"As long as I've known you, you always seemed to have a plan. Please tell me your plan isn't to give up and die once you leave."

Hex chuckled, rubbing his temples and trying to pretend that the spell hadn't given him a major headache. "I have a plan, Murphy. I just have no clue if it'll work. Not many places for a man without a body to go. How about I leave it there, on an upbeat note."

I nodded, knowing he was fully expecting to die.

"Remember, hope and happiness never die. . ."

I finished the sentence for him. "In Bulfinche's."

"No, ever. Bye Murph," he intoned and collapsed face first onto the bar.

"Bye Hex."

The Hex of my time woke up and looked up at me.

"Murphy? What happened? Last thing I remember was walking in here," he said.

"Well, for starters, you won. You're the new High Yuk," I said handing him the trophy. I'd point out the earwax later.

"I did? How?"

"It's a long story, but we have time."

It ain't over until all the loose ends are tied up.

     -John Murphy, Bartender at Bulfinche's Pub, and self-proclaimed master storyteller

Hermes came up with the perfect solution for what to do with General Swanson. He had left the party briefly and took the general back to the base, where everyone was still snoozing. Still naked as a jaybird, Hermes tied Swanson to the console of the missing missile.

When the base woke up and the next shift went to relieve their predecessors, they found the captains and the missile missing and the buck-naked general bound and gagged.

The general was debriefed at length by military intelligence. Normally, anyone with his story would have been laughed off, but he was the officer in charge of Project Skywatch. Also, no one on the entire base could remember most of the previous day, and all the surveillance tapes had been erased. Add to that a missing, fully functional Trident nuclear missile, and the military was freaking out. The idea of a government conspiracy to cover up the existence of extraterrestrial life was so widespread that everyone, including military intelligence, assumed it was true. The only explanation they could come up with that made any sense was that the entire base had experienced a close encounter. The aliens were believed to have stolen memories and the missile, not to mention the two missing captains. Their spouses were told they had died during a helicopter accident while participating in a military exercise. The general was believed to have been experimented on, and therefore having him in a position of power compromised national security. He was forced to retire, then taken into "protective" custody less than a week later, when he tried to approach the media with his story. Swanson has not been seen since.

Things at Bulfinche's went back to normal, or what passes for it. The staff and regulars had all returned. Dion still wouldn't talk about what had happened to him on Fools' Day and no one could get it out of him. There was a story there, so I'll keep trying.

About a week later, Toni was finishing up waiting tables during lunch when she came over to the bar with a question.

"Where's Fred? Did he forget to wake up?" asked Toni. She was trying to hide her concern. "I'm surprised you haven't rousted him out of bed yet, Paddy."

"Wouldn't make sense. Fred's gone out," said Paddy.

"I thought he had to work," said Toni.

"What? Could it be that you miss him?" I said.

"You wish, Murphy. I was just curious," said Toni.

"I gave him the afternoon off," said Paddy.

"Why? He have a hot date or something?" Toni asked, laughing.

"Actually, yes," said Paddy. Toni stopped laughing.

"Goatlegs has a date? Who'd go out with him?" she asked.

"She was about six feet tall, long platinum hair, and a figure that would make a Barbie doll jealous," I said. "And maybe even a waitress."

"I'm not jealous. Fred can do what he wants," said Toni. Then she used a common coping technique. "She sounds like a tramp, anyway."

"Actually, she's royalty," said Paddy.

"No way," Toni said.

"Way," I said.

"Why would someone like that go out with Fred?" Toni asked.

"I believe because she finds him attractive," said Paddy.

"Really?" asked Toni. Paddy nodded. Toni seemed distressed by this.

"You didn't think Fred was going to wait around forever for you, did you?" I asked. He would, but maybe if Toni thought differently, she might do something about it.

Toni didn't answer me. Instead she went to clear off a table and pick up her tip.

A few hours went by. Titania's date with Fred got me thinking, and I realized that with everything that had happened, Paddy hadn't been able to pull off any Fools' Day shenanigans.

"So Paddy, what was your prank going to be?" I asked.

"I may do it next year, so I won't tell you the whole plan. Suffice it to say that the IRS would be shut down, at least temporarily, and several surprised IRS agents will be caught in compromising situations and let's leave it at that," said Paddy smiling.

Just then, Titania and Fred returned from their lunch out. Paddy allowed Titania in the bar as a favor to Fred, but neither the boss nor the Queen was comfortable with the situation. Fred didn't want Toni watching them, either. Accordingly, they had dined out.

Titania had let her hair down, literally. She was also wearing a white dress that managed to look conservative and sexy at the same time. It was tight-fitting, with a high collar around the neck, but was open in the front to show off her assets. It was a bit chilly out, but Titania wasn't wearing a coat. Or any underwear, for that matter. Fred wasn't complaining.

Titania was holding onto Fred's arm. Both of them were laughing. They had a good time. Titania didn't appear to be putting any moves on the little guy, honoring his request to be friends. At least for the moment.

Toni had stopped what she was doing to stare. When Fred saw her, he stopped. Titania did the same.

"Hi, Toni," Fred said, with great naiveté. They truly had been out simply as friends, with no intentions on Titania or of making Toni jealous.

"Harrumph," Toni mumbled, turning away.

"This is the one?" asked Titania. Fred nodded.

Titania strode regally to the table were Toni was trying to make herself look busy.

"May I speak with you?" Titania asked.

"It's a free country," Toni replied.

"That is the fault of your rulers, but I'm not here to discuss government," said Titania.

"Then what are you here for?" asked Titania.

"To shake your hand," said Titania, extending her hand.

Surprised, Toni reached out and took it.

"The one called Fred cares for you very much. I hope you know how lucky you are. I wish you much happiness," said Titania.

"Thank you," said Toni, still off balance.

Titania turned to go, thought better of it, and turned back.

"Should you ever hurt him, I will make you wish you had never been born," whispered Titania. She turned and went to Fred's side before Toni could respond.

"It is time for me to go," said Titania.

"Are you sure you don't want to stay a little longer?" asked Fred.

Titania looked up and met Paddy's eyes. Their orbs had already been introduced, but that didn't change the situation.

"No, it is best that I take my leave. Goodbye, my friend," Titania said, bending down to kiss him softly on the lips. Fred had been hoping for a recap of their previous goodbye hug, but Titania decided to defer, due to Toni's presence. The Queen turned her attention toward the bar.

"Moran. Murphy. Lord Bacchus," she said, addressing Dion by one of his other many names.

She locked eyes with Toni and nodded, then left by the front door. She didn't need to use the nexus under the garage to get back home. She made use of a Faerie path that ended in Central Park.

"Toni, are you mad at me?" asked Fred.

Toni repressed her first instinct to make Fred pay for making her jealous. She realized Fred didn't have a malicious bone in his body. They were mostly made of calcium.

"No, I'm not. I was thinking, would you like to go out for dinner?" she asked.

"You mean you, me, and BG?" asked Fred, assuming that Toni's little girl would be included in the mix, as she usually was.

"Actually, I was thinking just you and me this time. That is if Paddy wouldn't mind babysitting?" said Toni.

"Not at all. It would be me pleasure," said Paddy.

"Hey, Toni, I'm off tonight. How come you didn't ask me?" I asked.

"Murphy, BG needs adult supervision. Half the time you need a babysitter, so I'm not going have you be the babysitter."

"But I told you I learned my lesson last time not to take the title literally. I won't actually sit on someone I'm babysitting," I said.

"Unless, it's an egg," added Dionysus.

"Right," I said.

"Ha, ha," said Toni. She never did much care for my jokes.

Fred was thrilled, but was back on the clock. He helped Toni finish cleaning off the tables. He still hadn't gotten the practical joke bug out of his system. What made it worse is, other than a pair of unwary customers, no one had fallen for any of his pranks, and it depressed him. He still carried the joy buzzer around in his pocket, looking for opportunities to use it. So far it hadn't worked. He slipped it on his hand again and went over to Paddy.

"Boss, I just wanted to thank you for giving me the afternoon off," said Fred.

"Think nothing of it. Besides, it's coming out of your vacation time," said Paddy.

Fred stuck out his hand for Paddy to shake. It was obvious that Paddy realized what was going on. I was waiting to see the joke or playful put down that would follow. The boss surprised me by accepting the handshake. The buzzer vibrated and Paddy pulled his hand away like he had been shocked.

"It worked! I got you!" screamed Fred, dancing for delight around the bar.

Paddy smiled. "Ye sure did. I didn't see that one coming."

Having "tricked" Paddy, put the cherry on the top of a perfect sundae sort of day for Fred. He was hoofing on air for the rest of the day.

"That was nice, what you did for Fred," I said.

Paddy grinned and winked at me. "We do what we can."

"And do it better than most."

PATRICK THOMAS – With over a million words in print, PATRICK THOMAS keeps busy writing the popular fantasy humor series Murphy's Lore (which includes Tales From Bulfinche's Pub, Fools' Day, Through The Drinking Glass, Shadow Of The Wolf, Redemption Road, Bartender Of The Gods, Nightcaps, Empty Graves, Startenders and Constellation Prize) as well as the After Hours spin-offs Fairy With A Gun, Dead To Rites and Lore & Dysorder. His Mystic Investigators series has grown to include the books Bullets & Brimstone and From The Shadows both with John L. French and Once More Upon A Time and the upcoming Partners In Crime both with Diane Raetz. He and John French also wrote The Assassins' Ball, the first book the Jack Gardner Mysteries. He has co-edited two anthologies - Hear Them Roar and the vampire themed New Blood. Patrick's syndicated humorous advice column Dear Cthulhu has been collected in Have A Dark Day and Good Advice For Bad People. A number of his books are part of the set and props department at the CSI television show. Laurence Fishburne's production company Cinema Gypsy Productions has taken a film and television option on Patrick Thomas' urban fantasy Fairy With A Gun. As an artist his work has graced covers for Dark Quest, Padwolf and Marietta, interiors and a cover for Space & Time magazine and comic covers for Ghostman. A mockumentary about him has surfaced on Youtube. To learn more, drop by his website at www.patthomas.net.

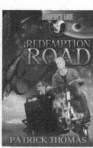